Lady Farquhar's Butterfly

Lady Farquhar's Butterfly

Beverley Eikli

ROBERT HALE · LONDON

© Beverley Eikli, 2010
First published in Great Britain 2010

ISBN 978-0-7090-9057-1

Robert Hale Limited
Clerkenwell House
Clerkenwell Green
London EC1R 0HT

www.halebooks.com

The right of Beverley Eikli
to be identified as author of this work has been
asserted by her in accordance with the
Copyright, Designs and Patents Act 1988

2 4 6 8 10 9 7 5 3 1

Typeset in 11.5/15pt Garamond
Printed in Great Britain by the MPG Books Group,
Bodmin and King's Lynn

For my father, Ted Nettelton. Also to my wonderful husband,
Eivind, and to Bernie, Frances and Linda for your
patience and insight.

CHAPTER ONE

1816

'YOUR REPUTATION IS in tatters, Olivia' – Aunt Eunice looked up from adjusting the stirrups of the little grey mare upon which her niece sat nervously – 'and you have lost everything! The time has come to take charge of your life.'

Olivia gripped the pommel with whitened knuckles. Opening her mouth to mutter that the truth was of little account when opinion was against her, she gasped instead as the docile animal shifted beneath her.

So much for the studied detachment she'd cultivated during seven years of marriage with Lucien. Her fear was as transparent as that of a frightened schoolgirl's. Now she was on a madcap venture doomed to fail, showing as much backbone in the face of her aunt's determination as she had when her late husband bent her to his will.

Grey storm clouds scudded from the west and the icy wind stung her face.

'An unfit mother, a faithless wife….' She muttered the words imprinted on her brain; the words with which Lucien had condemned her in his will. Then, unable to conquer her terror of the placid beast, 'Please, Aunt Eunice, must I do this?'

'You must fight for justice, Olivia.' The determined 'brook-no-opposition' expression that characterized Eunice Dingley's plain, leathery face brought memory flooding back. Olivia was obedient now but how well she recalled the altercations they'd had when she had

7

been a strong-willed child. How single minded had been her rebellion eight years ago as a headstrong debutante?

She had paid the price; it was why she was here.

Stepping back into soft mud that sucked at her boots, Aunt Eunice regarded her critically. 'Well, child,' she said with grudging admiration, 'you look well enough. Don't tear your riding habit when you fall off.'

Olivia winced as her aunt raised her hand to slap her horse's flank. 'What if he's like Lucien?' she hedged, bringing her mount around. 'Mr Atherton has already refused my request once. He must believe the stories—'

'He is a man.' Aunt Eunice said it as if that fact alone guaranteed Olivia's success. 'For goodness' sake, Olivia, we've already agreed this is your best course, regardless of what Reverend Kirkman thinks.'

The Reverend Kirkman. The knot of fear in Olivia's stomach tightened. The reverend had his own ideas as to how Olivia should win back her son.

This was not one of them.

She closed her eyes. Yet surely this was the best way? If there was any justice in Max Atherton's heart then truth and openness must triumph over the lies which had dogged her during her marriage and cost her the custody of her son?

A great black crow settled on the dry stone wall behind her aunt. Like her aunt, it regarded her with tilted head, eyes bright.

Her voice softening, Aunt Eunice laid her hand on Olivia's knee. 'Max Atherton came back from the Peninsular campaign a war hero. That, for a start, distinguishes him from his cousin. I've heard nothing to suggest he bears any resemblance to Lucien. Entrance him, Olivia, as you entranced that good-for-nothing husband of yours.'

'Mr Atherton believes Lucien's version of accounts. You read his reply to my letter.' It was not the cold that now made her tremble.

With a distracted frown Aunt Eunice smoothed Olivia's russet skirts. 'He has no other account to go by. He thinks he's doing what's best for the boy.' Squeezing her knee, she said briskly, 'Go, now! Take that tumble in his barley field so you can set the record straight.'

*

Max squinted through the blinding rain as he turned up the collar of his greatcoat.

It was hard to be sure from this distance, but the little grey mare sheltering beneath the elm tree at the far end of the paddock appeared to be equipped with a side saddle.

A lady's mount … but where was the lady?

His gaze raked the sodden field.

'No bran mash until we find her, Odin,' he murmured into his stallion's ear, sensing its reluctance to proceed in the face of the rising storm.

He'd been returning from his inspection of the new sheep he had been breeding in the northern paddock when his eye had been caught by a flash of scarlet. A female? Curious to make the acquaintance of any woman under forty in these sparsely populated parts, he'd watched the rider canter around the bend that separated his property from his neighbour's hoping she'd cross his path later. Instead, he'd happened upon her horse.

Lightning split the black sky and Odin snorted. Across the field, eerie in the strange light, the little grey mare gave a frightened whinny as it eyed them balefully.

'Steady, boy,' soothed Max, urging his mount forward.

Thunder boomed like cannon fire. The riderless mare bolted while Odin reared, forelegs pawing the air. Straining to keep his seat, Max scanned the field desperately for a sight of the woman, horror spearing through him as he caught a glimpse of russet beneath them; heard a faint female cry. Muscles knotted and straining, he hauled on the reins as he fought to control the terrified stallion.

Another crack of thunder. Foam sprayed from the mouth of the maddened animal which bucked again.

Before its four legs were on firm ground Max hurled himself from the saddle and ran to kneel at the woman's side as Odin bolted. Pushing back the folds of his multi-tiered coat which whipped his face, he felt for a pulse at the side of her neck.

She had cheated death but he feared the extent of her injuries. A bloody gash streaked the mud which caked her forehead; her body lay twisted. She did not stir as his hands checked the limbs beneath her skirts for breaks or other obvious injury.

Raising his head, he assessed the distance to Elmwood. He could see the battlements above the froth of rain-lashed trees which gave his home its name. In fine weather with no burden it might be a fifteen-minute walk. Now, with the ground a marsh and the wind and weight of sodden skirts it would be more than twice that, but he could not leave her to fetch help.

She was still unconscious when he lifted her. Turning his head from the sharp, icy rain which lashed his face and knotted the grass about his legs, he pushed forward, the wind keening like a banshee. His neck and shoulders ached and his breath rasped painfully. The heavens, it seemed, were using full force to hinder his efforts.

Once, he'd carried an injured soldier to safety under enemy fire; but there had been no storm and the artillery barrage had left them unscathed.

Now, the going was much harder. Glancing down, he was reassured at seeing the young woman's eyelids flutter and wondered if she were beautiful beneath all that mud. It no longer mattered. He'd been struck with a sense of purpose he'd not felt since he'd volunteered to fight for King and country nearly eight years ago.

Gradually the wind calmed and the rain became a gentle shower as the storm moved on. Reaching the tree-lined drive which led from the park to the formal gardens he tried to recall if Amelia had mentioned any newcomers to the neighbourhood. His sister's efforts to find him a wife after he'd returned from the Peninsula too battle-crazed to care suggested she would have.

'Max!' shrieked Amelia as she stood on the top step having sent two footmen to relieve her brother of his burden. 'Who is she? What has happened?' She had seen him from the drawing-room window labouring up the drive amidst the steady rain.

'Take her to my room,' he directed, resting his aching back against the wainscoting in the downstairs entrance hall.

'The blue room,' Amelia countered, adding, 'Don't be ridiculous, Max. What would she think to wake up in a gentleman's bed?'

'If she wakes,' Max said, glowering, because he wanted to have her in his room where he could watch over her, and where he had the tools to dress her wounds and set her bones, if necessary.

'Of course she'll wake,' Amelia said, sharply.

Thick dust sheets were spread upon the large tester in preparation. Amelia had wanted to strip the linen, but Max had decried such inhospitable practicality, reminding her it was not her house.

'And only yours, Max, for a few more years,' his sister muttered, as she made the counter order of dust sheets to Mrs Watkins, the house-keeper.

Ignoring her, Max also asked for a fresh nightgown, and a comb.

'One would think you were in the habit of attending to the needs of a lady, Max,' Amelia said, more archly than unkindly as her heels clicked across the boards to the window embrasure from where she regarded him with amusement.

'And plenty of hot water.' Rubbing his aching arms Max took a seat by the unconscious young woman's side. 'So you have no idea who she might be?' he asked, pushing back his cowlick. 'There's been no talk of visitors to the neighbourhood?'

Amelia shook her head. 'Do you think she's broken anything? Shall I check?'

'Her limbs seem in fine form,' Max replied, with a wry smile as he took up the sponge Mrs Watkins had just placed beside him. 'As for her face, she has a nasty cut.'

Amelia came up beside him. 'She's beautiful,' she remarked, for it was true, and Amelia never minced the truth. Or kept her thoughts to herself. 'But don't get romantic ideas into your head, Max, for she's probably spoken for, or is a widow with no money and six children, and you know very well you can't possibly take a wife to suit you unless she has at least two thousand a year.'

Gently, Max rubbed at a smudge of dirt along their visitor's jawline.

'I shall do whatever I please to suit myself, Amelia,' he said, gazing at the perfection of the unknown young woman's features: the gently curving mouth, the wide-set eyes beneath finely arched brows, the high, rounded cheekbones, 'for I answer to no one, and certainly not to you.'

The first suggestion that Olivia was nowhere familiar came from the scent of lavender. Without opening her eyes she sniffed appreciatively. Aunt Eunice was not fond of lavender but surely only she would have sprinkled it upon Olivia's pillow in deference to Olivia's partiality for it? Because Olivia was not well. Vaguely she acknowledged this, for the dull throbbing of her ankle and the sharper pain across her brow impinged upon the general comfort she felt nestled into what surely must be the softest mattress she had ever slept upon.

She opened her eyes with a start and struggled on to her elbows, her heart pounding at the confusion of her last memories.

Aunt Eunice had returned to their cottage. Wherever she was, Olivia was to fight this battle, alone.

The day was well advanced. Sunlight slanted into a large and airy room, handsomely decorated in shades of blue. She noticed a book upon the chest beside the bed. A book of poems. Byron? She squinted to make out the author and her head began to ache. Touching her forehead she felt the bandage.

'Good. You're awake,' came a voice from the doorway, and she twisted her head to see a young man advancing, his face obscured by the pile of books he carried. 'I was beginning to grow concerned.'

Bowing slightly, he introduced himself before taking a seat at her bedside and, to her astonishment, picking up her wrist.

'Your pulse is a good deal stronger,' he said. 'You appear to have twisted your ankle quite badly, but only you can assess the extent of that injury. The wound above your eye looks worse than it is. It should heal with no scar. In the meantime I thought you might enjoy some poetry.'

She was too taken aback to utter a word. Perhaps struck dumb with horror would describe it better, she thought, as she stared into eyes the colour of rain-washed slate. The dark, fathomless, unreadable eyes that had belonged to her late husband.

She swallowed. Max Atherton, her late husband Lucien's cousin: the man into whose keeping her son had been placed. With those eyes, confident and inscrutable beneath a high forehead, the straight nose and mouth she had once thought sensitive, it could be none other. He might be smiling but it was an act. Could only be one.

She gathered her wits. He must not see her fear. He would take advantage of it. Make her do things against her will.

Taking a deep breath she fought for control. She could not afford to make mistakes. Lucien was dead while Olivia had survived. She needed only the return of her son to make her happy, and she would fight for Julian to the death. He was the only reason she was here. She and Aunt Eunice had worked out every detail to prove her innocence, to make Max Atherton see the truth. Truth would be her ally, yet she felt the same cornered desperation she had when Lucien had confronted her.

She sucked in another breath. The secret of her survival lay in her ability to act. She could be whoever she needed to be.

'Mr Atherton.' She repeated his name, gaining confidence from the unmasked admiration she saw in his eyes. 'How very kind of you to come to my assistance' – she swallowed again, desperate to keep the fear from her voice – 'when I was so foolish as to take a tumble and thus put me in your debt.'

'On the contrary, you have enlivened what promised to be a very dull week – now that I know you are not mortally wounded.'

His smile was open, but his eyes …

She turned her head away. Any sign of vulnerability would put her in his power, but how could she banter with a man who looked so like Lucien it put the fear of God into her? How could she trust herself not to jeopardize everything for which she had worked so hard?

'When I looked down to see you lying trapped beneath my horse's hoofs, while he was rearing above you, maddened by the storm—'

The visions he conjured up were too close to her memories of being trapped beneath Lucien. His description could just as easily have been that of her husband's mad eyes blazing, foam and spittle flying from lips which had just bruised and bitten her.

She tried not to whimper.

'Forgive me, my dear Mrs Templestowe,' Mr Atherton said, his tone remorseful, his expression concerned as he bent over her. 'I have a deplorable habit of not dressing up the truth when it may cause pain. Too long a bachelor, I suppose,' he added with a smile.

'How do you know my name?' whispered Olivia.

'I made investigations around the neighbourhood and learned you were lodging at the White Swan.'

She had offered the publican her maiden name, for how could she present herself as Lady Farquhar in these parts before she had convinced Mr Atherton that the name was not synonymous with sin and vice?

The impulse to correct him died on her lips.

Surely, the pleasantness of Mr Atherton's smile was a calculated ploy to trick her into letting down her reserves?

He was smiling at her, now, the corners of his eyes crinkling into well-worn lines as if good humour were his natural state. But didn't grand manipulators have any number of ploys at their fingertips? Lucien had seemed the most charming of them all, and surely a man couldn't sink to depths of depravity deeper than those he had gleefully dug using pain and threats, violence and humiliation?

She had come here imagining his cousin was different and that the truth would answer.

Hiding her trembling beneath the bedcovers, Olivia forced her mouth into another cool, arch smile. 'Then you know you are harbouring a foolish, helpless widow.'

She was satisfied by the candidness of his look. No veiled, hidden knowledge lurking in those dark depths. Lucien loved to gloat, murmuring his depraved suspicions for which he had already condemned her.

He continued to smile. 'One who is guilty of nothing more than misjudging the weather.'

Shame welled up in her bosom but she kept silent. How could she possibly stare into those slate-grey eyes and tell him she was the shame-less widow of his late cousin? Like as not he would punish her so that not even Reverend Kirkman's plan, if that was ever put into play, would restore her son to her keeping.

She closed her eyes and fought the tears.

She'd wanted so much to tell her version of the truth and know the catharsis of exoneration.

She slept. Strength banished her lethargy and now all her senses were aroused by the need to find Julian.

So far there had been no sign of a child, anywhere. No childish laughter, no nursery-maid, no children's toys. The drawing room where Mr Atherton carried her would be out of bounds to children, but there must be evidence of a two-and-a-half-year-old boy, some-where.

Olivia thanked Mrs Watkins for the clean, dry clothes with which she supplied her. She was quiet as the housekeeper combed and dried her hair then helped her into the handsome blue velvet gown Max's sister had lent her. The fashions had changed since she had last paid attention to what she wore.

Where *was* Julian? Her heart thundered as she sat at the dressing table, forcing herself to sit still. Since the moment she had entered this house it had taken all her willpower not to leap to her feet and go dashing up and down corridors, like a madwoman, calling his name.

She nodded dismissal to Mrs Watkins and pressed her fingertips to her eyes. Why could Mr Atherton not have simply escorted her back to the White Swan?

If he *were* the antithesis of his cousin, Olivia had not the first idea how to appeal to the instincts of a man who was charming, kind and well meaning and would no doubt be horrified to learn of Olivia's past.

Olivia had learned how to play the devil.

However that was of no account. She would be gone by dinner time. Her mission now was simply to discover what distinguished Max Atherton from his late cousin so she could better craft her next anony-mous entreaty to have her son returned to her care.

Dropping her hands she stared, distracted, at her reflection, then rose gnawing her little fingernail.

What should she do? What *should* she do?

For so long she'd not made a single important decision on her own. Everything had been decided for her from what she did each day to what she wore.

Leaning toward the mirror she studied herself properly. The simple blue gown flattered her light hair and peaches and cream colouring. She looked young and – frowning – she thought, innocent.

Innocent? She gave a mocking smile as the familiar poisonous misery flooded thickly into her veins.

Carefully she smiled again: the kind of smile she'd practised so many times as a seventeen-year-old debutante determined to rise above the rest and waltz off with the season's most eligible catch.

Then she thought of young Julian, her darling baby, and her whole body throbbed with pain and longing. With a sob she covered her face with her hands. Forcing herself to breathe steadily, to slay the demons that mocked her from the darkness, she focused on the task at hand. Max *seemed* as unlike Lucien as it was possible to be. What if his kindness wasn't an act? The interest in his eye when he'd looked at her suggested he—

The flare of excitement she felt was quickly extinguished by self-disgust.

How she hated the effect she had on men. Turning quickly away from the sight of her reflection, she knocked the silver-backed hand mirror to the floor.

She froze. Her breath caught and dread engulfed her as she waited, ears attuned to the sound of approaching footsteps and a possible witness to her crime. Lucien had been violently superstitious. He'd have beaten her if she'd broken a mirror in his house.

She stared at the object at her feet, at its back of figured silver which gave no indication as to whether the glass were shattered. There was no sound of footsteps, but of course it was ridiculous to imagine Mr Atherton or his servants would keep such a vigilant eye upon her. Those days were gone, though it was often hard to believe it.

Slowly she bent. If the mirror were smashed she would leave immediately.

But if it was not …

Heart racing, not knowing what outcome she wanted, she turned the mirror over.

And stared into her unfragmented reflection.

A strange cocktail of emotions flooded her: hope and despair, excitement and terror, but overall a renewal of courage that perhaps this time she could use her charms to find happiness.

Mr Atherton had read her poetry. He had remained at her bedside for nearly an hour earlier in the day, chatting with her as if he enjoyed her company. And all the time she'd had a bandage on her head!

Perhaps she really could entrance Mr Atherton as she had entranced Lucien, and be happy for it. Then she thought of the dangers. Perhaps Mr Atherton's kindness was simply an act, a prelude to the seduction of his unexpected house guest. Lucien would have found such a challenge amusing.

Sickened, she retreated from her simple idea that Mr Atherton's inherent decency was such that he would be so overcome by the emotional reunion between mother and son when he finally produced Julian he'd understand the boy's place was with his mother, with Olivia.

She had no idea what kind of man Mr Atherton was. It was far too early to judge, though she was inclining towards the opinion that he was nothing like Lucien. That he was kind.

She bit her lips and pinched colour into her cheeks, checking her smile one last time. Yes, she looked pretty and ingenuous. There would be no sultry pout and sinuous sashaying as she made her entrance: the kind of entrance she'd used to captivate Lucien. Stupid, ignorant child that she'd been! Mr Atherton wanted a demure, honest young woman, and that's what she'd give him, though in truth she had no idea what she was, anymore.

When her host turned from where he'd been lounging against the mantelpiece and she saw only kindness and concern in those disturbingly familiar eyes she felt even further emboldened.

Admiration was something she'd had enough of to last a lifetime yet this man's was somehow comforting. She need no longer check over her shoulder in case Lucien was silently observing, interpreting the lust he saw in other men's faces as a deliberate lure she'd set for which he'd punish her in private, later.

The genuine pleasure in Mr Atherton's expression caused an unexpected lurch in the space her heart once occupied.

'Amelia's gown becomes you, my dear Mrs Templestowe. It's the colour of your eyes.' He advanced, his hands outstretched as if he'd known her far longer than a few hours. 'No limp?' He looked almost disappointed.

Olivia gave a little shrug and smiled. She strove to sound light-hearted, though her heart thundered. How strange that she should feel such an overt attraction to the type of gentleman she had once derided for being tame and unexciting. Well, anyone had fallen into that category when she had been seventeen, simply because he were not the dangerous and alluring Lucien, Viscount Farquhar whom she must have at all costs. She dropped her eyes, her shyness not an act. 'I must have just bruised it. I'm sorry for disrupting your plans for today, Mr Atherton. You have been very kind but as soon as convenient I will return to the White Swan.'

She saw his disappointment as he led her to the seat closest to the fire, saying, 'It is not often storms around Elmwood result in such charming strays. But look.'

She was still taking in the possibilities as he pointed to the window. He was attracted to her. She should not be so surprised at that. It was not vanity, simply a fact. When she was married to Lucien it was something to be frightened of. As a widow she had grown weary of the desire and derision she received, in equal parts, as if her beauty were somehow a mask for the corruption within. She saw that snow was falling fast in flurries of fat, floating flakes, but all she could think of was Lucien's lies. And how readily people had believed them.

'You can't possibly travel in weather like this, Mrs Templestowe.' Briefly he squeezed her hand before indicating the white, frozen landscape. 'For one thing, you're not dressed for it and, until my sister returns with the carriage, I have no way of conveying you to your lodgings.'

He looked rather pleased at the state of affairs. Nor could Olivia deny she secretly felt the same. Though not in the same, uncomplicated way. Out of the corner of her eye, as she pretended to gaze with dismay upon the thickly falling snow, she realized that acknowledging an attraction to this man would be deeply dangerous.

Impossible, even. She needed to appeal to his obvious kindness, and she believed she could do that. Anything more would end in tears for both of them. She acknowledged the truth with weary resignation. Regardless of the temptations, she could not pander to her heart. Certainly not in *this* instance.

'And here is tea.' On cue the door opened to admit the parlour maid bearing a tray. 'Surely you don't object to a dish of strong hot tea while we wait for Amelia and the boys? They are staying with me while renovations are carried out on their home which is not far from here.'

'The boys?' Olivia knew she'd jumped at the phrase with too much feeling. Her mind had not been in the present. 'There is more than one, Mr Atherton?'

'There are three,' he replied, rolling his eyes with a smile as she settled herself back into her green wing back chair. 'But only one is mine.'

Oh, no, he's not. Somehow, Olivia managed to keep her smile from faltering. 'How old is your little boy?'

'Julian is two-and-a-half. He's been with me the past year since his father, my late cousin Lucien, Lord Farquhar, passed away.'

'The poor child is an orphan?' Anger and mortification threatened to swamp her.

It was small consolation that Max Atherton hedged his reply and obviously took care with his words, as if he were uncomfortable at having to explain the situation further.

'The lad was put into my keeping to avoid contagion when his father succumbed to fever. When Lucien died the following month and the will was read I discovered to my surprise – amazement, really – he'd made me the boy's legal guardian.'

'So his mother also died of fever.' Olivia made it sound a statement. She gave a pitying sigh, masking her anger with an expression of regret, as if it were the only explanation since not even the cruellest husband would exercise his legal rights to deny a mother her child.

'The mother was unfit to rear the next heir to Lord Farquhar's estates.'

Yet not unfit to be Lord Farquhar's wife? A terrible rage blackened her vision. She dropped her gaze, unable to give voice to her real feelings, instead murmuring, 'How terrible. I think perhaps I recall having heard something about Lady Farquhar.'

Max sighed and looked even more uncomfortable as he fiddled with his cufflink. 'Alas for the boy, she was a fortune hunter; a vain, showy creature who trapped Lucien into marriage, ran into debt and led an altogether dishonourable life.'

'Yet she was a mother. I cannot believe she behaved so heartlessly towards her son. Did it surprise you, Mr Atherton?'

'I never met her—'

Olivia relaxed with grim satisfaction only to jerk forward in alarm at his next words.

'—though I saw her at a ball, once, two years after the pair eloped.'

She waited, breathless.

Mr Atherton indicated to her to pour. With shaking hand she lifted the teapot while he elaborated. 'She was with her husband, my cousin Lucien, but Amelia refused to meet her and as I was accompanying her I didn't make it an issue.'

'What did she look like?' Best to get it over and done with, if an unmasking were inevitable.

Max smiled as he accepted his tea and leaned back in the armchair opposite her. 'Beautiful. Like you, Mrs Templestowe.'

She swallowed; opened her mouth to speak but the words would not come.

He seemed not to notice. 'But obviously not a lady, like you, for her gown was ostentatious and' – he shrugged – 'the way she carried herself I could see the truth in the rumours.'

Lucien had decided what she wore. She had given up selecting her gowns herself, merely waiting and wondering in her dressing room whether he wanted her to flaunt herself like a trollop, or deport herself like a nun. With her husband's moods increasingly erratic towards the end, she had learned to accept his last dictate with the meekness of a child.

Still, it took all her willpower not to slump, defeated, into her chair. The fact that the sight of her, albeit from a distance, only strengthened his belief in the rumours was somehow doubly devastating.

Licking her dry lips she whispered, 'So you never sought her out after … after Lord Farquhar gave you her child?'

Max raised one eyebrow. The façade of genial, almost overeager host, slipped. Wearing a look of censure he suddenly resembled Lucien once more, and she clasped her hands together to stop them trembling as he added, 'One would expect she would make contact with *me*.' His voice was clipped, and his nostrils flared, as if he were speaking of someone utterly reprehensible. 'I suppose she did,' he eventually conceded, stirring his tea with a frown. 'But not until a good eight months had elapsed. I heard talk she had been gallivanting across the Continent in bad company until then.' He looked up, apology in his eye. 'I should not have spoken like that, Mrs Templestowe, yet I feel such a great anger on behalf of my ward as well as sorrow that he cannot know his mother.' He shrugged. Then his mood lightened and he smiled as if encouraging her to move on to another topic.

Olivia was not ready to let this one die.

'How would you receive Lady Farquhar if she did contact you and ask for the return of her child?' She tried to keep her tone offhand though her breath came in staccato bursts of anticipation as she waited for his answer.

Her host levelled at her a faintly quizzical look. Deliberating over his choice of words he said, 'I am bound to do whatever is in the best interests of the boy and as Lady Farquhar had taken a lover—'

'Surely not!'

Olivia's gasp of outrage was thankfully misinterpreted by Mr Atherton. 'I fear it is not as uncommon as you might believe, Mrs Templestowe, however discretion is required. It seems Lady Farquhar had neither discretion nor wit. My cousin was not a man to take such a matter lightly.'

On that they were agreed at least, Olivia thought silently as she racked her brains to think who her imaginary lover might have been. But then, Lucien had always imagined conspiracies when there were none.

Fear crept into the deepest recesses of her brain. No! She would not think of it. Lucien could not truly have suspected Julian was not his. Taking a deep breath she quickly dispelled any reflections of what some would consider wrongdoing. If she had ever done wrong, then Lucien's hand was behind it.

She listened to the chink of silver against china as he stirred his tea. His expression was distant. 'When I heard the boy had been made my ward I sold my commission and took up residence on this estate which I hold in trust for Julian until he comes of age.'

Olivia studied his face, searching for more similarities with Lucien. The physical family resemblance was there, particularly in the eyes, the straight nose and firm chin. Now that he was speaking of serious matters the almost self-conscious banter had gone. He was precise and direct and clearly decided on what he considered right and wrong. Very different from Lucien's arrogance.

Amidst the turmoil of her emotions, she felt a flicker of surprise. 'You gave up your career to look after a little boy?'

'I'd seen enough horror on the Peninsular to last a lifetime; was more than ready to leave the soldiering life and resume my agricultural obligations and' – he smiled – 'find a wife who would love this home and, hopefully, find me not too objectionable.' He cleared his throat. 'The boy needs a mother's love.'

Pointing at the plate of seed cake he exhorted her to try some, adding with sigh, 'Whatever Lady Farquhar's sins, her son's a lovely-natured little chap.'

She could not trust herself to speak. Raising her cup to take a sip her hand was trembling so much that tea spilled on to the Wilton carpet.

'My dear Mrs Templestowe, I think you are still in shock from your fall.' Unexpectedly Mr Atherton moved from the mantelpiece to take a seat on the arm of her chair, relieving her of her tea cup and setting it down upon the table.

Surprised and unsure what she should say as his hands gripped her shoulders, her heart quailed at his expression. There was blatant admiration in those slate-grey eyes and, like a traitor, her heart responded, just as it had with such dreadful results when she had cast in her lot with Lucien all those years ago.

But no, she could only be sceptical of such admiration. She was certainly no longer susceptible.

Yet his concern seemed genuine; and in addition to the admiration was something that looked dangerously like tenderness.

Tenderness? To succumb to tenderness would be too rash and much too dangerous. It was a trap!

And yet …

'I've no idea how long you lay in the mud, soaked to the skin.' His voice was like a caress, full of comfort and reassurance. He leaned across her to pull on the embroidered bell pull, seemingly unembarrassed by their proximity. 'I shall have a warm rug fetched for you. Let me feel your hands. Why, they're as cold as ice. I'll rub them for you.'

Olivia closed her eyes and surrendered to those dangerous, unfamiliar feelings: comfort, safety. Exquisite peacefulness.

Mr Atherton held the key to her future happiness: her son. If he admired her and she could *prove* to him she deserved it, surely happiness might follow?

Then insidious reality intruded and she had to steel herself against her despair, her defeat.

She thought of Reverend Kirkman, imagining his outrage if he learned of the venture on which she had so rashly embarked.

It was he who had cautioned patience. Patience, he had exhorted her, was what she needed when once again her impetuous nature threatened her happiness. Patience would be her salvation, he'd soothed her, when she'd leapt up from her chair at the reading of Lucien's will and later, when he'd physically torn her from her carriage, overruling her determination to drive the horses herself in order to reclaim Julian.

Olivia was pliant, her eyes still closed as she heard the maid enter, felt Mr Atherton tuck the blanket around her, making sure her feet were well insulated, bringing the warm wool up around her neck with tender, competent fingers.

'You must be very tired,' she heard him whisper, as he stroked a strand of hair back from her face. 'And still in shock from your accident.'

'Yes,' she murmured, her head falling to one side. Vaguely, she realized it was resting against his thigh as he sat on the arm of her chair. She didn't move it. Didn't want to.

Mr Atherton could get her what she wanted.

Her son … happiness.

If Reverend Kirkman would sanction it. She could be happy. She *could*.

She was in the midst of a dreamless sleep when it happened: the meeting upon which her whole life had been focused for more than a year, the reason she was here.

Jolting awake at the sound of a carriage drawing up before the front door, her ears seemed suddenly acutely sensitive to the crunch of the gravel under what sounded like a dozen little feet, and the joyful chorus of young voices.

Then the drawing-room door was thrown open unceremoniously and three small boys burst into the room.

'Uncle Max! Uncle Max!' they cried, as they leapt upon him.

Olivia opened her eyes. Gripping the side of her chair for support she stared at the three youngsters, all jostling for prime position on their Uncle Max's lap.

Fourteen months. It had been fourteen months since she had last seen Julian. The baby who had been removed from her care when Lucien had fallen ill was now a boisterous and sturdy toddler with a mop of dark curls and a sunny smile. His cousins were both fair-haired, a little older than he, but just as comfortable with their Uncle Max whom they were now pummelling with cushions.

'Boys! Boys!'

The nursery maid clapped her hands for calm. Olivia could only stare. Charlotte, who had accompanied Julian to his new home fourteen months earlier, smiled. She'd been told to expect Olivia but to say nothing. Her pride in her young charge was clear, however the small, thin woman who followed in her wake was less forgiving of the youngsters' unruly behaviour.

'Boys, your manners!' she cried, when she saw Olivia. 'Your uncle

Max has a visitor. And Max, you're no better, the way you encourage them.'

Mr Atherton exhaled on a long-suffering sigh as he stood up to greet his sister. 'Afternoon, Amelia. They make me feel young again and I missed them,' he said, his grin half apologetic. 'And Mrs Templestowe doesn't mind. She likes small boys. At least, you gave me to think you do.'

His laconic smile, as he turned back to her, suddenly became one of concern. 'My dear Mrs Templestowe, are you all right?' He took a couple of quick strides across the room and bent to clasp Olivia's hands.

'Amelia!' He swung round. 'Your vinaigrette, or burnt feathers, or whatever it is you ladies use. Mrs Templestowe had a nasty fall earlier and is still recovering.'

'I'm all right,' Olivia managed, faintly, as Max with great solicitude, patted her arm and eased her back into her chair.

'I'll send the boys away,' he said. 'Boys! We can play as soon as I've ensured our visitor is—'

'No, please! I'd love the boys to stay.' Olivia was aware of the urgency in her voice, which she hoped would be interpreted as politeness, as she struggled upright in her chair. 'Tell me your names, boys, if you please.'

The exuberance had been knocked out of them. Almost sullenly they ranged before her, fidgeting, anxious no doubt to be out of doors and away from this strange lady. Olivia's heart nearly broke.

Julian didn't recognize her. Even when she took his hand to shake it, solemnly, there was no recollection in his eyes. He was as restless as his cousins, turning his bright gaze upon his Uncle Max as if begging to be reprieved and dismissed from the room.

'So, you're Julian,' she repeated, forcing a tremulous smile. 'I'm very pleased to meet you, Julian.'

'Can I go now, Uncle Max?'

Not two minutes in her company and her darling boy couldn't wait to leave. She meant nothing to him.

She closed her eyes, briefly. Why should she? If his Uncle Max thought it, Julian thought it, too. She had abandoned him. Forsaken him. Without a second thought.

A terrible lump formed in her throat. She couldn't swallow past it. She felt the tingling, swelling in her glands as the tears forced their way up and out.

Releasing Julian's hand, she fell back into her chair. She tried to take a breath, choked on it, then shuddered, burying her face in her hands as she let out a strangled wail.

When rational thought returned, the boys had gone. Amelia, whom she'd barely even greeted with the requisite courtesy, was sitting on the sofa opposite her, regarding her over the top of her tea cup.

At least, she could see part of Amelia. The rest of her was obscured by Mr Atherton.

Dear Lord, she was squeezed up against him, her head upon his chest, her face wet with tears. She supposed she must have been sobbing like a mad creature.

He gave a short laugh when he saw her obvious dismay at the state of his coat sleeve.

'No cause for concern. I'm dressed like a country rustic and it's not as if I'm unused to ruined jackets, Mrs Templestowe, being so often in the company of snotty-nosed little boys,' he said, bracingly. He rose, perhaps realizing their closeness no longer appropriate now that her tears had ceased. 'Wonderful! A smile,' he said, his own warm and sympathetic as he gazed down at her. 'Seems as if a good cry was just what the doctor ordered.' He stooped to place a comforting hand on her shoulder, and his eyes met hers, their expression tender and enquiring. 'Would you care to tell me what that was all about?'

'Max!'

'It's not impertinence.' Mr Atherton sounded defensive as he turned to face his sister. 'If Mrs Templestowe is going to start sobbing in my drawing room for no apparent reason, then I believe it's a fair question to ask what might have upset her. You, Amelia, are wearing a most unbecoming bonnet, which is surprising, for you are generally in the first stare. If that is what upset Mrs Templestowe then I would be relieved to know the fault did not lie with me, for I was up before

Frensham was on hand to dress me. Perhaps I've committed some unpardonable crime in the manner in which I've mixed a green and black waistcoat with buff pantaloons. If the fault lies with me, I'd much rather be told.'

'You are entirely blameless, both of you,' protested Olivia with a weak smile, sitting up straight as embarrassment at her emotional outburst washed over her. 'It's just …'

Her words trailed into expectant silence. Stammering, she tried to come up with a plausible reason for her distress. 'Julian.' Her voice became a whisper. 'I lost my baby a year ago. When I saw Julian—'

She couldn't go on. She took another heaving breath, trying with all her might to resist another embarrassing deluge of sobs. Finally she managed a tremulous smile, blushing at being the focus of attention. 'I'm all right now,' she said, waving away Mr Atherton who looked like he was going to enfold her in his bear-like embrace once again. There was nothing like sympathy to bring on a bout of self-pitiful and self-indulgent wailing.

Yet hadn't all her efforts been with this portentous meeting in mind? Success seemed within her grasp.

There was Mr Atherton, the man to whom Lucien had entrusted Julian's future, and who was therefore responsible for Olivia's happiness, looking at her with transparent sympathy and admiration. As if she were the most precious and novel creature ever to have crossed his threshold. She acknowledged the look with a mixture of hope and dread. She was used to men's admiration but it had been a long time since she had courted it. Her beauty was a poisoned chalice. Mr Atherton was kind and decent. If she revealed to him her real identity he would be instantly disgusted. Even if he chose to dismiss the rumours that had blackened her name it wouldn't be long before he discovered the rottenness within. Lucien had tainted her. She knew better than anyone that the beautiful mask she presented to the world concealed a soul that was destined to writhe in the flames of Hell with her late husband.

Hadn't The Reverend Kirkman told her a thousand times?

It only strengthened her quest to regain Julian in this life. At any cost.

'I'll see that Charlotte is preparing the boys for nursery tea,' Amelia excused herself.

'It looks like rain yet again. My sympathies, Mrs Templestowe.' Amelia hesitated in the doorway, looking at Olivia as if she couldn't quite make her out. 'I cannot imagine what it must be to lose a child.'

CHAPTER TWO

I
F OLIVIA HAD been sleeping, the loud crash of thunder and rattling of
the casement would surely have woken her. As Max's new house guest
she had retired to bed two hours ago. The soothing pastoral scene upon
the wall had proved anything but that. In fact, she'd been staring at it
with increasing desperation when the enormous crash rattled the house.
It startled her so much she nearly fell out of bed.

Shivering under the quilt, she wondered if Julian were as afraid of
thunderstorms as she. When he'd been a baby she'd taken him into her
bed where he'd always slept, contented and oblivious to the wildness
without.

Now he seemed barely able to tolerate her. When Charlotte had
brought him down to say good night he'd climbed on to his uncle's lap
and twined his little arms around his neck for a good night kiss before
coming to stand, at Mr Atherton's instruction, dutifully before her.
With downcast eyes he'd parroted: 'Say good night to Mrs
Templestowe' before being released, with obvious relief, skipping off
with Charlotte to join his cousins.

Olivia recalled with pain his tense little smile, just before Charlotte
had led him away to bed. Her brief reunion in the corridor earlier with
Julian's nursemaid had reassured her she did not risk an unmasking for
the moment. Charlotte's joy was not in doubt, just as her loyalty had
never been. But when Charlotte had reassured her that Mr Atherton
was 'the most good natured of masters' Olivia had not been ready to

relinquish her fear that Mr Atherton's disgust at learning the identity of his unexpected visitor would override his supposed kindness.

Another crack of thunder was followed by what sounded like an eerie, distant cry. More than anything, Olivia wished the flash of lightning could bathe the room permanently in light.

What if Julian was lying in his bed, too afraid to find his Charlotte? Perhaps Mr Atherton had demanded that little boys needed to learn courage, and should not be offered comfort.

These, and similar fears, chased themselves around her head until she thought it would burst, until she had no choice but to force her fear into submission.

Rising reluctantly, she pushed her feet into slippers, threw her shawl around her shoulders, lit a taper and crept into the passage. She knew exactly where the boys were sleeping.

What mother would not?

But a tower room would be more exposed to the elements and if, for some reason, Julian had been placed into a bedchamber apart from his cousins, he would be terrified.

Olivia studiously ignored the probability that the boys would almost certainly be together, and that in this household no two year old would be abandoned to face his childish terrors, alone. It was her duty to ensure her little boy was not sobbing with fear.

Swiftly, she glided along several passageways, found the stairs to the tower, and was soon turning the handle of the room most likely to contain Julian.

No sound of sobbing greeted her. She pushed open the door fully and raised her taper high. The picture that greeted her was one of the deepest domestic bliss. All three boys were cuddled together in one large bed, eyes closed, oblivious apparently to the storm raging outside. An adjoining door was open through which Olivia could hear the gentle snoring of the nursery maid.

She stood for a few moments surveying the scene. Or rather, studying the face of her little boy. At least now she could gaze upon it to her heart's content.

Long, dark eyelashes swept his chubby, rosy cheeks. His thumb was in his mouth and he wore a half smile, as if he were dreaming of something pleasant.

Olivia drank in the sight that must sustain her until she was able to claim him for her own ... in three months? Two months? When would she finally be granted the legal right to be a mother again? she wondered with a pang.

It all hinged on Mr Atherton. She felt another pang. A very different one.

If only she had confessed her true identity the moment she'd opened her eyes: Mr Atherton was the most charming, good-natured of men.

Yet when honesty was required her courage had failed her.

She tried to dismiss the fear bound up in her lie. When the right moment came, she would tell him. Soon she would leave Elmwood and Mr Atherton – she felt a pang of regret – and from her home with her aunts she would compose a letter that struck the right note, asking for her rights as a loving mother to be respected.

For so long The Reverend Kirkman had convinced her that his plan to reclaim Julian was the only way.

Now that Olivia had broken free to follow her own instincts and had met Mr Atherton, already she felt the reverend's influence over her diminishing. Mr Atherton was open to reason, and weren't truth and reason the source of success and happiness?

A crack of lightning illuminated the room, the accompanying thunder making Olivia gasp with fear and Julian to stir in his sleep. She heard Charlotte's bed creak.

With her hand on the door knob she prepared to tear herself away, swallowing past the painful lump in her throat as she acknowledged the foundation on which her past and, now her future, were built: deception.

She felt the strong, cold fingers of her reality squeezing the chamber of her heart, moulding her mind. However much she liked Mr Atherton he could only ever be the means of restoring Julian to her. For her lie required more than a simple unmasking of her identity. Revealing the full extent of the truth threatened the future of her son.

*

No amount of thunder and lightning and howling wind could wake Max from a deep sleep.

Ghosts and goblins were another matter. Especially if they caused the floorboards in the passage outside his bedchamber to creak.

Someone was tiptoeing about the house in the middle of the storm, he realized, groggily. The thought that it might be a small boy sleep-walking or seeking comfort caused him to drag himself from the cosy comfort of his bed, draw on his thick silk dressing gown, push on his slippers and softly open his door. He did not want to alarm the little lad.

There was no point in lighting a taper. He now knew this house like the back of his hand, and the glow from his fire reached sufficiently into the passage for him to see clearly enough.

A crack of lightning and roll of thunder was accompanied by a high-pitched squeal of fright not two feet from him, and a taper wavered and nearly went out.

Max found himself staring into the terrified eyes of his new house guest, Mrs Olivia Templestowe.

For a moment he thought it was his sudden entry into her nocturnal path that had nearly frightened the wits out of her. However, when another flash lit up the entire house and the thunder created a din fit to end the world he saw that the young woman's terrors were wholly on account of the storm.

'Let me take that,' he murmured, removing the wavering candle from her grasp. 'What are you doing roaming the house at this time of night? Come, I'll take you back to your room.'

She looked lost and frightened, but her vacant gaze suggested she had not registered his presence.

He put his hand under her elbow and began to guide her in the direction of her chamber when another boom of thunder caused her to shriek again. This time she clung to him, burying her head against his chest.

Placing her taper on a low table, he put his arms around her shoulders and held her lightly. She was just the right height for him to rest his chin on top of the fine linen nightcap that covered her glossy light hair.

For some minutes she trembled while he fought the almost overpowering urge to enfold her in an embrace far more intimate. Her breathing was completely dominated by the storm: regular when it subsided, fast and shallow when the thunder roared and the lightning flashed.

Observing this fascinating phenomenon, Max was disappointed when she suddenly tilted up her head, crying out, 'Mr Atherton!' She looked shocked though she did not step back. 'I thought the boys might be afraid,' she added, dropping her gaze.

'Not nearly as afraid as you, it would appear.' He put his finger beneath her chin to tilt her head up again. They were the most amazing eyes he thought he'd seen: layers of blue disappearing into fathomless depths. And she was the most amazing creature he'd met. He could not make her out, and was looking forward to trying. 'You were very brave to venture out alone.'

'Brave?' she repeated in a whisper. He thought the look she cast him was rueful. 'I only wish I were.'

He realized he still had his arm about her. That she was looking up at him in almost childish entreaty and that she had made no effort to pull away. She was so very lovely. Far lovelier even than he'd imagined she'd be before she washed her face. And she certainly did not recoil from his embrace. He sensed she desired their closeness as much as he.

When she caught her breath at another roll of thunder he relished the chance to hold her tighter. Acknowledging the potential danger of their situation, he released her with a sigh. 'Come, I'll take you back to your room.'

She clung to his hand, resisting as he drew her along with him. Her face looked ashen in the next flash of light.

'Please don't leave me alone,' she whispered, when they reached her bedchamber. 'I am so terrified of storms.'

'It'll pass soon enough,' he soothed. Reluctant though he was to say goodnight, he knew they couldn't remain freezing in the passage much longer. Well, he wasn't freezing; his blood was fairly up just at the sight of her, but he could feel her shivering.

She closed her eyes, took a deep breath as she put her hand on the door knob and asked, 'You'll not lock me in?'

'Lock you in your room?' he repeated, trying to understand her. 'Good God, is that what your parents did?'

She shook her head. 'Not my parents,' she said, leaning against the door as if she were rallying all her fortitude. Another crack of thunder sent her lurching back into his arms and as she fixed him with her extraordinary luminous blue eyes he knew he was undone. That he was as enslaved as any man could be when she begged him in a low voice, 'Please don't leave me alone.'

He needed no more encouragement. Feeling like a fearless conqueror Max scooped her up and strode all the way back to his own room. Easing himself into the large, comfortable armchair by his bed, nicely warmed by the fire, he settled her across his lap. Her head, heavy with exhaustion, settled upon his chest and the staccato breaths soon became regular.

In minutes she was asleep.

CHAPTER THREE

WHERE WAS SHE? Olivia woke with a start as the maid drew the curtains.

The girl bobbed a curtsy. 'Master said as to leave you to sleep. Sorry, miss, but morning tea is in half an hour an' I thought—'

'Is it that late?' Olivia cut her off, jumping out of bed and drawing her borrowed shawl about her shoulders.

How could she have managed to sleep at all? she wondered, as she registered that she was in Mr Atherton's house. Then she remembered where, exactly, she had fallen asleep and her hands flew to her flaming cheeks.

Her heart gave a painful contraction.

'Julian!' she whispered, though her heart threw up a different name.

Being reunited with her son was the reason her heart was behaving so oddly, she told herself, as she quickly washed and dressed. It had nothing to do with the boy's uncle who had merely been kind and done what any host would to allay the fears of a nervous guest.

She banished the memory of his warm embrace. It was too dangerous to relive the exquisite sensation of relinquishing her worries in the arms of a man with honourable intentions. So overwhelming had been the feeling of comfort and safety that she had fallen asleep almost immediately. In his bedchamber. But not before she had succumbed to the comfort of his caress as his long sensitive fingers brushed rhythmically across her cheek, as if she were a precious child.

When had she last felt precious? Or deserved to feel so? she thought, choking back her self disgust. And that, really, was the crux.

With brisk, determined actions, she pulled on her stockings then waited passively while the maid dressed her.

Soon she would see Julian again, and that was all that was important.

But Julian was out walking with his nursemaid and cousins, she was told. The master, added the parlour maid, was in the drawing room, her tone indicating that this was where Olivia should direct her footsteps. Not towards a crowd of unruly little boys.

Arriving at the doorway at the very same moment as Mr Atherton only added to her awkwardness, compounded by his seeming inability to address her coherently. Lord, what must he think of her forwardness last night? she wondered.

'I trust you slept well, Mrs Templestowe,' he began, the colour burning his cheeks as he cast his gaze downwards, stubbed at a mark on the carpet with the toe of his boot and added in a burst of frustration, '*Must* I call you that?'

Dispersing her tension with a small laugh, Olivia replied with a wry smile, 'I think the outrageous manner in which I impinged upon your hospitality last night affords you the right to call me Olivia, if you prefer.'

For a moment their gazes locked, then they both laughed. It cleared the air, Max offering his arm to Olivia to lead her into the room just as Amelia made her entrance.

With the most cursory of greetings for his sister, Mr Atherton's gaze returned to Olivia's face as he took his seat beside her, murmuring, 'Did I tell you, Olivia, that I've made you an appointment to come walking with me after breakfast? There's something I want to ask you.' There was a gentle, teasing note in his voice which made Olivia want to lean towards him and caress his cheek as she entered into the spirit of light-hearted banter.

Instead, she felt dread take root at the look in his eye: a mixture of admiration and affection.

Fatal.

'I think you are a fraud, Olivia, for I can detect no sign of a limp, I'm pleased to note,' he said, casting first his sister, then Olivia, a broad, self-satisfied smile before tucking into a large helping of smoked haddock.

Olivia no longer had an appetite. Oh yes, she was a fraud. But as long as he failed to detect this she and her son had a future together.

Their post-breakfast walk was a gentle stroll around the rose bushes and the matter which Max wished to broach was Olivia's attendance at a house party he was hosting in three days' time.

'Please, will you continue under my roof in the meantime?'

His look was full of entreaty. She tried to resist it, tell herself it was far safer to leave immediately. She couldn't afford to further her acquaintance with Mr Atherton. She had to invent an excuse which precluded it.

But she could think of no suitable objection, other than an objection to the insistent voice of reason in her head.

Quite simply, she wanted to enjoy his company for as long as she could.

When had she last put her head on a pillow – much less a man's chest, God forbid! – and fallen into a sweet and dreamless sleep? When had she last felt so light with happiness at the mere caress or squeeze of a man's hand?

For the moment she ignored the truth of the matter, which was that she had to leave. Soon. Before she was in so deep she was doomed.

'What am I to wear to the ball if I'm not to appear like some little dormouse dragged in by your cat?'

He weighed this up with a frown, turning and clasping both her hands in his. 'Rather, some enchanting little squirrel,' he said, finally. 'At least, that's the impression you gave me when I dragged you out of the mud during the storm. No! That excuse won't wash with me. Amelia can get her girl to come and measure you and work her fingers to the bone so that you may step forth in finery that does your beauty justice.'

'Amelia's poor girl would never oblige your sister again.'

'Do I really look such a tyrant?' He smiled, leading her along a path through the manicured gardens towards the park. 'I value my reputation amongst my staff and the villagers and was merely trying to impress you with my willingness to ensure all your objections are quashed.'

The smile died on his lips as he halted once more, putting his hands on her shoulders to turn her towards him and asking quietly, 'I really would like you to come, Olivia.'

'Well, yes, I— what are you doing?' For suddenly Max's manner had become quite altered, his expression decisive as he caged her hand which had been lying loosely upon his arm, his footsteps purposeful as he marched her to the copse of trees which bordered the formal garden. Olivia had to run to keep up.

'Taking you deep into the shelter of those trees over there so we will not be observed from the house, or spied upon by my sister who has suddenly decided to prune the roses, by the looks of things.'

'Oh,' said Olivia, faintly, as she found herself shielded from the house by the thick trunk of a large elm tree on one side and Max's solid broad chest on the other.

'Oh!' she said again, as his right hand deftly untied the ribbons of her bonnet. Tossing it aside, his lips curved in a confident, appreciative smile as he drew her against him.

'Oh …' It was a final murmur of surrender as she melted into him. She felt her legs give way and her heart seemed to liquefy as his lips brushed hers, his fingers twining in the curls at the nape of her neck.

It was a soft, languorous kiss, too quickly over.

'Lovely Olivia,' he whispered. He held her away from him, observing her with tenderness. She didn't realize she was straining to move back into his embrace until he laughed, cupping her face and bringing his mouth back to hers.

Sighing, Olivia gave herself up to the unexpected, long-missed pleasure of being kissed by a man who knew how to stir her senses.

How many years since she had last felt desire? She'd forgotten how much she enjoyed surrendering to a sensuality over which she had no control, of casting away her inhibitions. His chest felt solid and dependable pressed against hers, his arms strong and safe around her, and he smelt good. Of sandalwood soap and horses.

'Darling Olivia,' he murmured, kissing her gently once more for good measure. 'You have a most extraordinary effect on me.' He shook his head as if to clear it.

'Mmm.' Olivia smiled and bit her lip, making no move to pull away. She was disappointed when he released her with a sigh so as to retrieve her discarded bonnet, but she laughed as he fumbled with the ribbons he tried tying beneath her chin.

'All thumbs,' she said, as once again he tucked her hand into the crook of his arm and stood looking down at her with a proprietary air. 'I suppose you're too much the soldier.'

'With a longing for the comforts of hearth and home. My soldiering days are well and truly past.'

She felt a chill and knew the time was nearly upon her that she must leave before she revealed too much of what she truly felt.

However his tone was light as he added, 'Though I daresay one can never quite escape one's past, can one?'

'I daresay one can't,' Olivia said softly, as she matched her footsteps to his, her pleasure in the moment gone.

The pine needles were soft and slippery underfoot and once Olivia fell against him. The sloping snow-dusted lawn, now in full sunlight, lay just ahead of them.

Max turned and again took Olivia by the shoulders, his expression pleading. 'Please say you'll stay for my very grand entertainment?'

Longing gripped her, despite her foreboding. For the first time in months she'd had thoughts other than Julian. She'd fallen asleep in this man's arms, revelling in the warmth of his embrace as much as the happy knowledge that her son lay sleeping nearby.

And now, once again, she'd surrendered to her instincts rather than reason and allowed her weak, fallible body to enjoy the pleasure of the moment with no thought for the consequences.

When would she learn?

But what could she say? When he was looking at her in a way that made her heart feel near to bursting with happiness and she wanted to hurl herself into his arms and beg him to kiss her again?

She gave a half smile and nodded, expecting to receive one of his open, easy smiles. It was a cruel burden to know that she would soon disappoint him.

Instead of the boyish laugh she'd expected, his expression was grave.

'Good.' He took a deep breath. His eyes glowed and, as she waited for his next words, she felt the warmth of his admiration, ignoring the knowledge, buried for now, that happiness was, as ever, out of reach. For how could she not want to hear the words that conveyed how she had altered his world in just a few short hours when it merely echoed what was in her own heart?

'I believe you've bewitched me, Olivia.'

She was silent. She had no response. Tying the ribbons beneath her chin more securely, touching the key that hung round her neck – Lucien's key; the key which had driven him mad in its failure to yield him what he wanted – she continued towards the house.

'Olivia?' His voice was full of concern. He put his hand on her arm to detain her. 'What is it, Olivia? What have I said?'

'It's nothing, a megrim,' she managed faintly, pushing on. Not the truth. That what he had said were the very words Lucien had used to accuse and condemn her?

Of course he would not have let her go and she would have been lying if she'd pretended she wanted him to.

'I've frightened you,' he said, coming to stand before her, not touching her. 'I've rushed headlong, following my heart, thinking only of myself, without even the delicacy to enquire after your bereavement, the true state of your feelings.'

'You've done nothing I haven't welcomed,' Olivia soothed, reaching up to touch his cheek. 'I lost my husband a little over a year ago and it was a blessed relief.' She wondered if he'd recoil; it would be easier if he did.

Yet she could not deny she welcomed his touch when he gripped her arms tightly, his expression full of sympathetic understanding as she added, 'He was a cruel man and I was not sorry when fever took him.'

She nestled her head against his chest when he drew her against him. She would stay there forever, if he'd let her.

When he raised her head with a gentle finger beneath her chin, they were facing the great house in the distance.

'I wish I could offer you all this.' His sweeping gesture took in the sun-kissed landscape, the handsome grey stone house with its battlements harking back to a much earlier age, its later additions making it a home rather than a fortress. 'But it is better to be frank. I only hold it in trust for my ward. When Julian is of age I shall return to my own estate.' He added, softly, 'I'm afraid my own home is a good deal more humble. Nevertheless, it is not the bricks and mortar that gladdens the heart but rather what dwells within.'

Resting his chin lightly on the top of Olivia's head as he held her to him he did not see the spasm of realization that shocked her to her very foundations. Did not register the strain in her voice as she ground out, 'I hope you do not resent the efforts you will expend on the boy's behalf, only to be turned out when he turns twenty one. I must tell you' – it was hard to say the words, looking upon all this that was once her husband's and that she might have held, herself, in trust for her son had Lucien not changed his will – 'I come with nothing, Mr Atherton.'

'What a fine match,' he said, swinging her back into the circle of his arm, his easy smile banishing his former sobriety. 'I was hoping I could not be accused of fortune-hunting. However, I was trying only to weasel from you your feelings, not what you had to offer. Promise you'll stay?' He kissed her lightly on the tip of her nose.

Her feelings. She wanted to wither in his arms with longing before she expired from shame; she wanted to scream at the injustice. Instead, she tried to swallow past the bitterness as she spoke the truth. 'My feelings? That you are the kindest man I've ever met.'

And the lie she was forced to utter. 'Of course I'll stay.'

With an effort she curved her lips into a smile as she gazed upon his strong features, his warm open expression. She wanted to commit them to memory.

For how could she see him again when the child she presented to the world as Lucien's heir denied the man she loved his rightful inheritance?"

*

'Is it to be the vermilion silk or the Pomona green?' With a decisive snip, another dead-headed rose dropped into Amelia's basket.

Had Olivia known Amelia was on her knees behind the rose arbour she would have chosen another route back to the house.

Max's sister had not gone out of her way to be friendly. Olivia suspected she considered her a brazen fortune-hunter and, indeed, she could understand Amelia's concern at her charming, good-natured younger brother making no secret of his susceptibility to Olivia's charms.

As Olivia hesitated over her answer, Amelia smiled suddenly. 'Try them both and we'll choose, if you like.' Rising stiffly, she added, 'I'll come to your room directly after luncheon. I don't know if Max told you we're expecting guests for tea.' Taking Olivia's arm she began to walk with her to the house. 'Miss Hepworth and her mother are visiting us from Bath.' She glanced at the sky. 'I hope we shan't have more snow. It's two hours when the roads are good and Miss Hepworth is an indifferent traveller.'

Olivia managed a sweet, responsive smile. Amelia was warning her off; telling her Max had another contender for his affections. Not that it mattered, she tried to convince herself, as Amelia led her away. She had no claim to Max's affections and never would have. But this new knowledge had come to her so recently and with such startling clarity that the pain was almost too acute to bear. She wished only she could find her way to her room and cry out her anguish in peace.

Stopping to rearrange a dead rose that was in danger of falling from her cane basket, Amelia said blithely, 'Miss Hepworth is a sweet girl.' There was the tiniest pause. 'With a nature that has not been spoiled by her fortune. I believe Max will see the wisdom of such a match.' The smile she slanted at Olivia was guileless.

But then, women such as this, Olivia thought bitterly as she concentrated on the toes of her boots as they walked towards the house, were always bursting with the stuff when they appeared at their most innocent. The man who had all but told her he loved her had been on the verge of committing himself to another when she had entered his life.

Another who was far richer and undoubtedly more worthy.

'I believe Max told you a little about how he came to have wardship over his cousin's son.'

Olivia was not surprised at the conversational tone. Max's sister was reinforcing her opposition using the subtlest of means.

Without waiting for a reply, Amelia went on, 'Max and his cousin, Lucien, were the sons of twin brothers. Or perhaps he's already told you the sad story?'

Still, Olivia did not answer. Of course she knew, but hearing it from Amelia highlighted the fact that she was acting a charade, being given information as a stranger would. Information calculated to highlight her point: despite her guilt, indignation flowered as Amelia expanded her theme.

'It's not just on Max's personal account that it was a tragedy Lucien's father was the twin born ten minutes earlier' – Amelia made no secret of her bitterness, now – 'since he was destined to become the gamester of the family.'

Olivia's throat grew dry. She understood the direction Amelia's veiled warning was taking, couched as it was in predictable homily: the desperate struggle of a once-great family to survive its past.

With unfocused gaze she stared ahead as they continued towards the house. She could not look Amelia in the eye just as she knew she could never look Max in the eye again.

Acid burned her throat. He might forgive her the one deception: but not the other.

If she could keep her tears at bay just two more minutes, she thought, increasing her pace. Lord, she'd become well practised at holding them back when Lucien had been alive.

Max was the innocent, in every way. He would never know how he had been cheated and she could never tell him. Not when it risked the future of her child.

'Like father, like son, Lucien followed his own father's dissolute ways just as Max, even-tempered and charming, favoured our father.'

Stopping at the base of shallow stone steps that led to the portico she fixed Olivia with her clear, level gaze.

'Now, of course, Julian will inherit Lucien's estates. With Max's guidance we hope he might resist the temptations which were the ruin of his father and grandfather. His father's weakness was gambling, his grandfather's was useless causes.' She gave a bitter laugh, adding, 'Thank God the estate was entailed so neither Lucien nor his grandfather could gamble *that* away. Our grandfather sold everything of value he could lay his hands on to raise funds for the failed Jacobite uprising of 1745. Now Max struggles to maintain Elmwood' – With a sweep of her arm she indicated the house and beautifully manicured gardens, the fields falling away on all sides – 'while he leases out his own much more humble estate. He needs to make a good match.'

She nodded at Olivia, her smile warm again. 'I will be up later to help you select your gown. You would look just as well in either colour. Certainly Max will think so. Your unexpected arrival has been a lovely diversion and I hope we shall be friends. Now, please excuse me, I must speak to Cook.'

She didn't even wait to see how her words registered with Olivia, slipping the basket over her other arm before running lightly up the stairs and through the doors which opened on cue.

Struggling to recover her composure Olivia turned back to the garden. She swept her eyes across the beautifully kept lawns, her vision blurring as she thought of that night a little over two years ago when Lucien had been away hunting and of the terrible storm during which her baby had been delivered.

Dear God, why had she not considered the implications of her actions before she came here? Before she met Max?

'Ma'am?' The housemaid's voice issued down to her. Olivia turned to see that she continued to hold the door open, her expression enquiring.

She dropped her eyes, mumbling, 'I must have lost my handkerchief during my walk.'

Retracing her footsteps she returned to the bench by the rose arbour. Some minutes later Charlotte appeared at the foot of the hill, taking a seat beneath a poplar tree while the boys played nearby with Max's King Charles Spaniel, Pansy.

Julian was trying to knot its ears upon its head but it kept rolling over before scampering in circles around the children.

Olivia stared. It was hard to breathe as she watched his innocent play. He was such a delightful child: dark, like Lucien, but even-tempered, sunny-natured.

How she longed to have him back, to be his mother once more, and how it tore at her heart to know he would not thank her for wrenching him from his happy home. She could see he thrived.

She blew her nose loudly, remembering the way the boys had laughed and shrieked with delight as Max had played with them yesterday.

She did not see Max until he was nearly upon her.

'Olivia?' He seated himself beside her.

She kept her head averted though she did not remove her hand when he took it and rested it on the seat between them. She needed to enjoy his touch a little longer.

There was a pause before he said, 'Amelia told you about our guest this afternoon.' It was a statement, not a question.

She nodded. Rather than try to exonerate himself he said, 'I was looking forward to her visit ... until you came along. You have rather complicated matters.' He gave a rueful laugh, adding hastily, 'I mean only to the extent that it would have been more fortuitous if I'd met you before Amelia made preparations for Miss Hepworth's house visit. She returns in a few days for the ball.'

'Amelia intimated you've already fixed your interest with the young lady.' Olivia stared dully ahead, her hand limp in his, her heart like a stone in her chest. 'That she comes with a fortune to match her pretty face.'

It did not seem out of place discussing the matter in such bald terms. She and Max had come a long way in a very short time yet she knew Max's defence made no difference. She had no choice but to leave.

He spoke carefully. 'It is true I paid her particular attention during the week we were in Bath together. Miss Hepworth's mother is ambitious for a match between us and Miss Hepworth, herself, appears not to be averse.' Though Max's voice was matter-of-fact his expression was worried as he looked at her. He added, 'I have never spent any time … alone … with Miss Hepworth.'

Olivia felt the heat rise in her cheeks as she brought her head around to face him. 'Do you think I am a fortune-hunter?'

His laugh seemed to drain the tension from him. To her surprise he hugged her against his side. 'If that were the case you would have chosen your target more carefully.'

'Elmwood is a very beautiful property.'

'My pride and joy, though, as I have told you, a property I only hold in trust.' He brought his face close to hers. 'But I bear no resentment at having one day to return to my own lands.' His grip on her hands tightened. 'I have thought a great deal lately about finding a wife whose sentiments were in harmony with my own. One who loves Elmwood but who is not so attached she would not be equally content with my smaller, humbler domain.' He chewed his lip. 'Or a small, humble farmer whose ambition is simply to breed the best wool in the county.'

Olivia couldn't let him go on. Not in this direction when her own desires followed his but her guilt tore her asunder. She longed for a quiet life. She yearned for a kind, uncomplicated husband who would love her without making excessive demands, and love her son.

Gently, she withdrew her hand. 'Amelia tells me your cousin gambled away much of the family fortune and that you need to make a good match to maintain Elmwood, much less your own estate.'

The words tasted like ashes yet she had to draw from Max his feelings on the subject.

Reclaiming her hand, he stroked her palm with his thumb. 'I know nothing about you or your past, Olivia.' He looked suddenly boyish, almost shy. 'I just find you utterly enchanting. If you are about to tell me you learned since nuncheon that you're about to come into a large fortune, there's no denying I'd be delighted, for you do realize that I wish to court you.' He brought her hand up to his lips. 'The fact that you bring nothing signifies nothing.'

Olivia tugged her hand away. Rising, she looked down at Max. 'Please, don't—'

'Adrian's a bear and I'm a rabbit—'

Careering up the lawn with his cousins in hot pursuit, Julian threw himself at Max's feet.

Max held Olivia's look, then laughing, rose and scooped her son up into the air just as Adrian arrived, roaring at his cousin's heels.

'We will talk about this later, Olivia.' Max reached down to give her shoulder a quick squeeze. The tenderness in his expression made her heart somersault. Lowering his head to her ear while his nephew squirmed under his arm, he said, softly, 'If you have nothing, Olivia, it stands to reason you need someone to look after you. Might I dare hope you could come to care for me? That you would, at least, permit me to pay you my addresses?'

Slowly, against her best intentions, Olivia nodded. She had always acted upon instinct but how could she tell him the truth? That she would soon be far away and had no intention of receiving his addresses.

The sweetness in his expression made her heart contract until Adrian lunged, tackling his obliging uncle to the ground.

Reaching down to stroke Julian's curls, Olivia feasted her eyes on him and Max for one long, last look before she turned and walked back to the house.

She was unprepared for the loud and urgent knocking on her bedchamber door before it was thrust open to admit Max. Leaping up from her seat at the dressing table her hand went to her throat.

She had never seen him look like this. For a moment he reminded her of Lucien and she shrank back against the edge of the walnut-inlaid table.

'Is it true?' His voice was harsh. He strode across the Chinese carpet and gripped her shoulders. The action was forceful, but the surprisingly gentle caress of his hand across her cheek made her close her eyes and lean into him. She felt the steady race of his heartbeat, heard the suppressed emotion in his voice as he rasped, 'Amelia says you're leaving. Why?'

Olivia winced, stepping back and turning her head so he could not see her own pain and guilt.

'You know why,' she whispered. Trying to inject lightness into her tone as she toyed with the silver-backed hairbrush lying on the dressing table, she asked, 'Did you enjoy your afternoon?'

Olivia had not been present for the tea party. She had pleaded a megrim.

'Miss Hepworth has returned to her home under no illusions as to how matters stand between us.'

When she did not reply he turned back from his contemplation of the garden. 'I am not on the look-out for a fortune.' Closing the distance between them he cupped her cheek and his voice was gentle. 'It's you I want.'

She did not move, though she had to steel herself against the tumultuous beating of her heart and the overwhelming urge to raise her face to be kissed.

Exhaling on a sob, she whispered, 'With the right wife you could achieve all your dreams, Max.' She had not meant to but need was making her act against her better judgement. Her hand reached up to twine behind his neck. Closing her eyes she ran her fingers over the rough short hair there. It was torture, knowing this would be the last time, but she could not help herself. 'You have ambitions, you need to make Elmwood prosper. Your agricultural experiments require money. None of that is possible unless you marry well. I am not a good match. I struggle to get by, living in the small cottage my husband left me, and my aunts' charity.'

She willed him to understand, and to let her go. 'I have nothing to offer you, Max. When the first flush of euphoria fades you'll quickly resent me.'

'So much for your opinion of my constancy,' he remarked, wryly. With a sigh, he strode towards the window. Leaning against the sill he twisted his neck to look at her. His eyes were dark with longing. Olivia nearly wept. His feelings accorded so well with hers yet was it not the truth that Max would positively despise her if he ever discovered how she had blighted his life, his prospects? Without even realizing it, she had nipped in the bud every ambition he might ever have harboured.

'These things will not bring me the happiness you would, Olivia,' he said simply. When she did not reply he added, frankly, 'We've only just met but I've never felt like this.' He straightened and his hand went to his heart. 'Can you truly deny what's here? I can't, and I won't let you either, unless you tell me right now I am nothing to you. I've never met a woman who makes me feel I can do anything, achieve anything; who makes me feel so alive. I felt it from the start. I knew you were the one for me even before you'd even washed the mud off your face.'

Her laugh was cut short by a sob.

'I ... I feel it too, Max, but I also know my fears are not as groundless as you believe. You've never asked about my late husband.' She took a deep breath. At least here was an opportunity to admit part of the truth.

Max said nothing but his look was of patient enquiry. How different from Lucien whose frustration would only escalate into anger.

Carefully, she put down the brush. 'We committed a terrible sin for which he never forgave me.' Yes, her words were registering. His brow was furrowed ... but there was no condemnation. She felt a jolt. He looked as if he had already absolved her; as if he could never believe her capable of anything worse than a schoolgirl's misdemeanour. How unlike Lucien. For a moment she contemplated telling him what really stood between them.

Then she thought of The Rev'd Kirkman and her resolve faltered.

Reverend Kirkman, Lucien's long time confessor, Olivia's advocate. The man to whom she owed so much.

He knew too much, too.

And he wanted Olivia. She swallowed painfully ... for his wife.

She brushed away a tear. The flame that burned so brightly between her and Max was doomed to flicker and die. At least her part truth now would give her an opportunity to leave with dignity.

'He was within days of marrying an earl's daughter. Her dowry was substantial but then ... passion banished reason and he eloped ... with me.' Olivia closed her eyes and drew in a rasping breath.

When she opened them again, Max's look of disdain reminded her so much of Lucien she covered her face with her hands. Except that

Max was looking as if her explanation for denying their love was as waterproof as a leaky sieve.

'So your future husband blamed you for the fact *he* persuaded you to elope.' He gave a short laugh. 'Is *that* why you think there can be nothing between us?'

'There's more,' she whispered.

If only this were the worst of it. If only she had a clean conscience. It was torture standing here before a man worthy of any woman's affections. Eight years on she could finally trust her feelings, but it was too late. She'd sealed her fate when she'd thrown in her lot with Lucien.

She hung her head as she continued, 'I had no dowry. Nothing to bring to the marriage. I was an orphan, my father drank himself to death and my mother died when I was very young, leaving her two older sisters to bring me up. I realized, early, that my beauty would have to count for everything.

'I was seventeen and, despite my poverty, proud and vain. I enticed my husband with everything I had – except the one thing he really wanted: my virtue. When I wouldn't give him that he married me and, fool that I was, I thought I had won him.'

Desperately she wanted to feel Max's arms around her, in forgiveness, absolution. But she also knew that was too dangerous. Not when she knew she had to give him up.

Max's voice made her raise her head. 'And he spent the next seven years making your life a misery because his brief lust overcame financial considerations. And as I obviously resemble your late husband you clearly think that if you accede to my wants I, too, will spend the rest of my days punishing you when Elmwood needs repairs, or I find myself without the funds to snap up the local borough in order to satisfy my political ambitions.'

Though he managed to inject a touch of humour into his tone, the edge of indignation made Olivia squirm.

Turning towards the looking glass she covered her face with her hands and whispered, 'Let me go, Max. At least for long enough to prove this is no youthful infatuation.'

He was at her side in an instant, pulling her against him in a fierce embrace. Olivia shuddered at the hard strength of him. Lucien, too, had once had a body of steel.

But there had been no kindness in *his* heart.

'Go, then,' he said, cupping her chin and forcing her to look at him, 'since it's so important you prove to yourself you're no seductive siren enticing me against my better judgement. But promise to return to Elmwood in a month. I already know that my determination to make you my wife will not have changed.'

Her head reeled and she sagged against him.

He had let her go. With dignity.

Yet he truly had wanted her for his wife. She nearly wept at the irony.

'Thank you, Max,' she whispered, relief making her light-headed.

He held her upright, his hands straying over her body, stroking her back, twining in her hair.

'There's just one thing more,' she whispered. Her mouth was dry. It was pure stupidity yet she couldn't help herself: she had always been a slave to her body. 'Kiss me.'

CHAPTER FOUR

'You have been punished enough, Olivia.'

With characteristic precision The Rev'd Kirkman replaced the fine, bone-china tea cup upon its saucer. Mesmerized, Olivia watched as he rearranged it until the handle was at perfect right angles to himself.

Then he looked at her, smiling. Expectant. He knew she was well aware of what this portentous meeting was intended to produce.

Aunt Catherine knew, too, and had been an eager conspirator, ensuring his favourite cake presided over the beautifully set table in the summerhouse. She'd fussed over Olivia like a mother hen that morning, producing what she considered the most appropriate gown for receiving a man who, nevertheless, had been a constant visitor for the past year.

The reverend leaned back, his gaze raking Olivia's dark-blue gown with its high-necked lace collar and demure cut. He nodded, approvingly. 'I had wondered what you might choose to replace mourning clothes.'

Olivia felt her face burn. 'You surely could not suppose I'd wear anything from' – she lowered her gaze – 'before.' He knew she had little enough money to keep up with current trends.

'Those days are behind you, Olivia.' He spoke briskly. 'Today marks a new chapter. Having made a careful study of Mr Atherton's character, I want to tell you that I have composed a letter that will, I trust, find its mark. Mr Atherton is a man of high moral integrity. He served with great distinction on the Peninsula and has lived an exemplary life since returning to manage Lucien's estates. Lucien's low way of life, I've heard tell, caused him great disgust, although I believe at one time the cousins were often together in Town.'

He was paving the way towards his proposal as Olivia had imagined he would, yet direct mention of Max, especially his upstanding character, made her wince. Mistaking the source of her longing, her despair, he said, 'You will, of course, recall the terms in which Lucien couched his wishes with regard to Julian.'

How could she forget? Julian was to remain under the guardianship of his uncle until Lady Farquhar could convince Max Atherton she was ready to acquiesce to a rigorous code of moral conduct devised by a husband of exemplary moral character. A pillar of the church who would wash away her sins.

He gave her a few moments. To squirm? Or as final reflection that Nathaniel Kirkman was just that man?

'My dear.' He extended his hand across the table and obediently she placed hers within it. 'The time has come to put an end to your suffering. You know I can return Julian to you, and you know, also, that the strength of my feelings overcomes any aversion to your' – he drew out the pause – 'shame.'

Olivia closed her eyes and shuddered. To what was he referring? The countless humiliations to which Lucien had subjected her, or…? Her throat went dry as she forced her brain to revisit the past. Not for the first time doubt tormented her. Could he suspect, or even know, the truth of Julian's parentage?

As she opened her eyes to face his familiar, inscrutable gaze she realized how important it was to find out. Then the familiar anguish dragged at her soul. What did it matter? Unless she were prepared to publicly declare her child a bastard there could be no future with Max.

'Trust me with your future, Olivia.' His smile over the top of his china cup was sympathetic; as if he understood her suffering and was offering himself to her as a great gift to lessen her mortal trials. 'Marry me, and I will reunite you with Julian.'

Julian.

Julian, not Max, was the cornerstone of her life. Reclaiming her darling baby was all that mattered and only Nathaniel Kirkman could gain him for her, for she had not the courage to travel an alternate path. Nathaniel's will was too powerful. He handed her his lawn, lace-edged handkerchief. She had not known she was crying; and again he mistook its cause.

'Under my tutelage you shall learn to subjugate your wanton impulses. Through me you shall tread a Godly path and find comfort.' His voice grew honeyed. 'I have the power to bring you true happiness, Olivia' – he waited for her to compose herself, for his words to sink in – 'through your son and humility of spirit. Now my dear, you have not answered me. I have the letter here. Am I to have it delivered to Mr Atherton?'

Olivia gave another sob.

An image of dark, curly-headed little Julian ought to have inspired her to respond in the affirmative. Instead, memories of Max's warm smile and his gentle touch blinded her to reason. His kisses had ignited a need she thought she'd conquered. She covered her eyes and tried to banish his image.

A fortnight, it had been. Two painful weeks since she had left him, and not an hour had passed without her yearning for him, yet she had spent barely two days in his company.

She felt Nathaniel's hand on her shoulder. She thought he might stroke her hair, or otherwise insinuate his touch upon her, but, as ever, he was the model of restraint and propriety.

He indicated for her to pour him another cup of tea. When he spoke again his tone was intimate, collaborative. 'Only you and I know *all* the terrible things you have done in Lucien's name, but there are enough who have been a party to those events which have tarnished your reputation; some would say, forever. I, however, believe you can be redeemed. And I believe it is God's will that I try.'

Another nail in the coffin which housed her hopes and dreams. Max had risked his life for king and country. Honour and valour distinguished him. He could never understand, much less condone, the things Olivia had been forced to do, the wicked, terrible things to which Nathaniel referred.

Still, she could not bend her will to Nathaniel's so easily. Her stubborn spirit which had been the undoing of her in the first place finally came to the fore.

'Your offer does me great honour, Reverend Kirkman,' she said, drying her eyes as she banished her emotion. With dignified calm she gazed at the man who would be her husband; a man to whom she owed a great deal and who had eased some of the pain of her marriage, but whom she had no wish to marry. 'Pray, allow me a day in which to consider it.'

He appeared unfazed and relief washed over her. She hadn't known how Nathaniel would react if she'd thwarted him. 'A very proper request, my dear.' He drained his tea cup, pushed back his chair and rose. Bowing, he said, 'I shall return tomorrow afternoon to receive your answer.'

She found her aunts waiting in the parlour like a couple of impatient schoolroom misses. They greeted her from the window embrasure which afforded an uninterrupted view of the summerhouse.

'Did he ask you, Olivia?' Aunt Catherine looked just like a little pea hen, the fluffy grey hair beneath her lace cap matching her dove-grey gown. Her kind, twinkling blue eyes were full of excited expectation.

'Did you accept?' Aunt Eunice's voice cracked like a whip, her interest completely counter to her sister's.

'Come now, Eunice, why won't you admit that marriage to the reverend is the best future Olivia could hope for?' Catherine appealed to her taller, more formidable sister.

'I said I'd give him his answer tomorrow.' Olivia sank into the chair beside the window and picked up the book lying there, as if her recent assignation was of little account.

'You will, of course, accept, dearest.' Aunt Catherine lay her mittened hand upon Olivia's shoulder briefly, before taking a seat on the sofa, opposite. Her myopic blue eyes blinked rapidly. 'He is quite set upon it, you know.'

'Should Olivia's feelings not take precedence?' Aunt Eunice's tone was dry, as she took a seat beside her sister. 'Let the girl alone,

Catherine, and stop trying to force a match if Olivia's feelings are not in accord with the reverend's.'

'Marriage to Mr Kirkman will enable Olivia to be reunited with Julian,' Aunt Catherine argued. 'He is guaranteed success. As a Godly, pious man he has the character required.'

'I'm hardly likely to do better. Certainly not in my current situation.' Olivia put down the book and sighed. The lines of worry etched on her aunts' faces reinforced the pain she had caused them.

She was no longer an impulsive child. It was time to act as an adult, and in everyone's best interests.

If she could only tame her spirit to obey.

Aunt Eunice sounded gloomy. 'Far better to remain alone, Olivia, than subjugate yourself to a man who makes your repentance and submission his mission.'

'Sister!'

'I've considered that.' Olivia cut through Aunt Catherine's predictable admonition. 'Yet if I cannot get Julian back any other way—'

'Mr Kirkman is not the only Godly, pious man on the planet. Have patience, Olivia.' There was an edge to Aunt Eunice's voice. 'Can't you wait until your heart is in accord with one of the many men who fit this broad description? Max Atherton is not the fiend his cousin was. You said so yourself. He'd surely grant you the latitude to find a man you preferred, even one whose Godliness fell a little short of the reverend's.'

'And what else do you know of Max Atherton, Olivia?' Aunt Catherine asked. 'You spent two days with him and his sister. Can you imagine how anxious we were, despite the assurances you wrote us?'

Olivia shrugged. It was too painful to dwell on Max and all that might have been had circumstances been different. 'Men of integrity,' she said, 'tend not to find women like me to their taste, Aunt Eunice. I fear that Mr Atherton will need to be doubly satisfied that my husband is a Godly reformer.' She gave a bitter laugh. 'Mr Kirkman undoubtedly fits that description.'

'Good Lord, Olivia, that is not reason enough to marry him.' Aunt

Eunice scowled. 'You talk as if you were so sunk in vice no decent man would have you in the same room with their wives.'

'They wouldn't.'

'But if they knew the truth—'

Olivia stopped her Aunt Catherine from continuing. 'Who is going to tell them?' She swallowed, the old bitterness banishing her blitheness. 'Who, in the world, is going to champion me?'

'Well, somebody should! Mr Atherton should, though it sounds as if your appeal fell on deaf ears. Your reputation has been tarnished by nothing but rumours.' Aunt Eunice tried to sound dismissive, but Olivia heard the defensiveness in her tone. She suddenly felt very protective.

'Aunt Eunice,' she said, gently, 'you know as well as I that the moment I'm introduced to anyone remotely respectable they won't see me as Lady Farquhar.' She shuddered as she recalled the shame Lucien had heaped upon her when he'd made her perform at his debauched gatherings. 'They will think only of Lady Farquhar's Butterfly.' She had started her speech defiantly. Now her voice dropped away. 'What man is brave enough to get beyond that stumbling block? I shall answer the reverend's question in the affirmative tomorrow. There can be no other way.'

CHAPTER FIVE

'MAX, YOU PROMISED you would accompany us to church this morning.' Amelia looked cross as she marshalled her boys, and her husband, into an orderly line before the front door. 'You'll be late! Why, you are still dressed for riding!'

Max hesitated at the top of the sweeping marble staircase and looked down at his sister in the hallway below. Jonathon, Amelia's long-suffering husband, raised his sandy eyebrows heavenward as if mentally and physically preparing himself for another spat between the siblings.

'Sorry, Amelia,' Max responded, carefully, 'but I am not prepared to be seen out with you dressed like that.'

Jonathon and Amelia swept their eyes over her cornflower-blue gown, topped on this chilly spring morning, with a smart white spencer. Jonathon looked startled, Amelia indignant. The two little boys giggled, scuffing their shoes on the marble flagstones.

It was the gown Amelia had lent Olivia.

Max descended a couple of steps and Amelia snapped as realization dawned. 'She was a little trollop trying to insinuate herself into your affections, Max. She thought you would make her gifts of more than simply my gown. Hasn't her continued silence made that clear enough? Though why you felt it necessary to break off your understanding with Miss Hepworth I don't know! She was the ideal consort.'

'She was very pleasing,' Max agreed. 'Ah, Frensham, I wondered where you'd got to with my valise.'

'You are surely not accompanying Julian to his new home?' Amelia stamped her foot. 'You agreed it would be kinder not to.' She closed her eyes as if marshalling patience. When she spoke again her tone was gentler. 'Your investigations regarding The Reverend Kirkman's character and your meeting with him satisfy Lucien's idea of an acceptable husband for that scandalous wife of his – you knew you'd have to return the boy, sometime.'

Jonathon cleared his throat. Max waited patiently, watching his brother-in-law's breath mist in the cold air, the profile of his weak chin thrown into relief as the sunlight slanted through a high window and pooled across the flagstones.

'Max,' he said, 'I know it's hard, but it'll be harder on you both if you do your leave-taking under the noses of Julian's mother and her betrothed.'

It was true. He'd thought it himself. 'I know it,' Max agreed, his shoulders slumping as he came down the stairs, 'but the lad hasn't stopped crying since he woke at dawn this morning.'

'Perhaps Charlotte will take his mind off his troubles better than you will, Max.' Jonathon clapped him on the shoulder as he drew level. 'Say your farewells here, as you'd planned. Pretend you're merely sending him off on a grand adventure and that you'll be seeing him again shortly.'

Max shook his head. 'Funny,' he reflected, 'I had no idea what to do with the boy when Lucien saddled me with him.' He swallowed past the lump in his throat. 'Now I've no idea what I'll do without him. Lord knows what I'm sending him to. I do at least owe him that! To find out, I mean. After all, Lady Farquhar was indisposed the day I met Kirkman. What do I know of Julian's mother? Considering the stories, it'd be negligent if I did not satisfy myself as to *her* character.' He looked appealingly at Jonathan and his sister who had just directed one of the servants to take their boys to church ahead of them.

'I'd share your misgivings if you were returning him to his mother's care, alone. But, Max' – Amelia's voice had lost its sympathetic edge – 'you've established that Mr Kirkman is a pillar of the church, a fine upstanding citizen who will lead by example. He has made it his mission to redeem this wretched woman. Come along, Max!' she urged. 'You're worse than a clucky mother hen. It'll take you five minutes to change your clothes and we can still make it to church in good time.'

'I hope you've made no promises to the boy's nursemaid.' Nathaniel tucked Olivia's hand into the crook of his elbow as they strolled across the vast expanse of carpeted floor. All around the edges of the room the furniture was shrouded in dust sheets, lending The Lodge, Olivia's old home, a neglected, shuttered air. Soon new tenants would make themselves at home here, the only means Olivia had of managing the financial upkeep on the nearby small dower house she shared with her aunts and in which Lucien had allowed her to live during her lifetime.

He frowned. 'We need to decide for ourselves if she is a fit and proper person to keep charge of the lad.'

'Charlotte has cared for Julian since he was born! Her loyalty is beyond question.'

Their gazes locked. Both of them knew this all too well. To Olivia it was a comfort. She swallowed as doubt stirred within. But to Nathaniel, Charlotte's loyalty could represent a threat.

To her relief he conceded, 'It is perhaps best to keep her close.'

They stopped just inside the dining room. Olivia closed her eyes. The smell of dust and damp were different from the beeswax and woodsmoke she remembered, but the draughty remoteness was just the same. She and Lucien had entertained regularly in this room. It had been the setting for countless lively, raucous dinners, charades and games of cards for ridiculous wagers. She shuddered as Nathaniel took her past the long, mahogany table which could seat thirty, and upon which she had regularly been made to dance.

All but naked.

Nathaniel ran his hand over its dust-sheet-covered surface and glanced at her.

The look in his eye told her he remembered, too.

But his tone was bland as he reminded her, 'Mr Charleston will arrive at the end of the month. I thought it appropriate Julian should be given some time, first, in which to settle in.'

Olivia did not say she wondered at the wisdom, even questioned the kindness, of putting a boy so young into the charge of a tutor whom she had not yet met. Years of being Lucien's wife had taught her caution; to think before she spoke. At least she had a little time to assert herself if she were unhappy at Nathaniel's choice of tutor. The most important thing was that Julian would be with her.

She must not think of Max. She squeezed her eyes shut. She would think of anything but Max, though recollections of his charming, easy manner and the kindness of his smile were constant reminders.

'Reverend Kirkman, forgive the intrusion—'

Olivia faltered. *The voice—! Oh, dear God, no!*

They were at the foot of the sweeping staircase about to ascend to the rooms above. Turning at the sound of footsteps and their visitor's voice, Mr Kirkman's face creased into a smile of welcome. Ushering Olivia forward, he extended his hand.

'Mr Atherton, delighted you chose to accompany the lad.'

Olivia could not bring herself to raise her eyes. She gripped Nathaniel's forearm, her gaze fixed upon the sweeping stairs as if they provided refuge. Heat and shame flooded her. She was exposed.

Yet was it no more than she deserved?

'Excellent, excellent. Pray, allow me to introduce my betrothed, Lady Farquhar. Alas, she was indisposed when we met.'

Dignified in the face of what must be his inevitable horror and disgust, Olivia slowly raised her head.

'Mr Atherton,' she said quietly, extending her hand, glad it was clad in neat fawn kid so he could not feel its clammy iciness.

She saw his shock, quickly smothered by good manners as he bowed, brushing the back of her hand with his lips, murmuring, 'What a pleasure it is to meet you, *Lady Farquhar*' – she could swear he almost bared his teeth as he added – 'having already met your *betrothed*.'

The turmoil he struggled to hide pierced her to the quick. A month on and she could be in no doubt that he had felt her deception, her disappearance, keenly. A vein throbbed at his temple. The simmering anger in his slate-grey eyes reminded her more of her late husband than the easy-natured Max she loved.

Concentrating on the points of her slippers she whispered, 'I must thank you for providing my son with such excellent care during this past year. Where is he? I have waited a long time for this moment.' It was pointless trying to communicate her feelings through her eyes. It was pointless trying to communicate her feelings through any medium when there could be no future between them.

After being told that Julian had been taken to the dower house where he was being greeted by his great aunts, Nathaniel, with a proprietary air, said smoothly, 'Lady Farquhar is a conscientious mother, Mr Atherton. You will recall from my letter that I have known her for the duration of her marriage and can vouch for her' – he hesitated, as if imbuing the word with meaning – 'softer side.'

Max glanced sharply between the two before focusing his stony gaze upon Olivia. 'It causes me great pain to part with the lad,' he said, adding with heavy irony, 'However only the *cruellest* of men would deny a child his mother's love.'

Focusing on the door at the top of the landing through which she wished she could simply disappear, Olivia nodded.

Max drew himself up. 'I was more than prepared to lend a sympathetic ear, Lady Farquhar, if you had chosen to petition me personally,' He paused. 'Instead, I see you are acceding, to the letter, the conditions laid out in my cousin's will.'

'I did write to petition you for Julian,' Olivia said faintly. She could not look at him. Could not bear his disgust.

'I seem to recall I suggested we meet in person.'

She could hardly say that Nathaniel had decided his course was the better one.

'Lady Farquhar and I shall be married just over the twelve months' mourning period.' Nathaniel's voice sounded overloud and pompous. 'I have known her, did I tell you, since her marriage to the late Lord Farquhar being as I was, in a manner of speaking, his religious adviser.'

Max nodded, still looking at Olivia. 'You mentioned it, sir.'

'Marriage is not an institution into which one enters lightly, as Lady Farquhar well knows.' Nathaniel patted Olivia's hand as colour burned her cheeks.

How she hated his cloying condescension.

Raising her head she saw Max's lips curl into a bleak smile. 'You are a fortunate man, Reverend.'

'Indeed, I am, and I wish you similar good luck.'

'I am in no hurry.'

'The marital state has much to recommend it.'

Max transferred his look from Olivia's blushing countenance to offer a nod. 'I'm sure you are right, though smarting after a recent rejection I am in no hurry to pursue it.'

The silence seemed endless. Striving for courage, Olivia inter-jected, 'You will recover. Perhaps it is your pride rather than your heart which suffered the injury, sir.' She strove for sympathy and hoped Nathaniel did not notice the trembling of her voice. 'Perhaps the lady had her reasons' – Olivia drew in a breath – 'and they had nothing to do with you. Perhaps she had already promised herself to another.' She forced the emotion from her tone and exchanged a smile with Nathaniel, as if she too felt no more than a distracted, passing interest in Mr Atherton's admission. Turning back to Max she added, 'Having shown such kindness and care towards your ward I cannot believe a disinclination towards your character was behind the lady's rejection.' How could she sound so distant, as if she were indeed consoling a stranger on a matter of the heart? A matter which was of no concern to her?

Max gave an eloquent shrug as he matched his pace with theirs in the direction of the front door. 'It no longer signifies.'

This was more painful than anything.

'You must accompany us for lunch,' Nathaniel pressed him. 'The dower house, where Olivia resides with her aunts, is just up the hill.' He smiled. 'Might I offer you accommodation at the manse? I know you've travelled many hours.'

Max inclined his head. 'That is most kind of you, Mr Kirkman, however for the boy's sake I will not linger. Lady Farquhar will be anxious to be reunited with her son and I would hate to' – he trans-ferred his gaze from Kirkman to Olivia as he added, coldly – 'intrude. I have already bespoken a room at The Jolly Miller.'

*

With a nervous glance down the corridor Olivia patted the thick veil for reassurance. Her throat was as dry as sandpaper as she drew back her hand and gave a discreet knock. It was madness to even be here. She would not deviate from her course. She would marry Nathaniel.

Yet she owed Max an explanation. She could not bear that he thought she was everything he had ever been told about Lady Farquhar. And worse.

'I wondered if you'd come.' He opened the door, standing aside so she could enter. His voice was as cold as his eyes. Nothing in his expression brought to mind the old Max: the untroubled, charming young man with his disarming air of ingenuousness.

'Max, I only came here to apologize,' she said in a rush. She wanted to make this brief. Her mission was to convince him she'd not set out to hurt him; that in fact her actions had little to do with him. She'd charted her course before they'd even met.

'At least do it so I can damned well see you and lift that hideous veil,' he said, closing the door behind them and leading her into the small room with its bed, washstand and chair.

Obediently she removed her bonnet, placing it on the washstand. She knew herself too well to try and pretend she wasn't waiting for some acknowledgement of longing or admiration. She told herself it would make her task so much easier if there were no sign of it, but when she saw the pain in his expression her own heart answered and her best intentions fled.

Quickly, she turned and went to the window. With her back to him she said tightly, 'Everything I said was true about my motives. I was prepared to do whatever it took to get Julian back. Please understand that I never meant to hurt you.'

'It just pleased you to toy with me.' He made no move to come to her. His voice was strained. 'Pretend, even, you cared for me a little.'

'No!' she swung round. 'There was no pretence and it's the reason I had to explain. Max—' She lowered her voice while she fixed her eyes upon his handsome, beloved face. 'I am not here to persuade you to take me back for I fully intend to marry Nathaniel. I just don't want you thinking my actions constituted any part of some elaborate, prearranged plot.'

He took his time replying. Picking up her bonnet he began stroking the folds of black netting. His tone, when he spoke, was one Olivia had never heard: bitter, ironic and hurt.

'Let me try to understand you,' he said, slowly, transferring his attention to her face. 'You came to Elmwood to try and persuade me to give you back Julian' – he paused with heavy emphasis – 'but instead of asking me outright you pretended to be someone else while all the time falling madly in love with me.' Tossing the bonnet on to the bed he raked back his hair, his agitation clear though there was no sign of it in his measured tone. 'Then, when I provided you with the perfect solution to all your heart's desires by offering marriage, you skipped back home to marry Mr Kirkman whom you've intimated you do not love, so as to regain Julian as per Lucien's will.' Sparks of anger flashed in his normally calm, grey eyes. 'And yet, you still maintain your feelings for me were genuine. What, Lady Farquhar, do you think that says about you?'

Olivia studied him while she struggled to respond. He looked young and vigorous, and so like Lucien it was hard to formulate an answer. So like Lucien might have looked had he been incarnated into a better person. There was the same dark cowlick that almost fell in a curl above his right eye. Lucien had encouraged it to fall. He'd liked its rakish look and the way it enhanced the devilish glint in his eye.

There was no devilish glint in Max's eye. Just raw hurt.

Yet again, she was the cause through her alluring, beguiling, enticing ways. For isn't that what she did? Seduced men for her entertainment? It's what everybody thought.

'Max, it's because you were sure to believe the rumours, sure to think I was that kind of woman that I did what I did,' she whispered, taking a step closer, holding the back of a chair for support.

He appeared unmoved. Warily, from the centre of the room he watched her. His voice was still cynical though she could hear the strain he tried to disguise as he replied, 'Actions speak louder than words, Olivia.'

'What would my reception have been, Max, had I announced myself to you as Lady Farquhar?' Pain sliced through her. 'If I'd dressed and deported myself demurely you'd have considered I was acting a part. You'd have waited for me to slip up, reveal myself for the scheming seductress society believes me. You'd not have let me have Julian.'

He ignored this. 'You did not object to my advances, Olivia. Perhaps you've forgotten that.' A muscle twitched at the corner of his mouth. 'Foolishly I believed at the time you felt something for me.'

'How can you imagine I was pretending?' she cried, bringing her hand to her breast to press against the sudden pain there. 'I assumed my maiden name, but that was all. Everything I said, every action was honest. My only wrongdoing was concealing my identity. Everything I said, every response towards you, was real.'

He gave her a searching look, then, with a sigh, moved to the door. 'Thank you for your apology,' he said, tonelessly, his hand on the door knob. 'I imagine that took some courage.' He inclined his head in dismissal. 'As you pointed out yourself, though, it doesn't exactly alter the fact that you deceived me and are about to marry someone else.'

She didn't know what to do. This was not how it was supposed to end with Max calmly showing her the way out. Once the soft click of the latch consigned her to the passageway with Max on the other side of the door the one spark of love that had ever honestly flickered in her breast would be snuffed out and she'd be more alone than she'd ever been.

Yet wasn't that what she'd engineered, herself?

'I gave you my heart,' she whispered, stopping in front of him. 'I'd have given you everything.'

'I'm sure many men would gladly have accepted, Olivia. I, however, was looking for something more permanent.' He glared at her. 'Something honestly given with no strings attached.' He stepped back as if afraid of coming into contact with her.

His words pained her though she acknowledged the truth of them. Biting back her first response which was to defend her actions she stepped as close to him as she could without actually touching. She'd leave, not because she wanted to, and not before she made one final stand. She could not bear to leave without his forgiveness.

'I responded as I did because you were kind.' Tentatively she rested her hand lightly on his lapel. 'From our first encounter you made my comfort and welfare your concern. I had not experienced such thoughtfulness.'

He looked at her hand with suspicion, turning his head away to stare through the half-drawn curtains. The casement panes were dirty and the room bathed in gloom but his pain was clear.

On her account.

'My husband spent our entire marriage punishing me for' – she made a derisive sound – 'forcing him to the altar when I was a foolish debutante.' How badly she wanted Max to understand. She withdrew her hand. Max brought his head round. His eyes glowed with some emotion she could not recognize. She could not bear to think it was disgust. 'When your feelings for me went beyond mere kindness I responded with every fibre of my being. I wanted you, Max. I wanted you so badly, but I had not the courage to reveal myself as scandalous Lady Farquhar, branded so unfairly by her husband as a harlot, an unfit mother.'

'If you considered me so' – he swallowed, adding derisively – 'kind, why not lay bare your scandalous past so you could defend each charge to my satisfaction?' The suspicion returned to his manner. 'Such as the truth behind Lady Farquhar's Butterfly?'

It shouldn't have felt like a slap in the face after all this time. She should have expected it, and it should have been she who brought it up.

Rage at the long and lingering injustice bubbled up so that she hissed, 'Lady Farquhar's Butterfly paid my husband's gambling debts.' She was so upset she didn't know if she could continue. But she must. She clung to the door knob for her knees had gone weak, the pounding in her brain threatened to obliterate her lucidity. She was so angry even the shock and understanding that registered suddenly in Max's eyes was no catharsis. When he put out a hand to help her she drew back.

'One night Lucien lost more heavily than usual.' Each word was an effort. Her defences were in place. Max would not dare touch her while she glared at him with as much poison in her heart as if he had been his hated cousin. 'Perhaps he was more than unusually affected by the drink. He must have made some reference – coarse and ironic, no doubt – about the birthmark on my breast to his gambling partners. A birthmark he fancied was shaped like a butterfly. I was sitting at another table with several of the men who weren't playing Faro. None of the wives was there. It was not a respectable gathering, but Lucien thought I was decorative.' Drawing herself up in an effort to salvage her pride, she shrugged. She would manage to control her emotion sufficiently to recount the rest as if it was a sordid moral tale in which she had but a passing interest. It was a trick she'd perfected as Lucien's wife.

'Finally he rose and called me over. I stood by the table, awaiting his pleasure while he and the other men looked me over like a horse. They were leering and sniggering. I was terrified, humiliated, but there was nothing I could do. Then Lord Grimble nodded at Lucien and said he thought sampling Lady Farquhar's butterfly with a kiss would be bargain enough at which point Lucien ordered me to disrobe.' Her voice trembled. 'Right there, in front of them all.' She squeezed shut her eyes. 'I was too afraid to disobey. Lucien was so ingenious at inventing the cruellest tortures. Besides, I thought one of the men in that room would surely protest.' Olivia swallowed as she rested her head against the door. She felt the memories close in on her. Felt her breath start to leave her.

Then she was in Max's arms and he was crushing her tightly against him, kissing her hair, her eyes –

– her lips.

Chapter Six

SHE RESPONDED LIKE a wilting flower receiving rain. Her heart opened like the floodgates of a weir to receive ... hope? Happiness?

Except that there was no hope and, as ever, happiness would be fleeting. Still that didn't stop her twining her arms behind his neck and responding to his kiss with all the ardour of their last encounter. She could not deny her passionate nature when it was aroused.

Older and wiser, she knew the price of happiness. Since she could not afford it beyond the moment she intended to take all she could while it was offered: Max's arms around her, his hard, strong young body all muscle and desire, binding her with his need.

His kisses were incendiary, inflaming her with a desperation to throw all caution to the wind and seal their love upon the four poster in the centre of the room, and she would have had she been able to offer him marriage.

But, of course, there could be no taking it to the next level while she was a woman, betrothed, on a visit intended to explain and reinforce this uncomfortable truth.

When she felt his reluctant but undeniable withdrawal it was like mourning what she'd been unable to mourn before.

'If I told you I believe everything you've told me' – breathless, he chose his words carefully, his dark eyes searching hers as he still held her against him – 'would it be worth my asking you, again, to marry me?'

Olivia covered her face with her hands and stepped out of his arms. This was not supposed to happen.

He looked so desperately, heartbreakingly sincere, his expression so full of yearning she had to force back the tears. And trammel down the desire to throw herself back into his embrace.

She couldn't let him see the answering want in her own eyes. Stumbling towards the light, she again sought the sanctuary of the window. Here she could support herself against the cold glass, stare out into the grey afternoon light and wonder, briefly, why she had been cursed with the kind of beauty that made men want to possess her and punish her in equal measure.

For Nathaniel wanted her as badly as Lucien ever had. She was not fooled by his restrained manner. He would fight Max for her using every unsavoury titbit of scandal, every damning piece of character evidence at his disposal.

And he had plenty of it. Nathaniel was a formidable adversary. Max's kindness and honour were no match for Nathaniel's ploys.

Yet hadn't Max just accepted, at face value, everything Olivia had told him in exoneration of her behaviour? Didn't that mean he'd forgive her the rest? All he wanted was the truth. Surely it was worth the risk?

She gripped the window sill as she stared vacantly into the stable yard. All she need do was say: 'I will be yours if you can forgive me the fact that Julian is a bastard who has usurped your position as the rightful Viscount Farquhar.'

She gathered her breath. She could say it.

Then she remembered that not only her happiness hung in the balance. Declaring Julian a bastard meant condemning him to society's scrapheap. He would be entitled to nothing: no social standing, no financial support.

She crumpled against the window pane. She could not do it. She wanted Max above all except the wellbeing of her child. She simply couldn't take the risk.

'Olivia?'

She had to answer him. Soon. Even as she turned, her mouth

opening to respond, she hesitated, the truth balancing on the faintest of breaths.

It was as her gaze registered the empathy and compassion in his expression that she knew she'd say no.

Not because of Julian; not because of her fears for him, for Max had honour and decency, she knew that.

But because of her own deficiencies.

She did not deserve him. Max was good and pure of heart. A gentleman, not a cruel tormentor. It wouldn't be long before those eyes which melted her soul with their gentleness would soon kindle with disappointment.

What did it matter that she had not deserved Lucien's treatment? The fact remained: he had corrupted her. What did it matter that she had wept every night at the seductive, wanton acts she'd been forced to perform with a smile? The fact remained that she'd danced all but naked in a transparent shimmer of gauze on the dining table and men had lined up to kiss her breast with its famous butterfly birthmark.

Regardless of how much she bared her soul to Max now, she did not think she had the fortitude to bear his increasing disappointment, his dawning realization of her unworthiness.

'I'm so sorry, Max,' she whispered. They were the hardest words she'd ever said. A slap in the face for him and the death knell for her own hopes of happiness. She swallowed. 'I cannot renege on my promise to Nathaniel. Please try to understand.' She turned her face a fraction, caught the flare of surprise in his eyes, the blanching of his skin indicating, more than words ever could, his wounding.

She went on, resting the small of her back against the window sill, 'For more years than I care to remember Mr Kirkman has salvaged my dignity in situations too awful to revisit.' She swallowed again, almost elaborated about the table dancing and everything else, but bit back the words at the last moment. He'd need to know if he were to be her husband. Since that wasn't to be, at least let him leave with a less tarnished image of herself.

'I'd like to know what the worthy reverend was doing at Lucien's debauched gatherings in the first place?' Max ground out, as he regarded her from the centre of the room.

Olivia gave a helpless gesture. 'Lucien liked to balance vice with piety.' She took a deep breath. 'Nathaniel accepted Lucien's invitations because the only way he could help me was to be in attendance. Usually with a linen sheet on hand to wind around me as the music stopped whereupon he'd whisk me upstairs while I sobbed upon his shoulder. I think he disapproved of Lucien's wicked ways, but what could he do?'

It was true and this, if nothing else, should have decided her. After a lifetime of vanity rewarded by her fall from grace she ought to have accepted the time had come to pay her dues to him.

Feeling like an old woman, she picked up her bonnet and retied it as she moved towards the door, with one final look at Max. 'I owe Nathaniel so much. An unspoken understanding has existed between us from the day Lucien died that once my mourning period was over Nathaniel would claim me. He intimated as much as he outlined my best course in reclaiming Julian.' She paused, her hand on the door knob. 'I am only doing my duty.'

In two strides Max had crossed the room and taken her by the shoulders. 'Duty? What has love to do with duty?' he rasped, his face close to hers. 'Nathaniel has no claim on you. He merely did what any decent man was obliged to do.'

Olivia wriggled out of his grasp, pulling down the veil as her hand groped for the door knob. Salvation demanded she make her escape now. No matter that it tore her heart in two she had to do this.

'And Julian?'

His voice was thick with a mixture of anger and misery as he let her pull out of his arms. 'If you marry Nathaniel I will not see you again; would not want to, for it would be more than I could bear. But what about Julian?' His voice cracked. 'When Lady Farquhar made no effort to contact me, I, fool that I am, allowed myself to become attached—' He took a breath. 'You read me well enough to know that I would never exercise my authority to keep the boy with me.' He dug the palm of his hand into his eye socket as he dragged out a breath. 'Am I to lose everything?'

'You may see him whenever you wish,' Olivia whispered, her

wretchedness threatening to consume her. She could not bear to see him like this.

'Provided Kirkman sanctions it,' he muttered.

Olivia gulped, nodding. Then, opening the door herself, she stepped out into the corridor and fled.

'I thought Mr Atherton was leaving this morning.' Aunt Catherine looked anxiously between her niece and her sister. 'Mr Kirkman has just sent a message to say the two of them will be joining us for dinner.'

'Mr Kirkman sent the message?' Olivia put down her sewing and frowned at her aunt who shared the meagre warmth of their little fire from her favourite seat opposite.

'Apparently he's been entertaining Mr Atherton. They rode to the abbey ruins earlier and—'

'Olivia?'

Olivia jerked her head up at Aunt Eunice's sharp tone and cursed herself for allowing her feelings to be so transparent. She wasn't glad he was coming, and that, clearly, was what had excited her aunt.

'I … just feel anxious. What if he's decided to renege and take Julian back?' she said, feebly, as she returned to her stitching.

'Mr Atherton appears as unlike his cousin as is possible.' Aunt Eunice regarded her with interest. She had always known how to read her. 'Catherine, why don't you tell the kitchen? One extra place is hardly worthy of all your frowns, Olivia. Mr Atherton seems a very easy-to-please gentleman. I doubt he'd be too concerned if we served him bread and dripping on account of the short notice.'

Olivia said barely a word as her aunts welcomed Max into their fold before ushering everyone through to the drawing room for some Madeira before dinner.

She wished she could simply disappear, taking Julian with her, and never return. She'd leave them all in a heartbeat, she decided, watching Aunt Catherine fawning over Nathaniel, and Aunt Eunice's sharp eye roving over all, as if trying to understand that which Olivia wished heartily to keep from her.

Why had Max come? Why hadn't he just let her get on with her life according to their understanding of yesterday? Despite her long experience in play-acting she did not know how she would manage to behave towards him as if he were a mere stranger she had met the previous day. As for Max, what did he even know of play-acting? He was as transparent as the gossamer gowns her late husband had liked her to wear.

She was terrified.

Smiling faintly, she refused the seat Nathaniel offered her as they congregated in the drawing room before dinner, going instead to the corner of the Wilton carpet to kneel with Julian and Charlotte to play with the tin soldiers Max had bought for his nephew.

The little boy seemed as subdued as she, though perhaps a little more responsive towards her than he had been during the few days she had spent at Max's home. Quietly they lined up the soldiers in a neat row and distractedly Olivia stroked her son's soft dusky curls, listening to the drone of conversation and feeling sick with dread.

Would Max expose her visit to Elmwood in front of Nathaniel? She doubted that was his motive. Wearily she accepted he was making one final bid to win her back.

Misery overlaid all. She couldn't bear it. She'd well and truly accepted her fate.

'—isn't that so, Lady Farquhar?'

She jerked her head up at the sound of her name. All eyes were on her. Max's, most particularly. Without his good-natured smile and the gentle humour that softened his features he looked frighteningly like his cousin.

'I'm sorry, did I alarm you with my sudden question?' Max frowned in polite enquiry.

Olivia's heart pounded like a drum. The tin soldier fell from her grasp. 'You look so much like Lucien,' she whispered.

It took a moment for him to register this. There was shocked silence. She put her hand to her mouth. Mentioning Lucien in her household was akin to mentioning the Devil.

Max smiled and although it was not his usual open, kind smile, his resemblance to Lucien dissolved upon the instant. 'Forgive me, I keep forgetting my cousin was your late husband.'

With a nervous cough, Aunt Catherine said, 'You do indeed bear a striking resemblance to the late Lord Farquhar.'

Max's cool tone was tinged with surprise. 'It is not usually remarked upon.'

'For there is no resemblance when you smile, Mr Atherton, and I think you are generally a good-natured gentleman.' Olivia gave a shaky laugh.

'Please don't stand on ceremony with me.' Max gave a rather thin smile. 'We are surely sufficiently close to call each other by our Christian names.' Was it only Olivia who heard the irony?

She blushed and turned away as an image intruded of Max's hot feverish kisses and her equally feverish response.

'You were away, was it six years, Mr Atherton?' Aunt Eunice intervened, indicating to the servant to bring the Madeira.

'My regiment was sent overseas shortly before Lucien and Olivia were married. I returned to live at Elmwood after Lucien's death.'

Aunt Catherine took an appreciative sip of her aperitif. Entertaining was a rare treat. 'It must have been a shock to have been given the wardship of your nephew though it's apparent you've done a commendable job looking after him.' Grey ringlets bobbing, she beamed at him.

All eyes turned to Olivia at the sound of her stifled sob. Aunt Catherine gasped an apology. Aunt Eunice sounded glacial. 'As you can imagine, it is a sore point with Olivia that her late husband publicly proclaimed her unfit to take charge of her son.' She stared down her autocratic nose at their visitor who sat in the best chair by the piano, facing the ladies. 'A child requires a mother's love above all else.'

'I appreciate that.' Max spoke softly, his eyes roving over Olivia, his mouth a thin line. 'And I can see Julian is in good hands. I would be the last to deny the boy has a very' – the tiny pause was not lost on Olivia – 'loving mother.'

There was a knock at the door. Olivia froze in the midst of having her hair brushed in preparation for dinner. She clenched her fists in her lap as the door was thrust open.

'Young lady, I think you've some explaining to do!'

Instead of Max, who had every reason to make such a demand, though his presence in such a manner would have been extraordinary, a glowering Aunt Eunice swept into the room.

'That'll be all, thank you, Dorcas.' Olivia nodded dismissal at the maid and waited until the door was closed before she said, defensively, 'You sent me on a mission to reclaim my son. I carried it out successfully.'

'This man, Lucien's cousin, Julian's guardian—' Aunt Eunice shook her head before continuing, 'You led me to believe Max was as unsatisfactory as Lucien and you were only too glad to get away. My eyes tell a different story.'

Olivia turned back to the looking glass, her voice dull. 'I can't imagine what you mean, Aunt Eunice.' She looked stonily at her reflection, unwilling to meet her aunt's eyes. Dorcas had just arranged her hair with a tumble of golden curls threaded through with pearls on either side of a centre parting. Her gown of gold and cream satin set off her skin to perfection and around her neck the little key that Lucien had given her on his deathbed nestled in the hollow between her breasts.

'Don't tell me you've gone to such pains with your appearance on Mr Kirkman's account?' Aunt Eunice ground out. 'The way you've rigged yourself up you'll have the two of them engaged in fisticuffs at the dining-room table.'

Olivia turned, indignant. 'Miss Latimer delivered my new dress this afternoon. I had no idea Max would be accompanying Julian.'

'Just as Max had no idea that the woman who clearly turned his life upside down and with whom he is undoubtedly in love, was Julian's mother. Ah, Olivia, it was ill done of you.' An uncharacteristically sorrowful look replaced Aunt Eunice's anger as she rested her hands on Olivia's shoulders. She shook her head, slowly. 'Have you learned nothing since you married Lucien? Not even to trust your instincts?'

Olivia swung round on her stool. 'You think I'd trust Max with my heart? Max is Lucien's cousin. He looks like Lucien; he *glowers* like Lucien. Surely you saw the way he looked at me. No doubt he has a temper every bit as evil as Lucien's. You *hated* Lucien! Yet you would have me wed his cousin in preference to the eminently suitable, well-regarded, upright and pious Mr Kirkman?'

'There are many men I'd rather you wed in preference to Mr Kirkman, though your Aunt Catherine begs to differ.'

The dinner gong sounded and Olivia leapt to her feet. 'Nathaniel can't abide unpunctuality,' she said, desperate to escape her aunt's scrutiny. The last thing she needed was Aunt Eunice pressing her to accept Max's suit over Nathaniel's.

At the dining-room door she nearly collided with Max. Bowing, unsmiling, he offered her his arm.

Olivia met his assessing gaze with a distinct lack of composure before turning towards the table where Aunt Eunice was seating herself beside her sister.

Max helped her to her chair. 'You're even lovelier than I remembered, Olivia.' He spoke softly. 'The last month has been a long one.'

Miserably she bent her head in acknowledgement of the compliment. And the gentle reproach.

'I hope Nathaniel deserves you.'

Raising her eyes to his she could discern no malice, nor did his tone or expression hint at sarcasm. 'Max, I'm sorry—'

'Ah, Mr Atherton, Olivia, good evening. My love, you are a vision. Isn't she a vision?' Mr Kirkman, seating himself beside Olivia, looked smugly at Max who proceeded to his chair opposite.

Olivia turned her head away from Nathaniel's possessive smile, uncomfortably conscious of his thigh within a hair's breadth of her own. The way he fussed over her comfort seemed calculated to emphasize to Max his exclusive ownership.

'I expect, Mr Atherton – I mean Max,' she amended, with a contrived blush, 'will be off early in the morning if you've more than three hours' riding ahead of you. Shall you break your journey in Bath?'

'You could, of course, extend your visit.' Aunt Eunice gave Max an expansive smile. 'Nathaniel must attend to business tomorrow. You could help Julian settle in. Isn't that a good idea, Reverend?'

The reverend's nod accompanied a weak smile, as Aunt Eunice went on in answer to Max's appearance of consideration, 'Excellent. Well, there's no need to remain at the inn when there's plenty of spare room, here.'

'That is, if Olivia has no objection to my presence under her roof. I would hate to distress her if I remind her so much of her late husband.'

'Only when you glower, Mr Atherton.' Olivia smiled sweetly, looking up from her plate.

Max raised his eyebrows. 'Good! In that case any likeness will hardly be remarked upon as I'm renowned for my good temper.'

Aunt Catherine gave a little sigh of happiness as her glass was refilled. 'What a wonderful state of affairs. Julian shall doubly benefit from the tender care of a doting uncle in his earliest years, and the wise instruction of his new stepfather as he grows to be a man.'

Max cleared his throat. 'I trust I might continue to see Julian often in the future.'

'Of course—'

Olivia's prompt agreement was interrupted by Nathaniel. 'Forgive me, Mr Atherton, but I believe it to be in the boy's best interests if there is no contact for some months.' He gave one of his lengthy, considering looks with which Olivia was so familiar, adding, 'Julian needs to settle in to his new life.' He turned at Olivia's stifled protest and patted her arm. 'I want only what is best for the boy, my love. If you can persuade me otherwise, I'll happily accede.'

Olivia refrained from any rejoinder as she acknowledged the devastating effect of Nathaniel's words. Max's affection for Julian was plain and although it would be best that Olivia not see Max again once she was married, she had promised Max continued access to the boy.

She was relieved when dinner was finally at an end.

She woke late after a fitful night. Her eyes felt gritty and her head buzzed with fatigue. Attending to her appearance, she wished she looked the picture of radiance Max had thought her last night, even though she knew it was a shameful wish. Running quickly up the stairs to the nursery, her heart contracted when she discovered the room empty. She hurried along the corridors and into the garden calling for Julian.

Perhaps Max, unable to contain his anger at her deception, had kidnapped him. If he had changed his mind about relinquishing Julian he certainly had enough ammunition to bolster the case against her.

Footsteps in the snow leading through the park gates only increased her fear, but just as she'd convinced herself Max had indeed made off with her son she heard voices.

Advancing slowly, as quietly as she could, she listened.

'Your mother loves you very much and she *is* your mother so it's her turn to look after you.' Max spoke softly. As Olivia could hear nothing from Julian she imagined Max was succeeding in soothing the lad. Raw grief rose up in her breast as she waited on the other side of the holly bush for the right time to announce her presence.

'Not every boy is lucky enough to have such a beautiful and kind mother, Julian. Do you know how many little boys would long to have a mother like yours?'

She heard a little hiccupping sob and was hard pressed not to add her own. Max's bond with Julian was so much stronger than her own. She understood how hard it would be for her son. For both of them. Never had she felt so wretched though she consoled herself it was further proof Max would be better off without her. It was one thing to make men fall in love with her; quite another to live up to their expectations. Lucien had called her his little cream puff: delectable to look at, he'd said, but without substance.

'And your new stepfather is a very upright and important fellow. At least in these parts,' Olivia heard him add in a none-too-flattering undertone. 'A reverend, no less! A very lucky reverend, young Julian, for he has got himself the most beautiful wife in all England. I daresay your Uncle Max is just an idle wastrel in comparison.'

'What nonsense!' Olivia brushed past the bush and frowned at Max. 'I suspect you wanted me to hear that so I would feel obliged to contradict you.'

Max rose, setting Julian down at his feet. Stooping to put a hand on the boy's shoulder he suggested with wheedling enthusiasm, 'Why don't you collect us some pine cones? Your mother and I have some things we need to say to one another.'

'What a good idea, my darling boy.' Olivia smiled at Julian, trying not to take his sullen rejection too much to heart as she put out her hand to stroke his curls before he ran off. With difficulty she said, 'What do you think needs to be said that hasn't been said already?' She wanted to channel her confusion into anger, but the way he was looking at her, his eyes smiling, a curl to his lip that was more gently challenging than malicious, threw her completely. 'I've said I'm sorry. I've admitted I used you shamelessly to get to Julian and I deeply regret what happened.'

Max took a step forward, his smile broadening. With a quick glance at the disappearing Julian, he tucked an errant curl behind her ear.

'What, exactly, do you regret? Falling in love?' He touched her cheek with his forefinger, trailing it slowly down to her collarbone.

Heat rose in her cheeks and her bosom heaved as she strained in a breath. His touch curdled her insides. Damning her susceptibility she said on a shaky breath, 'Lucien made no bones about my deplorable character.' She focused her gaze upon his gently curving mouth, wishing more than she'd ever done to feel the touch of his lips upon hers once more as she whispered, 'He would have said wicked, carnal attraction was between us, nothing more.'

Max chuckled. 'I'm more interested in what *you* would have called it, though I have my answer just by the way you are looking at me.' He cupped her face and brought his own closer. 'You are afraid to risk your heart a second time, Olivia, but I am not Lucien,' he whispered. 'Lucien was a jealous madman who did not appreciate the greatest gift he was ever given. You! For I see little evidence of the character flaws Lucien elaborated upon.'

'You'd discover them in good time.' Olivia sagged against Max's steadying arm. Covering her eyes with her hands, she fought tears. 'He lived with me for seven years—'

'And destroyed your self worth. Olivia …' Max wrapped his arms gently about her shoulders and stroked her hair. The gentle drone of his voice was catharsis, blocking out the awful reality to which she'd soon return.

'I barely slept last night,' he murmured. 'I thought of all I knew about Lucien. He took my initiation into his hands, you see, introducing me to his favourite gaming hells and other dens of vice. I was six years younger and, at eighteen, a willing disciple, though the novelty quickly wore off.' He paused. 'A year before, Lucien had seemed kinder. I suppose because he was in love.' He drew out the pause, adding, 'But something happened. He became the tyrant his father was. I heard he'd made a pact with the Devil; that he believed there was a fortune stored beneath the floorboards. He was insane, I understand that, just as I understand, better than you think, what your marriage must have been like. Lucien respected no one. I can imagine how he treated you.'

Closing her eyes against the intensity of his look, she swayed. She felt dangerously exposed, afraid of revealing more than she could afford.

When he broke the silence his words carried an edge of frustration. 'You say you owe The Reverend Kirkman your hand in marriage. Can you really do that, Olivia, when you know it means sacrificing your life's happiness?'

When still she did not speak, could not, he went on, 'My guess is that Lucien made you feel so worthless you don't believe you deserve happiness.'

She flinched, forcing herself to meet his eye. 'I am no better than Lucien painted me,' she said, weakly. 'When you discovered the truth you'd hate me.'

With a grunt of irritation he shook her gently. 'You are no longer a wilful debutante or an innocent pushed reluctantly into marriage, Olivia,' he said. 'You are a grown woman with experience of the world and a will of your own.'

Silence stretched between them. When he spoke again, his voice was steady, matter-of fact. 'You delight me, Olivia.' He smiled as if he truly thought her the most exquisite thing he'd laid eyes upon. 'Every moment I am with you fills me with pleasure. We can make a wonderful future together – you, me and Julian.' He waited, his smile refusing to fade as the silence grew.

She knew she need only nod and it would be enough. She turned her head away, watching Julian in the distance as he played in the late April snow, her heart knotted with pain and self disgust as Max tried one final gambit, 'If you thought to send me away with tales of your shocking past and your misplaced sense of duty towards a man who did what any decent man would do, Olivia, you've failed.'

How dearly she wanted to accept his offer and step into his arms. They rested at his sides but she knew she need take only one small step and he'd wrap her up in them, and her life would be just the way she wanted it. Everything she could ever desire would be hers. If only …

'Oh Max,' she said, at last, brokenly, her misery threatening to crush her. 'If only I could explain.'

'No, my dear.' He stepped back, his look curiously empty as he avoided her outstretched hands. 'If you cannot give me your love, I do not want your sympathy.' Formally, he offered her his arm. 'Let us fetch Julian and return to the house.'

Dinner was a lacklustre affair. Only Nathaniel seemed to enjoy himself. He'd imbibed more wine than usual and had taken control of the conversation. Even Aunt Catherine, his greatest admirer, seemed to be losing interest in his learned dissertations.

Halfway through pudding she twisted in her chair to raise the curtain hem so she could look out of the casement.

'Gracious, I do believe it's still snowing.'

'Surely not.' Aunt Eunice pushed back her chair and went to the window. 'The wind has picked up,' she said. Unnoticed above the babble of conversation it could now be heard howling through the treetops.

'It's a veritable storm.' Aunt Catherine's voice was tinged with concern. 'I'm only glad you're not caught up in it during your journey home, Mr Atherton,' she said, before frowning and looking at Nathaniel. 'You'll have to stay until it subsides, Reverend.'

Olivia felt the dismay rise within her. The idea of being incarcerated with both Max and Nathaniel for any length of time was more than she could endure.

'How wild it is.' Even as Aunt Catherine spoke the keening of the wind seemed to rise in pitch. A dreadful crash sounded in the distance and Olivia jumped.

'Just a tree branch, my dear.' Nathaniel patted her arm and Olivia tried not to recoil at his touch. Was it only just now, since she had met Max, that he evinced such a reaction? He had comforted her plenty of times in the face of Lucien's treatment.

She closed her eyes, squirming at the idea of having him under the same roof and realizing how paradoxical was the sentiment since she would soon commit herself to him, body and soul, for the rest of her life.

Max offered her a bolstering smile. She smiled in return, blushing at the sharp look Nathaniel directed at her.

Carefully she put her knife and fork together and leaned back to allow Dorcas to remove her plate. Her cheeks still felt hot.

'Olivia, surely you still have some of Lucien's clothes packed.'

Nathaniel in Lucien's clothes? She didn't know whether to laugh or gasp. All eyes were on her and for the second time in as many minutes she felt the heat burning her bosom upwards.

'Of course,' she managed, unable to stop her glance sweeping the man beside her from head to foot.

'Perhaps I can be of assistance,' Max offered. 'I brought several changes of clothing which may help lessen Olivia's distress.'

Olivia cut through the sympathetic tut-tutting. Nathaniel dressed in something belonging to Max was even worse to contemplate. No, she told them, she had a whole trunk of Lucien's nightshirts and other elegant items of apparel. If Nathaniel was happy to be seen wearing shirt points from two seasons ago he could have them all.

'I'll see what I can find, Nathaniel,' she said smoothly, as dinner was cleared away. Rising, she nodded to the gentlemen as she and her aunts left them to enjoy their port.

It was a relief to be out of the room. Clearly the wind was not going to abate. Clearly Nathaniel had no choice but to remain.

In her dressing room she rummaged in one of the large trunks by the window only to realize she had packed all Lucien's things in the attic. She'd never thought to look at them again. Had sworn she never would.

Taking a candle, she followed the corridor which led to the nursery. At the doorway she stopped to gaze in pained wonderment at Julian's sleeping face. Her beautiful boy. The child she had cradled at her bosom and cared for until Lucien had decided she was no longer fit to rear him. Now he was hers again and Olivia was the guardian of his future. His happiness. She clenched her fists. She would fight for him to the death. Choking on a sob, she turned away. She would sacrifice even her greatest happiness if it ensured Julian's future.

At the end of the passageway a narrow staircase – more of a ladder, really – rose steeply to the attic. It was a relief to climb beyond reach of Aunt Eunice's hectoring, Aunt Catherine's quizzing and Nathaniel's unnerving presence.

And she would be far more composed if Max were not there, either.

In the darkness above she set the candle down on a horizontal beam. If her fears were not so earthly her heart would be leaping about as erratically as the candle flame, she thought, as she settled herself on a large tin trunk and stared at the ghostly shadows that danced by the flickering light.

She had never been a nervous girl. Skittish, in her way, but determined and stubborn. When she'd run off with Lucien it would have taken a hurricane to have pushed her back. No amount of reasoning or threatening from anyone would have had any impact on her decision to go with him. He was London's catch of the season and she, penniless Miss Templestowe, had whisked him from under the noses of every other designing miss competing for his affections.

But she had never enjoyed his affections.

She cupped her chin in her hands and stared at a large painting of Lucien as a child. She'd consigned it to the attic after he'd died. He must have been about three for he was still dressed in petticoats with a blue sash about his middle, his arms wrapped around the neck of a King Charles Spaniel. How angelic the pair looked posing beneath a cherry tree. She could imagine it was Julian with Max's dog, Pansy. The young Lucien's hair was dark and curling, his eyes blue, like Julian's. It was fortunate Julian had the same colouring, she reflected. The thought caused another pang. He was the reason she could never be with Max but how could she regret the past when her little boy had given her life's greatest joy – and pain.

She rose, the floorboards creaking beneath her feet, as she bent to open the trunk.

'Make sure the nightcap matches.' The whisper startled her and she leapt back, heart pounding, a scream dying in her throat before she realized it was him.

'Max!'

His head appeared through the gap in the floor, 'You dare not risk his ire if he's not turned out fit to face a congregation.'

'I think Nathaniel is a little less concerned with his appearance than Lucien was.' She was more relieved that Max's good humour had returned than afraid of being alone with him. 'Lucien, as you can imagine, was not best pleased if his valet's taste in matching waistcoats did not accord with his own. I think he went through valets faster than clean shirts.'

Max leant against a cross beam, watching her as she rummaged through Lucien's clothes.

'And indeed, I do have plenty of nightcaps to match his nightshirts.' Olivia smiled wickedly as she scrutinized one of them. 'Lucien would not have dreamed of – or in – anything else.'

'A veritable slave to fashion,' remarked Max, stepping over a pile of old shirts and peering into the trunk. 'Why did you keep so many?'

His nearness sent tremors through her. Breathing deeply she fought the longing to sway against his side. 'These are just the ones from the year he died. Lucien discarded everything at the end of each season.'

'Good Lord,' remarked Max, looking down at his own blue and gold-figured silk waistcoat while he fingered his shirt points. 'I know I'm up to the mark in this rig-out, but I'm glad I don't need to subject myself to Lucien's scrutiny. The Lodge must have had the best-dressed servants in the village.'

'Lucien didn't believe in charity.'

She turned her head, pretending to be unaware of the way he was looking at her. She had not meant to sound bitter. She must not play the victim and risk whipping up his chivalry. Good Lord, it was madness even to be alone with him.

He was showing admirable restraint, but she…? She was as weak as dishwater, she knew it.

Cautiously, she straightened. Max had seated himself on another trunk at right angles to her, his attention caught by the painting of Lucien with his parents. In the flickering light he looked devastatingly handsome, irresistibly desirable. Her heart started to hammer. How quickly the comforting feeling she had felt in response to his kindness turned to desire.

Beware, the voice of reason chimed in her head. The ladder beckons. Leave with your dignity intact and the only possible decision open to you, unwavering.

She closed the trunk, topping the pile of garments she had selected to lend to Nathaniel with a blue and white striped nightcap. Moving back, she had to stoop so as not to bump her head on the sloping beam above her.

Max turned back from his study of the painting and smiled. 'Julian looks very like his father,' he remarked.

'With your easier temperament, thank God.'

He put his hand out and touched her wrist, saying, 'Julian is a lovely child. There is nothing in his nature that brings Lucien to mind.'

She felt the charged impulse travel up her arm, through her nerve endings and deliver its powerful jolt to the core of her heart. He felt it too, she could tell, just as she could tell he was equally aware of her answering reaction.

There was a tense breathless pause, lasting less than a second as their silent communication found a mutual answer.

She could not help herself. Could not deny the cravings of her body when he tugged her so she landed on his lap; could not stop herself responding with an ardour to match his when he took possession of her mouth, so easily plundering her useless resolve to resist him. His molten kisses consumed every last atom of resistance, sweeping away her fears of discovery, of the secrets between them. They lay in a small, unaffected part of her brain. Forgotten. For now.

She cupped his face as she kissed him back, drinking in all the love and courage he offered, wanting to be everything he desired.

'Lord in Heaven, Olivia,' he gasped, as he branded hot kisses the length of her throat, following the low cut neckline of her dress, 'I've never wanted anything, anyone, like I want you.'

His words ignited her answering need for a love that was not tainted like Lucien's had been, like Nathaniel's would be.

But reality was a whisper away.

Oh God, Nathaniel.

Then Max's hand stole across the outline of her breast to stroke the sensitive skin at the hollow of her neck and Nathaniel was forgotten beneath the onslaught of Max's redoubled ardour and in her rush of desire for him she forgot herself and whispered the truth.

'I've never wanted anyone like I want you, Max.'

For just an instant he stilled. 'Prove it,' he murmured through his kisses.

Prove it?

Shock banished her pleasure. She gasped and tried to wriggle out of his arms.

As his hands fell away she straightened, her hand going to her throat. Removing the chain from around her neck she handed it to him.

'The key to my heart,' she said. She looked down at her hands, now resting in her lap. 'Lucien gave it to me with those same words, though in truth it was the key which denied him the treasure he believed was hidden somewhere in the house. I only wish I could offer you something of substance.' She could hear the longing in her own voice, the pained acknowledgement that this was the end of everything between them.

His disconcerted look was quickly replaced by a laugh, short and tinged with irony as he said, 'The key to a chamber which will soon be occupied by someone else, it would seem.'

He set her from him, rising and going to the picture once more. 'Lucien has much to answer for,' she heard him mutter, before she felt his light touch as the pendant was replaced, once more, around her neck.

She glanced down, noticing it felt heavier, that the key was larger.

'The key to Elmwood.' His voice sounded almost distant behind her. 'It is your home if you ever choose to make it so.' He rested his hands upon her shoulders and she felt longing and pain curdle in her belly. 'If only I believed you were the scarlet woman Lucien painted you and that you were merely toying with me, I could understand.' His voice grew harsher when she said nothing.

'My God, Olivia, I know this was more than fumbling self gratification for you.' He came round to stand before her, looking down at where she sat.

'Your feelings came from the heart. Like the encounter before. And the one before that.' His face darkened with anger.

She could not bear it. Not the anger, nor the thought of losing him.

Oh, *why* had she done this? How could she have allowed herself to be so weak?

The flickering candlelight accentuated the shadows beneath his eyes. She could conjure him into Lucien if she wished. Pretend he would beat her into submission, violate her – oh, never her face, for what would the guests think? – unless she agreed to what he wanted.

She opened her mouth to speak. To tell him she would marry him. To lie to him so as to keep him off her back until he was gone and she could then exorcise him out of her life.

But she could not be so dishonourable.

'Then I will try to explain.' Hunched miserably into herself she noticed his surprised hesitancy as he cocked his head.

Yet how could she tell him? How could she explain the myriad brutalities which had resulted in those very actions which stood between them.

Julian.

How could she explain Julian?

'I'm listening,' he prompted after a long silence.

She swallowed, watching the forefinger of his right hand, its silent tapping against the crossbeam the only outward sign of his agitation.

She squeezed shut her eyes. For so long she had acted in *reaction*. Lucien's brutalities had prompted so many self-preserving defences.

Now, she felt exposed. Speaking the truth without it being violently torn from her seemed an impossible feat.

All she could do was lay the groundwork and hope that by the time she reached the end he'd have more understanding.

'Lucien was desperate for an heir.' It was feeble, but it was a start.

'I can hardly blame my cousin for that,' Max said, drily. 'Most men want an heir.'

Oh Lord, this was not going well.

'Our first child died within the hour. Lucien blamed me for the fact it was not baptized.' She swallowed, remembering his fury when he came into the bedroom to find her cradling the dead newborn. 'It was a difficult birth,' she went on, blocking out the pain, 'and I' – she turned her head away – 'was not ready for another, but Lucien would not heed the doctor. After that there were two miscarriages. Lucien blamed me.'

Glancing up at him she saw that his expression had lost its censure. Max settled himself beside her on the trunk and took her hands between his.

'Go on,' he said gently.

'Nathaniel said it was God's punishment on Lucien.'

'I trust he informed Lucien personally of this judgement.'

Olivia nodded. 'It didn't help. Lucien was even more brutal to me, though he continued to confess all his sins to Nathaniel.'

'An interesting position for your intended.'

Olivia gripped his hand and glared at him. 'Nathaniel was the only person Lucien allowed to show me any kindness.' Defensiveness made her hoarse. 'It was like a game to him. He encouraged it. He'd humiliate me in front of his guests, then wait for Nathaniel to cover me up and carry me away.' It was painful just to remember. 'Yet if any member of the company tried secretly to come to my aid, Lucien made sure they regretted it.' She gulped, turning to face Max once more. 'A young man stayed with us for a time. From Bavaria ...'

She couldn't go on. By the time Max's arms were across her back she was hunched over, sobbing silently.

'Forgive me,' he whispered, stroking her.

His touch was soothing, comforting as she remembered. She wanted to enjoy it forever. But of course, her obligation was not yet fulfilled.

'I had recently lost a child and Lucien was very angry. This young man and I spent much time together. Lucien found us reading poetry and took it into his head that we were' – she swallowed convulsively – 'betraying him. He beat Pieter to a pulp before my very eyes, and then … he punished me.'

Eventually Max asked, gently, 'What happened?'

'Nathaniel appeared and organized everything.' She shuddered. 'Pieter was covered in blood, groaning, the servants too afraid to go to his aid. Nathaniel tended to his wounds and dispatched him.' Olivia couldn't meet his eye. 'I don't know where he went. I never saw him again. When Nathaniel found me I was unconscious on the floor.' She looked at her feet, then held her arm to the candlelight. 'My dress was torn and I was covered in blood for his signet ring had sliced through my wrist. Lucien came back when Nathaniel was bathing me. He stood in the doorway and watched for a long time. Then he laughed and said I was between the Devil and God and whom would I choose? I told him it was a relief to me we didn't have a son because I couldn't bear seeing him turn out like his father. Then I said that while everyone believed I was unconscious I had had a message from our first born who was burning in the fires of Hell. I said little Lucien had informed me the Devil said he'd soon see his father because Lucien, too, was damned. Eternally damned.' Olivia gave a convulsive swallow. 'Lucien was terrified by the prospect of eternal damnation.' Another shiver made her convulse. 'I'd have said anything to stop him laying his hands on me again.'

'My poor Olivia,' murmured Max.

'It worked.' Olivia gulped. 'Lucien kept away from me after that. He held fewer parties.'

'Were you still required to add a … decorative touch?'

Olivia shook her head. 'I was with child again and quite ill throughout—'

'Olivia! Are you up there?' Aunt Eunice's voice carried up from the base of the ladder. 'Nathaniel has been ready for his bed this past half an hour. Surely you must have found one of Lucien's nightgowns by now?'

Olivia turned to Max as she rose. She felt panicked, her story only half told. 'Perhaps you'd better stay here.'

'Oh no, skulduggery is not part of my repertoire,' he said, as he prepared to follow her down the stairs to greet their reception party: the aunts and Nathaniel Kirkman.

CHAPTER SEVEN

━━◦◦◦⟨◦◦━━

M**AX STOOD BEFORE** the casement of the little chamber he'd been allotted and stared into the garden. Like ghostly soldiers, the poplars swayed in the pale night and the wind emitted a thin, eerie sound.

Sleep would elude him, he knew. There was no point even trying. Olivia's story appeared like an unfinished tapestry: loose threads everywhere.

She'd been leading up to a confession, but what was her crime? Or the worst of them? She'd been a victim for seven years. Survival would trump morality. Is that what she was telling him? What could she have done that was so shameful she'd chosen to keep silent and lose the man she had, finally, openly, professed to love?

He had no choice but to wait until the morning for answers, but would she be as willing to divulge all after a night in which to consider the consequences?

How would Max, himself, feel when confronted with the truth?

For he was beginning to fear the worst.

The storm was building. He must check on Julian as was his habit, but for the first time his thoughts of the boy evinced a shudder.

The nursery was in the west wing, far removed from the rest of the sleeping quarters. Quietly, he made his way along the corridor, pausing at the passage that intercepted it. He raised his candle high to identify the figure which had emerged at the end. Reverend Kirkman. Quickly, he stepped back. Hadn't he been accommodated at the other end of the house? he wondered, waiting for him to pass Olivia's bedchamber. If it were Kirkman's intention also to visit the nursery Max would delay his visit until later.

But he was not going to the nursery. Max heard the faint creak of the door to the only bedchamber along that passageway: Olivia's.

'Heavens, Max! You made my heart nearly stop.'

It was Olivia's Aunt Eunice arriving via another corridor, though it was hard to imagine anything had the power to make Aunt Eunice quake in her boots.

'You're checking on Julian, too, I see.'

Max forced a smile. And forced himself not to brush past Aunt Eunice and into Olivia's chamber on the heels of Kirkman.

'It's a habit,' he said, distractedly, unable to drag his eyes from the glow of candlelight that filtered from beneath Olivia's door. 'Julian isn't fond of storms.'

'Olivia always hated them,' Aunt Eunice remarked, taking Max's arm and steering him towards the nursery.

'I know.' Max glanced down at her, resigned to the fact he could not play sentinel until the other man emerged. 'She used to be locked in her room on such occasions.'

'Olivia slept with me or Catherine during thunderstorms.' Eunice slid accusing eyes across to Max. 'Lucien locked her in her room.'

He should have realized this, of course.

'Once he locked her in for five days on nothing but gruel and water.'

Despite what he'd learnt of Lucien's treatment he was still horrified.

Aunt Eunice met his dismay with a hard look. 'Martha, Olivia's maid told me. She went to The Lodge with Olivia when Olivia married and continued to pass on news even after she married the publican, Mr Mifflin.'

'Five days?' Though after what Olivia had told him he'd believe anything.

'Lucien saw conspiracies in everything she did. If she displeased him, he punished her. I believe on this occasion she'd walked to church with a neighbour, a handsome young man who admired her. The young man got a bloodied nose; Olivia got five days' incarceration. No doubt she learned to choose her companions carefully.' The old woman's voice grew bitter. She slowed her footsteps as they approached the nursery wing. 'He whisked my beautiful niece off her feet, squandered her happiness, sapped her of her spirit and stripped her of her son. And there was nothing I could do for she severed contact when she defied me to be with Lucien.'

She stopped, staring at the door before them. Even in the softening glow of candlelight the woman looked much older than she had earlier this evening. Her grey hair hung in a thin plait over one bony shoulder and her mouth quivered.

'Olivia was the child I never had.' Her voice caught. 'Georgiana, her mother, was the baby of the family. The favourite, for she inherited our Aunt Jane's entire fortune, only to squander it on a fortune-hunter who left her to die alone as she gave birth to Olivia.'

Max patted the woman's arm. 'Olivia's lucky to have had you, then.'

'Perhaps it was a mistake to protect her so much.' There was self doubt in the bleak look she sent him. 'In her childhood we spoiled her, cosseted her, turned her head with compliments.' She sucked in a breath. 'Then she met Lucien.' Max saw her tremble with the force of her hatred. 'Lucien taught her about life's cruelties. He had no mercy, even in death. And now our beautiful Olivia is about to sacrifice herself to that pompous old drone I've had to suffer the past year!'

She fixed Max with a gimlet look. Earlier he would have met it with an equally defiant one, declaring he had no intention of allowing such a thing to happen.

Right now he didn't know what to think.

His lack of conviction must have been apparent. Disappointment kindled in her eyes. 'I know she loves you,' Aunt Eunice whispered, as she gripped his wrist with one bony hand. Her look communicated her silent hope that Max would be Olivia's valiant defender.

Max stared at the floor, his resolve to be that man marred by the fear of what he'd discover when Olivia finally confessed the truth. 'She doesn't believe she deserves happiness,' he said, as he wondered how great her crime must be before that became indeed the truth.

*

Olivia jerked upright at the tentative rap upon the door. A wild rush of anticipation flooded her as she ran to it, turning the doorknob with a smile that reflected her burgeoning hope.

Max. He was not a man who'd let suspicions fester. Only the truth would answer and she'd give it to him. Damn the consequences.

'You'll pardon the intrusion, Olivia.' With his trademark frown and ponderous manner Nathaniel brushed past her, covering her hand with his own as he gently turned the doorknob, closing the door behind them.

'Nathaniel, you can't—'

Ignoring her, he put his hand upon her shoulder and led her away from the door.

She didn't like the way he was smiling at her.

Twisting out of his semi-embrace she crossed her hands in front of her chest, knowing the sheer fabric of her night rail left little to the imagination.

'So coy with me, Olivia, when we are soon to be wed?' he asked.

'I'm not going to marry you, Nathaniel.'

There. That's all it took. And she had said it. Now what could he do to her? She need only scream once and the entire household would descend upon the room in an instant.

With both hands now upon her shoulders he steered her backwards towards the bed. 'So it is as I feared.' She saw the anger in his eyes though his voice was calm.

'I shall scream.' But she could manage no more than a pathetic whisper and she was trembling so much it was all she could do to remain standing.

She was trapped between the high bed and Nathaniel who was leaning over her. In Lucien's striped nightshirt. Nathaniel was short of stature and more thickly set although he was by no means an unattractive man. He could set many a feminine heart aflutter, Olivia knew. More pious ones than hers.

'Don't do this, Nathaniel,' she pleaded. She could feel the hardness of his desire pressing against her thigh through the fabric of her nightgown before he pushed her upon her back.

'What? Take you here like a common harlot?' His eyes shone with derision, but at least he kept his feet on the floor. 'Under your own roof with your aunts down the corridor? Credit me with a little more finesse. No, Olivia, I mean only to discuss the situation in which we find ourselves. I think that under the circumstances it is quite proper you would entertain your betrothed when he has concerns about your future happiness' – her skin crawled at his heated breath on her neck – 'and the happiness of your son.'

It was hard to control her ragged breathing. She struggled beneath him before giving up, wishing she could manage more conviction as she whispered, 'Did you not hear me? I said I am not going to marry you so we have nothing to discuss.'

'Since this is the first I've heard of this new state of affairs I'd say we had plenty to discuss.'

Looming over her, his expression was difficult to read. Olivia closed her eyes against the anger, the wounded pride. She had not expected intimidation.

'I take it Mr Atherton is behind your change of heart. Clearly you've deceived me. You've met him before.'

Olivia inclined her head a fraction. No point denying it. However it stood to reason Nathaniel would take it badly being superseded by Lucien's cousin.

'I love Max.' It was catharsis to say it though whether or not Max still loved her or *would* still love her was another matter. At least telling Nathaniel that the truth was finally out in the open meant he would surely not continue to press his suit.

She was wrong.

He kept her pinioned upon the bed, his body heavy as he angled one knee beside her thigh to gain better purchase. 'I have waited eight long years to make you mine.' His whisper sounded more like a desperate snarl than a reaffirming caress. 'We've had an understanding since before Lucien died.'

Self-preservation battled within. She could not let him dominate her, terrorize her, as Lucien had.

She struggled again, managing to free one arm which she used to push him away, hissing, 'No, we have not!'

'Then we have misunderstood one another for my offer and your acceptance of it in the summerhouse seemed to me the only logical outcome of a long and difficult courtship.'

He released her then. She curled up her knees and swung round to gain distance but he sat heavily on the bed, pulling her across his chest and catching her beneath the knees to swing her on to his lap.

Olivia went rigid as he forced her head against his shoulder. The garment was musty from its months consigned to a trunk without air but she could smell the faint essence which reminded her so strongly of Lucien. And beneath it, the animal smell of her suitor, roused by anger and pride.

Nathaniel grasped her by the chin and twisted her face to look at him as he repeated roughly, 'Do not play the coy maiden with me just because another contender for your affections has presented himself. One that you prefer.' He clamped his hand round her neck and pulled her head back on to his shoulder. 'You know you cannot have him,' he hissed, as his hands caressed her throat.

'You can't force me to marry you,' Olivia rasped. She was close to swooning. Unable to struggle to any effect, she lay limply in his arms.

'There are many compelling reasons for a match between us.' The tenseness seemed to drain out of him in response to her passivity. Nathaniel sighed as his fingers explored the contours of her neck and chest. He gazed out of the window. 'Surely, my dear, you gave up fairy stories when you married Lucien.'

Olivia tried to swallow through her fear. 'Nathaniel, I ... I'm very fond of you but—'

'Don't think I'll be satisfied with a sop like that,' he sneered, bringing his face close to hers. 'We were meant to be together. Everything has been orchestrated for this union.'

'I want to be with Max. If—' She tried to be brave. 'If you force me to do anything against my will I *shall* scream, I promise you!'

'I'm not so stupid, Olivia.' Rising abruptly, he pushed her back down upon the bed. 'Look at you!' His voice dripped with derision. 'Eight years ago you were the toast of the town. A diamond of the first water. Now, you're just a shell. Your reputation is in tatters and the charm and gaiety that captivated society just a memory. Oh, to me you're still lovely to look at. I had hoped to restore to you what you had lost through your own foolishness. I had hoped to redeem you. No doubt Max thinks a vacuous plaything will do very well until he finds the kind of wife he's really after.' His lip curled as he delivered his verdict. 'An innocent, simple creature, pleasing to the eye with no damning past to threaten his manliness.'

She would not let him see he had found his mark. 'Max has honour and he knows his own mind. He wants *me*.'

'I've no doubt he wants you, Olivia,' chuckled Nathaniel. 'Most men want you. *I* want you. But does he want to marry you? And if so, was that after you threw yourself at him … but before you confessed to him the truth?'

Olivia gasped and covered her eyes, twisting away from him. Had they been empty taunts she could have borne them.

'Ever the slattern, Olivia.' Bending over her, he trailed his forefinger across her collarbone, skimming the tops of her breasts. 'Like satin,' he breathed. He traced the arches of her eyebrows. 'So beautiful yet so stupid,' he added, moving his mouth to her ear. 'So stupid because you cannot let your mind master your body. Unlike me, my darling Olivia, else I'd be walking away, satiated right now. But I shall leave that for another night. Our wedding night.'

Olivia started to cry; short, shallow gasps, tears streaming down her face. His shadow as he leaned over her was as oppressive as the weight of him had been. She hiccupped. 'How can you want me if you despise me so much?'

'Despise you?' He considered the question as he tugged loose the bow of her nightdress then retied it more tightly so that she was respectably covered. 'And love you in equal measure. I shall be your salvation, Olivia.'

'Max knows *everything* about my past,' Olivia whispered, recoiling from his touch, wishing for Max's embrace to wash away the sordidness she felt.

'Everything?' His brow furrowed as he sat. Hunched on the edge of the mattress he reminded her of a calculating toad who has just received a blow. He looked genuinely perplexed and Olivia revelled in her sudden power until he delivered his *coup de grâce*. 'How can he still want you when he knows your dark and dirty little secret?' His astonishment was not feigned and Olivia's self-disgust made her crumple inwardly as he added, 'He honestly forgives you for what you have stolen from him?'

The look on her face must have revealed the truth for suddenly he was standing, his arms around her as he drew her to her feet, supporting her as she swayed. His voice was triumphant as he cried, 'Always the dreamer, Olivia. You say you told him the truth. Ha! You've barely scratched the surface.'

She felt the wetness of her tears on the back of her hand as she wiped her cheek, raising her head from his shoulder where he'd forced it. This time she did not resist as he threw back the covers, lifted her gently on to the mattress and tucked the blankets around her.

'There, there, my love,' he soothed, bending over her, offering her the milk Aunt Catherine had warmed and brought her a short while before. 'Drink this. You've had a nasty shock, discovering your beauty isn't always enough to get you what you want. Soon I will be your husband: friend, not foe. With every weapon at my disposal I shall ensure Julian's future remains secure.' On stockinged feet he padded towards the door, turning when he reached the middle of the carpet. 'Don't worry, Olivia.'

She turned her head from his triumphant sneer.

'You may not love me, but your secret is safe. We both know guarding that little powder keg is essential … for the happiness of *all* concerned.'

An empty shell.

Is that what she was?

Shivering, curled up in her narrow bed she listened to the mice in the wainscoting and the rattle of the casement. Hours later the chirping of birds announced the dawn.

How desperately she had tried to find the words to unburden her soul, to tell Max the truth when they had been in the attic. How close she had been.

And she would have followed through on her promise of the truth in the morning had it not been for Nathaniel's visit.

Max was the light in her life. He made her believe the truth could be overcome.

Nathaniel's visit reminded her it could not.

Quietly, she sobbed, hunched beneath the covers, racked with despair. What should she do? She was torn asunder by her feelings for the three males beneath this roof but Nathaniel held the trump card. It wasn't just his insidious threats of revealing the truth about Julian. Before Nathaniel's visit Olivia had resolved to do just that, herself.

It was his judgement. With time Max would regard her as Lucien had – venality masquerading in a cloak of beauty.

A thwarted Nathaniel would turn her sins into moral outrages and evidence of corruption not even the most besotted suitor could countenance.

Head pounding, she tried to crystallize her thoughts.

With the brightening dawn her courage returned.

At the heart of every decision she'd made since Julian had been born was his future.

Marriage to Nathaniel ensured the safety and welfare of her son.

But how would Julian judge *her* when he was grown?

A woman too afraid to trust her instincts? Too weak to stand firm against threats and coercion?

Miserably, she reflected on the two men who held her hostage: Max with his love and the fact he deserved an unpalatable truth she was too afraid to risk. And Nathaniel with his threats and his *promises* to hide the truth.

Drawing in a rasping breath she struggled upright on her pillows, her heart racing.

The truth lay at the heart of everything.

Only the truth would answer. Aunt Eunice had sent her to Elmwood to 'set the record straight' so she could regain her son but from the outset she had lacked the courage to tell Max the truth.

Yet Max's love had held firm in the face of her shameful deception.

Why? Because he believed she was pure of heart.

She was!

She shivered, her mind engaged in a battle between hope and fear. Unless she conquered her fear she'd never realize her dreams.

Nathaniel had made her believe Max represented Julian's greatest threat; that only he, The Rev'd Nathaniel Kirkman, had the power to protect Julian's future. He'd used veiled threats to conjure up a future unimaginably perilous for young Julian.

Oh God, she thought, her pulses racing, why had she not seen the truth before?

Max was not Julian's greatest threat: Nathaniel was.

CHAPTER EIGHT

A FIRE WITH ANTICIPATION, Max waited for her at breakfast. After a night in which doubts and fears chased firm resolves to forgive her everything, he now needed simply to see her.

One frank smile and a murmured reinforcement of her feelings for him would be sufficient. He freely admitted he was enslaved.

Olivia had suffered appallingly during her marriage to Lucien. However shocking the truth, she was the victim of forces beyond her control.

With an effort he forced down his smoked haddock – and the impulse to jerk his head round to Aunt Eunice on his left and give her the reassurances she had wanted last night: that regardless, he would be Olivia's knight in shining armour. He would protect her to the end.

And he would.

He just wished he could reassure Olivia, but her chair remained empty and he was barely able to hide his disappointment when Dorcas appeared with the announcement that Olivia was still sleeping and seemed feverish.

Finally the moment of departure was upon him. He could delay it no longer. Olivia's aunts, Eunice and Catherine, exclaimed their pleasure at his company, pressing him to return soon. Kirkman merely nodded stiffly.

A thick covering of snow whitened the curving driveway that led to the main road. He'd said his farewells at the front step, exhorting everyone to return to the warmth of indoors.

Now, from astride Odin, Max gazed up at Olivia's casement window. In three seconds he would be out of Olivia's life, but not for long.

Hadn't she avowed her love for him? Surely all she required was affirmation of his understanding and forgiveness. Even if his worst fears were confirmed....

Ignoring his apprehension he held firm, reminding himself of what was at the heart of Olivia's forthcoming admission: she was not to blame.

He lowered his head to whisper encouragement to his horse, twisting in the saddle when he heard the crunch of footsteps upon the gravel. Light, running footsteps.

Wearing nothing warmer than a flimsy Norwich shawl over her dress, Olivia was hastening across the few yards which separated them.

Lord, she was beautiful. With her hair hanging past her shoulders in two plaits she reminded him of one of the Vestal Virgins in a book of illustrations he'd had as a child.

Having been tormented by Olivia's unfinished tale, the myriad possibilities as to why she was unable to commit herself to him – each more lurid than the last – his heart now soared. Her haste and the look in her eye could mean only one thing: she was here to confess and crave his understanding.

And she would have it.

Drinking in those spectacular blue eyes and the full, curved lips he could kiss forever, he would forgive her anything.

'Max! You ask why I believe I cannot marry you.' Her voice came in breathless gasps. 'There is no easy way to say it and no time to dress up the truth but if you will hear me out—'

'Come with me now,' he urged, reason turning him into an impetuous schoolboy as he reached down from the saddle for her. The urge to protect her thundered in his breast. 'If you are frightened of Kirkman, don't be, for I will let nothing harm you. Ever.'

Tears formed on her lashes. It could have been the cold and the exertion but he did not think so.

'Oh Max!' Her voice disappeared on a cry of pain. 'I have wronged you so greatly but Lord knows it was not my intention at the time.'

'Hush.' He dismounted and drew her, unresisting, into his arms. 'Confess your secret, but you already have my absolution. I can see Lucien's lies for what they are.'

'Lucien's lies have nothing to do with this. It is what I have done.'

Brushing his lips across her brow he corrected her. 'What Lucien *made* you do, Olivia. With me you need no longer be afraid.'

She pulled out of his arms, wiping her streaming eyes with the back of her hand. Taking a deep breath she half turned, but her words were clear, misted in the icy air as she gasped, 'Max! Though I have done wrong, things are not as they seem.'

'Ah, Olivia, I am glad to see Mr Atherton is receiving the send-off he deserves.'

They hadn't heard him approach. Flinching, Olivia swung round as Max's shock hardened.

Mr Kirkman placed a proprietary hand upon Olivia's shoulder and confronted Max with obsidian eyes.

'Olivia will miss you very much, Mr Atherton.' It came out a purr. 'She told me so last night.' His hand slid down her arm to clasp her small fist.

She made no move to push him away.

Max stared with confusion at the woman he loved. He wanted to repeat his offer. To take her with him, but her expression was suddenly closed as she half raised her hand in parting.

'God speed, Max,' she murmured. A spasm of fear crossed her face then boldly she took a step forward and placed her hand on his shoulder.

He had to lower his head to hear her.

'I shall write, Max,' she whispered. 'I shall explain everything.'

I shall write.

The rebirth of hope gave him new strength. On impulse he halted Odin on a bend of the drive which led to The Lodge.

A gravel path led to the family crypt a few yards away. Dug into the side of the hill, halfway to the dower house, it had been a favourite hiding place during a memorable holiday when he'd been a small boy.

He decided to pay his final respects to his cousin. He'd try to remember Lucien as a boisterous playmate and pleasant companion rather than the violent despot who had tyrannized Olivia for seven years.

But the door to the crypt would not yield. Lichen-encrusted and swollen with age it seemed an impenetrable barrier between the past and the present.

Max stared at it, wondering if his body would be interred within the stone sarcophagus beside his cousin. Imagining Olivia, in black, reclaiming freedom only to lose it to the possessive churchman.

With a surge of angry longing he tugged at the key on its thin chain which he had placed around his neck.

'The key to her heart' she had said, just as the chain snapped and the key fell with a dull jangle to the flagstone upon which he stood. A cruel echo of Lucien's meaningless words.

Bending down he picked it up and, without thinking, inserted it into the lock. It turned smoothly and the door swung open, admitting him to the hallowed precincts of the final resting place for all the Viscounts Farquhar for the past 400 years.

And their faithful dogs, he amended with a wry smile, as he stepped into the gloom.

A high window, just above ground level, admitted the weak spring sunlight and, as his gaze slid from the stately sarcophagus where Lucien was interred to the tiny sarcophagus beside him, he felt a rush of sorrow and sympathy for Olivia.

How must it have felt to have been consigned to no more than a vessel that must produce the next heir? Derided, abused and worthy of less consideration than the King Charles' Spaniel Lucien showered with affection and which now lay in state in its miniature resting place beside him.

Olivia had been granted life tenure of the dower house with almost nothing to live upon, after being stripped of the one being that gave her life meaning: her child.

'Ah, Lucien, it was ill done of you,' he said, running his hand over his cousin's inscription before turning away.

If only Mr Kirkman had no rightful claim upon Olivia he would stride up the hill and demand that Olivia return to Elmwood with him now. That he forgave her everything and he knew how to make it all right.

He pulled the door shut, blocking out the past but unable to change it.

For Kirkman's involvement altered everything.

Nathaniel drew Olivia back to the house with him before Max had disappeared round the bend of the drive. How desperately she longed to prolong the moment before his beloved form was no more than a memory, but Nathaniel was a force too great to resist, alone.

Pleading a megrim as soon as she was indoors she gathered ink and paper from the drawing room while Aunt Eunice cornered Nathaniel, begging him with uncharacteristic interest to regale her with the details of the sermon he was writing for his forthcoming sermon in Nuningford.

Nuningford. A week from now.

Gazing from the casement window in her bedchamber Olivia watched Max's straight-backed figure disappear round the bend that led to the main road.

She drew in her breath, her nerve ends tingling before setting her writing box on her lap and beginning the hardest letter she had ever written.

Max, her knight in shining armour.

Max, whom she loved more than she'd believed possible, whose love for her gave her strength and purpose.

How would he feel about her when he read her confession?

My dearest Max – she could feel the blood surging through her veins as the pen scratched over the rough surface – *I promised you the truth and you shall have it. There is no easy way to say this—*

The truth.

Dropping her pen, Olivia rose and went to the window.

The truth would change everything: Julian's security, Olivia's future and quite possibly Max's love for her. But the truth was the only way to remove Nathaniel's shackles and to move on with her life.

Looking down at her white knuckles and the ink spots on her fingers, she reaffirmed her resolve. If she continued to evade the truth she would be worse than the creature beyond redemption Lucien had painted her. And if she had any chance of earning Max's continued love and respect she had to take the risk now.

Returning to her writing desk she continued.

The truth is that Julian is not Lucien's legitimate heir. He is not the boy born to me that terrible stormy night when Lucien was away hunting and my physician was delivering a breech birth many miles away....

The pain and horror of that night was engraved upon her mind. Charlotte and Martha had attended her as she had convulsed with birthing pangs upon the four-poster in which Lucien had been born, and his father and grandfather before him.

The raging storm had prevented the message being delivered to the physician for several hours. Charlotte had soothed her, reminding her that Martha had delivered her six siblings after news came that the squire's wife was dying. The river was swelling and it was doubtful the physician would be able to cross when his painful job was done.

Picking up her pen, Olivia continued.

Our child was born strong and lusty. Charlotte and Martha put him to my breast and we celebrated that at last Lucien had his heir and perhaps I would have my peace.

Olivia forced herself to continue.

But the boy died within the hour. He started to labour in his breathing and in terror I had Martha fetch Mr Kirkman. Lucien needed to be reassured that this child would not burn in the fires of Hell.

Unable to continue, Olivia pushed back her chair and took a restless turn about the room. Twisting her hands, she tried to compose herself, formulate her words so that Max might understand the terrible grief that consumed her that night; her fear of Lucien's anger and the maternal cravings which would grasp at any means of giving her the son she and Lucien wanted so desperately.

Even if it meant a terrible deception.

Slowly she lowered herself into her seat and picked up the pen once more. With thundering heart she dipped it into the inkwell.

The moment had come to commit to paper the words that would be the ultimate test of Max's love.

Nathaniel came promtply. In his arms he carried a babe, wrapped in swaddling clothes. Its cry was as lusty as my own child's had been, less than an hour before. But my own child was now silent. Blue and silent and the reverend was too late.

I fought Nathaniel as he removed my beloved infant then watched in wonder as this new child latched on to my breast.

Julian.

Olivia sat back so the tears would not spoil the ink. Wiping them away with the back of her hand, she wrote,

Julian is Lucien's child by his village mistress who delivered the same night. When I saw the eyes and the shape of his jaw I knew Mr Kirkman spoke the truth: that Lucien was his father and that he would die unless a wet nurse were found soon.

It took a moment for Olivia to compose herself before she could continue.

Forgive me, Max, for doing what any bereaved mother would surely do.

From the moment I suckled the child, knowing its mother was dead, I could not give him up. A precious gift had been put into my safekeeping and it was my God-given duty to protect him ... to the death.

Julian was not born within the sanctity of marriage but he is Lucien's child, nonetheless. Lucien's fury would have known no bounds if he'd returned to learn his son had died before he was baptized.

I confess that while my love for the child was instant and sincere I was also guilty of cowardice. I did not know how I could survive much more of Lucien's brutality in his determination to father an heir.

Olivia put the pen down and ran the back of her hand across her brow before she was able to finish her task.

Darling Max, I paid no thought to your rights when I acted as I did. Only since I met you have I understood the enormity of my actions which have denied you your birthright. This letter sets out the truth and also begs your forgiveness. I would not hurt you for the world.

You have brought the sun into my life and given me hope where none existed before. I love you like I never believed possible and can only hope your kindness and compassion will temper the disgust you have every reason to feel on account of my continued lies.

The time for lies is past, now, and I offer this full accounting so that you may decide how best to proceed in order for you to reclaim what my actions have wrongfully taken away from you.

Whatever you decide, please know that I shall understand and continue to love you.

Meanwhile I wait in fevered anticipation for a sign indicating your feelings and outlining the course of action you wish me to take in order to redress the wrong I have done.

For now and always, I remain your loving Olivia.

She had to allow herself to hope; to believe that Max's compassion would ensure she would *not* be accompanying Nathaniel to Nuningford the following week.

After sprinkling sand on the parchment she folded and addressed the precious missive just as Dorcas entered to bring her some comfrey tea for her aching head.

'I'll take that with Miss Catherine's letter to her Cousin Mariah, shall I?' asked Dorcas, setting down the mug of steaming tea and picking up the letter.

Olivia turned her head away so as not draw attention to her excitement. 'Thank you, Dorcas.'

'An' what shall I tell your aunts who are worried for your poor head?'

'That I shall be down for luncheon,' she said. 'The rest has done me good, as I'm sure the tea will.'

Dorcas placed the letter in her apron pocket and picked up the breakfast tray she'd brought her mistress earlier that morning. It remained untouched.

At the bottom of the stairs she met Mr Kirkman who had just put on his gloves and greatcoat.

'I hope Lady Farquhar recovers her good health soon,' he said, as he reached for Aunt Catherine's letter which lay upon the silver salver on the hall stand.

'She seems better, sir,' Dorcas said.

Hesitating, he looked at her as he put on his hat. 'I believe, Dorcas,' he said, 'you have something from your mistress which is to go out with Miss Catherine's letter.'

Smiling, he held out his hand.

It was noon and Max was hungry when he dismounted in the stable yard of The Pelican less than an hour later, tossing the reins to an ostler.

Olivia's parting had reaffirmed the promise that existed between them. The promise of a future that could withstand the perilous present and the lies of the past.

Olivia was true of heart and her heart belonged to him.

'Regular beauty, ain't he?' The stable-lad's tone was admiring as he stroked the horse's steaming flank. Hopeful, too, as he asked, 'We'll be stabling him for the night?'

'Only an hour or so,' replied Max, nodding as the publican appeared on the back step lacing his hands across his impressive belly as he welcomed him.

Max shrugged off his greatcoat as he entered the low-ceilinged room. He'd expected to find it empty but a returned soldier muffled against the cold sat drinking in the shadows.

'Don't mind Dorling over there. Known him since we was lads together afore he joined 'is Majesty's Service,' said the publican, with a dismissive wave in the soldier's direction while he poured Max an ale.

Dorling, eyes not meeting theirs, jerked his head in acknowledgement, his expression sour.

'Never bin the same since his daughter died,' the publican explained in a stage whisper, as he pushed Max's drink across the counter top and lowered his bulk on to a stool behind. 'So,' he added in regular tones, 'you've just come from the big house, I gather. Me wife, Mrs Mifflin, used to be lady's maid to Lady Farquhar.' There was pride in his tone.

'To the good lady,' muttered the soldier, raising his tankard.

Max's response was cut short as the publican slammed his fist down on the counter.

'You keep yer thoughts to yerself tonight, Dorling, or you'll be kissin' Jack Mifflin's great fist,' the publican warned, wagging a menacing finger in the old soldier's direction. 'Mr Atherton 'ere is a guest of the Misses Dingley.' The pewter ware rattled and a great log in the fireplace shifted noisily in the threatening silence.

Max raised his eyebrows but kept silent. The publican's response seemed excessive, especially as he heaved his great bulk to his feet and continued to glower in Pat Dorling's direction.

Dorling looked almost smug.

'Guest of my lady, eh? He who is smitten shall be smited.' The old soldier cackled at his obscure joke, baring an incomplete set of yellowed teeth. He squinted at Max. 'Acquainted with Lady Farquhar already? I's sure you was amply rewarded, a handsome gennelmun such as yourself.'

Steadily, Max regarded the odorous creature, the tattered scarlet uniform visible beneath his greasy greatcoat. The dirty, unsteady hand that reached for his drink told its own story. The man was drunk and had some grievance against the elderly sisters and their niece. Perhaps he'd been a former employee, dismissed for his fondness for the bottle. Perhaps he'd harboured a *tendre* for Olivia and been given his marching orders.

'Observe the respect due to Lady Farquhar,' he warned.

The publican settled himself back upon his stool. 'Or you'll be out on your ear,' he threatened.

'Even without your good lady to issue the orders?' Dorling fixed Max with a baleful look, adding, 'Ain't allowed to cross the threshold when Madam Viper's around.'

'Well, you'll 'ardly get much sympathy from that quarter, mouthing off at them refined ladies at the dower house when you know my missus'd give 'em 'er last farthing if they'd only say the word, poor as church mice they all be. Now be off with yer afore you say summat you really regret.'

'Ah, Jack, that ain't no way to treat a friend of forty years an' more. Leastaways let me finish me drink wot I paid good money for, then I'll go, quiet as a lamb.'

The man laced his fingers round his mug, settled himself more comfortably in his corner chair and looked morose. 'I hear The Lodge is all shut up now.' He sighed. 'The widow Farquhar hadn't the funds to keep it up so it's kept in dust sheets until it's leased again, or the boy comes into his inheritance. Ah, there was merry times there afore the merry widow were a widow.'

He sucked his gums loudly in the silence, his quick darting eyes showing he knew how to play to an audience.

Max shifted in his seat, his discomfort growing. Could this pock-marked old soldier suspect the secrets Olivia hugged so closely to herself? The secrets she had promised to reveal to Max and which Max had sworn to forgive – he licked lips, suddenly dry – on the basis that Olivia was a helpless, unwilling victim of circumstance?

'Lady Farquhar has mourned her late husband a full twelve months, sir,' he said. His voice held a note of warning.

'Oh, aye, she's entitled to find herself a man to her liking, I'll grant you that,' Dorling conceded readily enough. 'Spoiled for choice, no doubt, with all them gennulmen who've tasted 'er wares lining up at her door. Me being one of 'em, but o' course she don't remember me' – he gave another plaintive sigh and fixed his rheumy eyes on Max – 'when I were just one o' so many.'

'Out!' roared the publican at the same time as Max rose to his feet, his hand going to his hip where once his scabbard hung; but it was more than a year since he'd swapped soldiering for farming and he no longer carried a weapon.

'What would a man like yersel' know of such a lady? You've insulted Lady Farquhar and I'll not have it. Get out!' roared the publican, towering over the little man whose disgusting appearance belied his insinuation.

The soldier rolled his red-rimmed eyes and made a smacking noise with his lips as he kissed the tips of his fingers in an extravagant gesture. He did not move. 'I's told you afore only seems you were a lot more eager for the details than seems to be the case tonight.'

Though a part of him hated himself for doing so Max needed to hear the worst from a stranger: from the lips of a coarse and common soldier who, under normal circumstances, should think himself lucky to kiss the hem of a lady so superior to himself.

Dorling drained his mug and pushed it across the counter with a nod for it to be refilled. He sniffed. 'No doubt you gazed at the great lady with awe, sir, though I'd challenge you to 'ave said no to a taste of Lady Farquhar's butterfly if it were presented to you on a platter.' In the horrified silence he added with relish, 'Aye, literally.'

Max felt the bile rise up in his throat as the publican yelled, 'Slander!' and wrapped his large, meaty hands around the little man's neck.

'God's honour, 'tis the truth,' gasped Dorling.

'Let him repeat the story he no doubt tells any who'll listen,' Max said coldly as he finished his ale. 'Then it's my turn to wrap my hands around his neck.'

Reluctantly, the publican released his erstwhile friend. The little man chuckled as he resumed his seat, jauntily nodding his thanks as he picked up his tankard.

'I were invited to the great house on account of my skill wi' the cards and it pleased Lord Farquhar to put on a little entertainment for the assembled company.' He leered at the two men, his beady little eyes greedy for their shock, undeterred by their hostility and contempt. 'Just so happened it was his wife that were the main event. Served up on the most enormous silver platter all covered with fruit. Aye, sirs, fruit and cream with the lady revealed in all 'er splendour when the cover were removed. Then the music started and she did 'er little dance upon the table with the company roarin' an' cheerin' their approval.' He puffed out his chest. 'You think the likes of me ain't fit to lick 'er boots, but let me tell you, I licked a damned sight tastier morsel that night.' He bared his yellow teeth in a parody of a grin as he said with satisfaction: 'Lady Farquhar's Butterfly. Taught 'is Lordship some rare tricks wi' the cards that night and were 'appy not to 'ave to pay for the privilege of rolling that cherry round on me tongue like the others to whom 'is Lordship were indebted—'

The smack as Max's fist connected with his jaw was stifled by his bellow of fury as he threw himself upon the man. Gathering him up by the scruff of his neck he slammed him against the doorframe. Dorling squealed like a rabbit being skinned, but his expression was defiant as he glared at the two men who brandished their fists above his nose.

'You think a lady's above reproach just because she puts a fancy title in front of her name?' He wiped the back of his hand across his mouth, grimacing at the blood. 'Well, me blessed Meg, God rest 'er soul, were a hundred times more of a lady when Lord Farquhar took a fancy to 'er an' do you think she had any say in the matter? Now she's dead on 'is account while me lady who laughed and danced upon the table like a tuppenny whore sails on to greener pastures.'

With an air of injured dignity he shrugged himself free and headed for the door, rubbing his jaw. 'Anyone'd think you had designs on the lady, yersel',' he muttered, with a narrow-eyed look in Max's direction. 'Reckon you 'as to be mighty plump in the pocket if she'll flutter 'er lashes, or anything else, at you.'

'Lady Farquhar is to become a clergyman's wife,' the publican said, brandishing a heavy pewter mug as he waved the man out.

Dorling turned, disbelief warring with ribaldry. With a guffaw he gripped the doorframe to steady himself.

'Well, don't that beat all!' He shook his head. 'Not that clinging little Reverend Kirkham who sprinkled holy water on 'er ladyship's footsteps before 'e spirited her away after each debauch?'

Sick to the stomach, Max watched as the publican dealt the old soldier a parting kick.

'Reckon it was the clergyman what fathered that child o' hers!' Dorling taunted from the doorway. 'Ain't no wonder 'e wants to marry her!'

Max steadied himself against the back of a chair.

'Ain't no more than wot the designing trollop deserves! Cursed my Meg, she did, and stole the reverend's sister from 'is lordship!' Dorling's eyes were pinpricks of malice. 'Well, 'e's welcome to 'er, 'e is. Lord Farquhar took away her son on account of her loose morals and t'was no more'n she deserved, but my Meg didn't deserve what she got. 'Twas the reverend wot let my Meg die *and* the child she bore, leaving me wi' now't!'

Chapter Nine

For five days Olivia existed in a haze of hope but as the week drew to a close a heavy resignation descended upon her.

She saw the dubious glances her aunts exchanged when Miss Latimer held up the bolt of dun-coloured fabric she'd selected for her wedding gown, and was unmoved.

'That will do nicely.'

If she thought only of the fact that marriage to Nathaniel was still – as it always had been – her only alternative, she could survive.

She clasped her hands at her breast. The spark of hope which had flickered so brightly since she had met Max had died inside her. Her confession had killed his love.

His silence was killing *her*.

Nathaniel had played his trump card and Max had conceded. There could be no more testimony of his change of heart than his silence to the letter of confession she had written him.

Olivia gazed at her little boy who was playing with some wooden pegs under the table and her heart swelled with love.

Then constricted with fear.

What would happen now?

Perhaps Max would publicly declare Julian a usurper. The repercussions went further than public humiliation and an uncertain future. The small allowance Olivia was allowed as custodian of the child would be cut off.

'Do you not think the gown will be a little ... plain?' Aunt Catherine ventured.

'It's not in your usual style.' Eunice touched the drab coloured sarsanet and sighed. 'Though I suppose it's been eight years since I saw you clothed according to your own taste.'

'My own taste?' Olivia's lips twitched. It was a relief for her mind to travel beyond the grief that held her hostage. 'Do you remember the sparks that flew as we fought over the gown in which I was to be presented?' She ran her eyes over the fabric and the sketch which Miss Latimer was holding up. It held no interest or meaning for her. Marriage was a bargain, after all. Few women married for love. What did the reasons for her impending nuptials matter? She and Julian needed a roof over their heads and now that Nathaniel was getting his way he may well be kind to them both. 'I thought you'd be pleased at my new-found sobriety.'

'You're going to be a clergyman's wife, not take holy orders.'

'Is there no pleasing you, Aunt Eunice?' Olivia sighed. Once she'd have flared up and flounced from the room. Now she strove for meas-ured calm and her words contained a note of sorrow rather than recrimination. Indeed, she felt little real emotion. It was as if her heart were contained in a glass box. Now that her future had been deter-mined she told herself she had little further interest in it.

'Let us walk Miss Latimer to the garden gate and then take a turn around the garden,' Aunt Eunice suggested with clearly an ulterior motive.

'So you can try yet again to talk "sense" into me?' Olivia whispered with deceptive sweetness, as Aunt Catherine helped the seamstress roll up the fabric.

She took her aunt's arm and, smiling at Miss Latimer, ushered her to the door.

'So, young lady, Nathaniel is determined to mould you to his own fashion, just as Lucien did. And once again, you're following like a little lamb.'

Olivia's step faltered but she made a quick recover and continued resolutely along the pathway which had been swept clear of snow.

'I can tell you are trying to provoke me into a passion, Aunt Eunice,' she said, calmly, 'therefore I shall not dignify that with an answer.'

'Good Lord, Olivia, if ever there was a girl to try one. I don't know what your mother would have made of you.' She heaved in a breath. 'I expect you'd have been at each other's throats, you're so alike.'

Olivia felt emotion surge through her veins. She did not want to talk of her mother, just as she did not wish to speak of Max.

'Olivia.'

Olivia was surprised at the urgency in her aunt's tone. Even more so when her aunt gripped her shoulders and held her clumsily against her for a brief moment before letting her go.

Resuming her footsteps, head bent, she went on, 'Why do you persist in this madness of atoning for …' Her words trailed off, though she did not slow her pace. Finally she added, 'For I wish I knew what, exactly.'

'Nathaniel has offered Julian and me a future.' Olivia hurried to catch up with her aunt, still taken aback by the uncharacteristic show of affection as she struggled with the question. 'I thought I was marrying for love when I eloped with Lucien. I do not intend making the same mistake twice.'

'You married Lucien to be perverse because Catherine and I were so opposed to—'

'Are you suggesting I'm marrying Nathaniel simply to be perverse? How little you understand me, Aunt Eunice.'

Her aunt looked at her sadly. 'Yes, how little I know you, Olivia. How little I knew your mother.' Shaking her head, she went on, 'If it's about money, we can manage. Come with us to Bath, Olivia. Enjoy yourself for a change.'

Olivia bit her lip as she looked past her aunt's old, weary face, now bright with hope, to the fir trees beyond, limned with pink and gold light as the sun faded. Last week it had been a supernatural, ethereally beautiful scene, gilded with promise as she had walked this path with Max. He made her feel anything were possible. Even happiness.

But happiness had been fleeting. She should have known it.

Bone-jarring shards of pain stabbed at her once more. She had told

Max *everything*. Seven days it had been and she had received nothing but silence. What choice did she have but to continue her current course?

To go to Nuningford with Nathaniel? To hear the sermon he had written for her on shame and atonement?

She shuddered as she thought of the man who swore to safeguard Julian's future, Olivia's future and …

Closing her eyes she sucked in a shaky breath.

… and the secret she had disclosed to Max, but which had been received by cold, stony silence?

The hope in Aunt Eunice's eyes faded at Olivia's lack of response. 'If I thought you loved Nathaniel I'd have no reservations, but you don't.' She gave a grunt of frustration. 'Ask him to release you. I don't know what hold he has over you, but he will never make you happy.' Squeezing her shoulder she tried again. 'Your cousin Mariah and young Lucy would love to see you again. They asked if you would come.'

Olivia shook her head. 'I am twenty-six years old, Aunt Eunice. Old enough to decide that marrying is in the best interests of my son.' The enticing thought of going to Bath was stifled by her acceptance of her obligations: her visit to Nuningford to hear her husband-to-be preach.

She had no choice for she had to ally herself with someone who would provide for her son.

'I'm sorry, Aunt Eunice,' she said with genuine regret, 'but I cannot accompany you to Bath.'

They returned to the house to find Julian in tears and an exasperated Nathaniel leaning over him.

'Whatever's the matter?' Olivia hurried over and sank on to the drawing-room carpet so she could take her small son on to her lap.

For the first time he did not push her away, but clung to her, sobbing as he buried his tear-stained face in her shoulder.

Olivia held him tighter. How precious he was. The greatest gift of her life. A huge lump formed in her throat.

'Puppy …' he gulped. 'I want puppy.'

She turned to where a soft mewling sound came from a cane basket. A pair of large eyes, as tragic as Julian's, regarded her from over the top.

Nathaniel, frowning, reached across from his chair brandishing a piece of parchment.

Stifling the gasp that rose to her lips, Olivia took it, hoping he did not notice her shaking hand.

Max had written.

Barely able to contain her excitement, her eyes skimmed the sparse four lines of text: instructions for Julian on how to care for his new friend and the reassurance Max would see him when his new stepfather deemed fit.

Shocked, her hands dropped to her lap, the parchment fluttering to the floor. There could be no more blunt way for Max to indicate his withdrawal from the contest for Olivia's affections.

Turning her head from Nathaniel's scrutiny, she gave the puppy a distracted stroke. Julian was loving it a little too enthusiastically but she was imprisoned within a cocoon of grief, heedless of all but the pain which shredded her heart.

The extent of her shock made her realize that despite his silence she had still held out hope. The crisp, business-like tone and reference to her marriage as a *fait accompli* now made it clear there was no hope.

Forcing herself back to practicalities, she schooled her manner into one of quiet reason. 'Why should Julian not be allowed to keep the dog?'

She must concentrate on the soft warmth of her child and the joy of feeling needed.

The look Nathaniel sent her reminded her she must watch her tone. With characteristic care he smoothed his coat tails as he rose. Standing, he regarded her, steadily.

'My dear Olivia, while I have nothing, personally, against Mr Atherton and can understand his gift was well intentioned I do not believe it is in Julian's best interests to have such a potent reminder of his life with his uncle.'

Olivia opened her mouth to protest. Her impulse was to flare up at him, tell him that of course Julian could keep the dog. She was his mother!

Nathaniel's expression changed her mind. A tight, warning smile turned up the corners of his mouth while the expression in his hooded dark eyes was implacable. He was not angry. Yet. But she could see this tussle for domestic authority was a litmus test for the future.

She dropped her eyes, hugging Julian closer to her. He was whimpering, but seemed content to be in her arms.

Never had she felt more keenly the responsibility for his future, his security and happiness.

He looked to her to protect him. She felt the pride, the joy, the burden of it churn in her heart. Resting her head upon Julian's she breathed carefully past the panic.

She was Julian's only barrier against a harsh and unpredictable world. Max had failed her. While he had given eloquent expression to his change of heart he had left her in fearful suspense as to what he might do next.

Nathaniel was still looking at her. Waiting. He had assumed the mantle of protector to the wronged and aggrieved Lady Farquhar long ago.

The arbiter of all domestic decisions, too.

Still clutching Julian to her chest she said as evenly as she could, 'Max says in his letter he'd promised Julian a puppy from his dog Pansy's litter when they were parting.' She found she was clenching her hands. She hated to do it, but she was prepared to beg. 'Please let Julian keep the puppy,' she whispered.

Wrenching himself out of Olivia's arms, Julian was like a miniature tornado as he head butted her stomach. 'Puppy, mine! Puppy, mine!' he wept. Holding him at bay, Olivia watched fearfully the play of emotions cross Nathaniel's face.

Would he punish the child for his stubborn resistance to accepting his decree? Nathaniel did not understand two year olds. He may well consider this a disciplinary matter.

To her relief he elected not to choose this path. Sighing, he turned to leave. 'I shall consider it while I prepare my sermon this afternoon.

In the meantime, see the dog is taken to the kitchen so Julian does not get too attached to it.'

He left her sitting in the middle of the carpet with Julian sobbing in her lap and Max's letter gripped between her fingers.

So Nathaniel had seen nothing untoward in opening the parchment which clearly had not been intended for him?

In a trance she stroked the dark curls of her baby: the fruit of her husband's betrayal, the son whose future only she could protect.

Through the fog of despair came a flicker of hope. Perhaps Max had suspected Nathaniel would intercept any correspondence between them. Perhaps he would communicate privately with her.

Tell her he loved her? That he forgave her everything?

Fear returned.

Perhaps he would coldly demand she announce Max publicly as the new viscount and prostrate herself as the woman who had denied Max his birthright?

Kissing Julian's silky curls she acknowledged he would not be so cold and she would do whatever was required for Max to take up his rightful position.

She owed him that.

But without his support she would be a disgraced widow, her reputation even more sullied, struggling for the protection and financial resources needed to ensure the futures of herself and her son.

In such circumstances she had no choice but to marry Nathaniel.

She was not surprised that her downcast spirits reflected Nathaniel's dominance, putting him in a benevolent mood that afternoon.

Setting down his tea cup, he announced with great ceremony during afternoon tea, 'Let the boy have the puppy. He'll forget where it came from soon enough.'

Olivia rewarded him with a teary smile. Just as Max had forgotten all but the treachery he laid at her door.

As soon as tea was over Nathaniel ordered Julian down from the nursery so he could with even greater ceremony present him with his new puppy.

'My sermon for the Nuningford congregation shall focus on compassion and gratitude,' he said, resting his hands on Olivia's shoulders as he and the aunts watched Julian cavorting around the drawing room with the playful little bitch he'd named Molly. 'You have inspired me.' Guiding her head round so she had no choice but to look at him, he asked, 'You are happy, my dear?'

There was no undertone of malice, no hint of threat. It was as if their conversation in Olivia's bedroom had never taken place. As if Nathaniel were the most genial of men and Olivia the most willing of widows.

'Of course.' She twisted her chin out of his cupped hand so she could watch her son. Whatever she did was to ensure her child's future.

His uncertain future.

'You have certainly made me so.' His voice was a low murmur nearly drowned out by the boisterous shouts from the other side of the room. 'I praise God he set you on the path to righteousness and fulfilment from which Lucien diverted you' – he paused, adding heavily – 'using me as his instrument.'

Olivia shuddered.

'Oh, my dear Nathaniel, just look at them!' gushed Aunt Catherine, beaming as if Nathaniel were the architect of Julian's happiness.

Olivia stepped out of Nathaniel's grasp and went to kneel by her son. 'You must thank Mr Kirkman for his kindness,' she said putting an arm about the child.

He shrugged it off and bounded after the puppy. 'Thank Uncle Max,' he lisped, before hurling himself on top of the wriggling animal.

CHAPTER TEN

❦

Normally, when the daffodils first popped their golden yellow heads from the almost frozen ground Olivia would experience a great surge of hope. Spring was here and the hunting season, only a few months hence, would mean she'd see less of Lucien. The world in general looked more promising.

Now, as she watched Nathaniel heedlessly trample those innocent harbingers of hope as he inspected the ropes that tied their trunks to his carriage this chilly April morning she felt nothing but despair.

Not for the first time she wondered at her strength of character in allowing him to trample her dreams and wishes in the same way he was trampling the clumps of daffodils that lined the gravel drive.

Yet what alternative did she have? She was in a perilous situation. Her social isolation was bad enough, but poverty stared her in the face.

With Max offering no guide as to what was in store for Julian, let alone herself, marriage to Nathaniel was the price she must pay.

'Ah, Miss Dingley!' Greeting Aunt Eunice with a self-satisfied smile as she issued out of the house in company with her sister, the clergyman added, 'I have with me my sermon which you recently evinced a desire to hear and with which I shall amuse the congregation at Nuningford. I think Olivia shall find the journey passes in seemingly far less than the two hours the coachman estimates in this fine weather.'

Olivia gulped. Two hours in Nathaniel's presence. Two hours listening to him prosing on about compassion and gratitude.

She could not do it.

Not to herself. Not to Julian. She imagined her boy as a young man forced to submit to Kirkman's uncertain temper. Forced to be humble and grateful.

Nathaniel would trample over him. Trample over any youthful exuberance he might show like he was trampling over her and over the clumps of pretty yellow daffodils.

'Will you get off them!' Starting forward, she gripped his sleeve and tugged.

She heard Aunt Catherine gasp, and the shock in Aunt Eunice's warning, 'Have a care, Olivia!'

Surprisingly, his voice was low and calm as he turned. 'Forgive me, Olivia, for paying such scant regard to your favourite flower.' He raised her palm and kissed it with a smile. 'Are you ready?'

'I'm not going.'

She heard the same mutinous tone she'd used as a seventeen year old when she'd defied her aunts to be with Lucien.

Aunt Catherine stepped forward and put a comforting hand on her shoulder. 'Of course you must go, Olivia.'

Blackness blurred her vision. It was terror. The terror she would lose her nerve before she had shown the courage she might never show again.

'No! I shan't go to Nuningford!'

Aunt Catherine gasped. A spasm crossed the Nathaniel's face as he took her forearm and steered her round to the carriage door. 'Wedding nerves,' he said crisply. 'Perfectly understandable.'

'I'm going to Bath!' Olivia resisted like a nervous filly, flinching at his touch, unable to look him in the eye. 'I'm sure the Nuningford congregation will be as awed by your sermon as I was last night, Nathaniel, but I am going to Bath with my aunts to stay with my cousin Mariah. And I'm taking Julian with me!'

'Julian can come with us if it means so much to you, but you are coming to Nuningford.' Though his voice was smooth it held a nasty undertone, one with which Olivia was becoming increasingly familiar. 'Mrs Snyder is waiting. She is looking forward to accompanying us and does not like to be kept waiting.'

'Puppy! Molly!'

Olivia closed her eyes at the happy shouts of her son and the crunch of gravel as he pursued his new friend. Julian would not take kindly to being incarcerated for the next two hours.

Turning, she saw the puppy bounding towards them, its tongue lolling, its ears flapping in joyful abandonment. It seemed to take as much pleasure from the game as Julian. Glancing back at Nathaniel she could see he was consumed entirely by the need for mastery over her; that he was oblivious to the child and the dog. She winced as his fingers dug into her forearm while he opened the carriage door with the other hand.

She recognized the determination in his angry look. What chance had she against the strength of his will?

'Don't imagine that animal is coming as well,' he snarled.

She saw the boisterous pair careering in their direction, pleasure transcending all. Her heart soared at their innocence. Her son had an ally; the puppy would be a beloved companion.

Turning back to Nathaniel her heart leapt with fear. Oh God, Julian was too young to recognize the malice that dominated his step-father-to-be.

'Nathaniel, no!' she screamed.

He paid no heed.

'No!' she cried again, watching in disbelief his well-aimed kick.

She saw Julian's confusion, heard the muted noise of Nathaniel's boot connecting with the soft underbelly of the small creature. Wincing, horrified, she closed her eyes at the sound of its sharp, truncated yelp.

'Puppy!'

Julian's scream rang out, the aunts turning in unison to see the puppy's little body thrown into the air, a tiny ball of white and brown fur somersaulting against the blue sky before it came to rest limply in a clump of daffodils.

'I will never marry you!'

Courage flowed through her. She must be true to her instincts. Nathaniel was evil. He would bend her to his will, just as Lucien had. He would destroy her, as Lucien nearly had.

And he would destroy Julian.

Glaring at Nathaniel, she held her confused, shuddering son against her skirts and hissed, 'Not if you were the last man on earth. I will never marry you and nor will I be your victim as I was Lucien's.'

Nathaniel took a menacing step forward. When she refused to retreat, his look became conciliatory. It had no effect. Her mind was made up. She was her own master, just as she was master of her son's future. She might not be able to safeguard his comfort and security but she could ensure he grew to be a man of conviction who respected her for hers.

Fortunately Julian was too young to understand.

He tried to coax life into the little creature with whom he'd only just become acquainted and cried when it wouldn't play with him. Olivia comforted him as best she could, pulling him on to her lap and rocking him when his realization that he'd lost his playmate for good was too much to bear.

Nathaniel showed no remorse and his anger left Olivia unmoved. Even his reminder that Olivia and Julian faced a future of uncertainty and penury had no effect.

When Olivia remained steadfast in her refusal to accompany him 'so they could at least discuss matters' he finally climbed angrily into his carriage and departed.

Olivia then made plans to despatch the little dog's body, directing Dorcas to dig a hole in the garden, but Julian screamed when he realized the puppy was to be covered with soil.

Struggling to hold the hysterical child, she stopped the maid and together they crouched over the still warm body. Julian quietened then, hopping off her lap and picking up a limp ear.

'Lucien had a dog just like this one,' Olivia said, stroking its silky coat.

'I remember, ma'am,' said Dorcas, wiping her red face with her apron. 'It were called Molly too. How the master did dote on 'er.'

Olivia said nothing. It was no place to remark that Molly held a far greater place in her late husband's affections than she had ever done.

With a sigh she scooped up the little dog's limp body and turned towards the house.

'Take Julian to the nursery and change his clothes,' she directed. 'He'll be coming to Bath with us. I'll take the puppy to the crypt. Molly can rest beside Lucien's beloved Molly.'

'You'll need 'elp down there, Miss Olivia,' said Dorcas. 'I'll run and fetch the key.'

'It won't be locked,' Olivia called, already heading down the hill. 'You take Julian. It's best he doesn't come with me.'

Hugging the soft bundle in her arms, Olivia went over the decisive parting she had made with Nathaniel. It didn't matter that he had not meant to kill the animal, but it was enough. Enough to throw off the fear and uncertainty he had exercised over her for so long. Enough to forge a new direction. She would go to Bath with her aunts that afternoon and she would never see him again. She was determined upon it. She and Julian would be free.

Excitement pulsed through her as she headed down the hill towards her old home, despite her joyless task. She was a widow. She belonged to no man. It was true she had no money, but somehow she and Julian would manage.

The crypt door swung open with just a gentle push. Set into the side of a grassy knoll it was a gloomy place a few minutes' walk from The Lodge, though enough light streamed through a window high in the wall for her to see. Lined up like silent sentinels of the past she gazed upon the stone sarcophagi of her husband's ancestors.

And that of her husband.

Gently placing the little dog upon the lid she fingered the inscription. How grand, how noble it made him sound when he had been just a man. A man driven to madness through longing for what he could never find; if indeed it existed at all.

Faithful Molly's tiny sarcophagus was positioned at his feet. Bending, Olivia tried to move the heavy lid but, despite it being so small, it refused to budge. Straightening, she scanned the rows of neat stone caskets. Above Lucien lay his grandfather, the equally infamous 5th Viscount Farquhar. Perhaps the only difference between them was that Lucien's grandfather had tyrannized three wives before his sudden death during the uprising of '45 while Lucien had tormented only one.

Lucky Olivia had outlived *her* tyrannous viscount.

With a wry laugh she bent to move the lid entombing the King Charles' Spaniel whom Lucien's grandfather had no doubt esteemed more than any consort.

This time she encountered no resistance. With only a little effort she was able to shift it sufficiently to make a gap large enough for young Molly's corpse.

She stood up and went to fetch the dog from Lucien's sarcophagus.

'Poor Molly,' she whispered, closing her eyes as she nuzzled its soft coat. 'You had such a short time to enjoy life, and yet I do believe you have given me the freedom I might never have had were it not for your sacrifice. I'm sorry.'

How lonely, she thought, as she lowered the animal on to its bed of dust and old bones. She remembered thinking the same, despite her anger, when Lucien had been interred.

She bent to close the lid, pausing as the cloud which had obscured the sun was suddenly dissolved by its heat, sending its dazzling rays through the grimy window. A flash of something bright caught her eye. Something that was not dust and bones. Cautiously, she put her hand into the sarcophagus, wishing she were wearing gloves as the feel of damp organic matter sent shivers up her spine.

They were not shivers of revulsion for long.

Her fingers, probing through the blanket of dust, encountered something smooth. Smooth and disc-shaped. Cold and flat.

Tingles of excitement tore through her as she closed her fist upon a handful of them. Her breath caught in her throat. Could it be? There was no need to ask. She knew exactly what she had unwittingly stumbled upon. The 5th Viscount's treasure.

With a whoop of joy Olivia plunged both arms into the dark space beside Molly's body and brought up a handful of gold coins.

Too many to hold. Raising her hands to the light she closed her eyes and listened to the dull chinking noise they made as they slipped through her fingers and hit the flagstones. The enormousness of her discovery was difficult to comprehend. Her brain throbbed with wonder, disbelief and finally settled upon reality: the repercussions. It did not matter that the treasure did not belong to her. They would bring her joy, nonetheless.

Dropping the coins upon the lid of Lucien's grandfather's crypt she again plunged her hands into the dust and darkness. Dust comprised only a thin layer. There had been no attempt to hide the coins. The sarcophagus was filled with them.

Dizzy with hope and joy she had to sit down, gazing in wonder at the gold in the flat of her palms.

'Max's birthright,' she murmured. It was hard to breathe through her excitement, to gather her thoughts. Her discovery changed everything.

After a while her thoughts settled. She knew what she must do. This afternoon she would accompany her aunts to Bath. It served as a good halfway point. Refreshed, she would continue the next morning to Elmwood.

Elmwood was two hours' carriage ride beyond Bath.

Elmwood – where Max would be waiting.

Hope blossomed once more.

Returning most of the coins to the crypt she closed the lid, keeping five which she would present to Max.

She might have unwittingly denied him his birthright but she was about to atone with more than just a public avowal of the truth.

Her interest on her shame would be ensuring his gilded future.

CHAPTER ELEVEN

—◦⦿◦—

HUGGING HER NEWFOUND knowledge to herself as the carriage rattled towards Bath and her aunts dozed in each corner, she could barely contain her excitement.

Oh, she was used to keeping secrets. For more than two years she had kept the greatest secret of all: a secret that would condemn Julian to an uncertain, if not perilous, future.

But this secret offered her salvation.

A future with Max.

Sagging against the corner cushion of the carriage with a sleeping Julian across her lap her mind spun with possibilities.

Max would be able to indulge any whim or fancy he chose, whether it was experimenting with wool growing or standing for Parliament.

Even Amelia would welcome her with open arms. Miss Hepworth might come with a fortune to match her pretty face but Olivia had discovered Max's fortune.

And Max loved *her*.

Her instincts told her so, just as she now considered it entirely possible Max had not received the letter she had written him. She had to believe this.

The more distance Olivia put between the dower house, especially as they passed the manse where Nathaniel lived, the more she felt her old spirit returning.

It wasn't just the gold. She had done it: she had thrown off the yoke that made her as much Nathaniel's whipping post as she had been Lucien's.

Whatever happened, she and Julian would survive. Her son would survive with his spirit intact because she had shown the strength needed to make it so, albeit thanks to the brutal kick which had killed Molly.

Careful not to disturb the sleeping child in her arms, she leaned forward. Aunt Eunice was stirring, straightening her lace cap as she blinked open her eyes.

'Aunt Eunice,' she whispered, another surge of excitement coursing through her, 'I do not intend seeing Nathaniel ever again!'

'But there are just weeks until the wedding!' Aunt Catherine, who had just woken, herself, sounded close to tears. 'What happened was a terrible accident. Think of your reputation, Olivia!'

'What of it?' Olivia managed to keep her voice from wavering though it was true. She would be branded a jilt; more ammunition against her for those who believed Lucien's slurs.

Dabbing at her eyes with a scrap of lace, Aunt Catherine sniffed. 'All we want is your happiness, Olivia, but how can any woman be happy if she is not received in society? Despite this morning's accident Nathaniel has been good to you—'

'Because it profited him!' Aunt Eunice's voice was harsh.

'I shall not marry him and I shall *never* change my mind,' Olivia said firmly, even as visions beset her of a vengeful Nathaniel using every dirty trick at his disposal to wrest from her all that she held dear. But with Max in possession of the truth Nathaniel's power was void.

The boy was stirring. With a yawn he pulled out his thumb and his eyelids fluttered open. Olivia waited tensely for him to recoil when he realized where he was but he did not. Instead, he settled himself more comfortably on her lap, rubbed his eyes with one grimy fist and offered her a smile.

Her heart somersaulted. Love, like molten liquid surged through her veins. She hugged him against her, kissing the top of his head and breathing in his warm, little boy smell.

'Julian, sweetheart,' she whispered, 'Mama's not marrying Reverend Kirkman.'

'Marry Uncle Max?' With his thumb firmly in his mouth the words were indistinct but understandable.

Olivia gave a weak smile as she closed her eyes against the scrutiny of her aunts.

Would it be enough? Fear rubbed at her earlier confidence. Would revealing to Max the whereabouts of his grandfather's lost fortune be enough to restore what had once existed between them? Max regarded principle and morality more highly than material goods.

'A mighty fine sentiment, young man,' Aunt Eunice said approvingly, 'and one I endorse sincerely.'

Olivia held Julian more closely. 'If he will have me.'

'Of course he'll have you!' Aunt Eunice cut in sharply. 'He's as moonstruck as any green boy, that's clear enough!'

Aunt Catherine put her head on one side. 'He is Lucien's cousin, of course, and you do not know him as well as you know the reverend—'

'What does that signify, Sister,' interjected Aunt Eunice, 'when Mr Atherton displays all the heroic qualities needed to set a female's heart aflutter as well as kindness and common sense?' She paused, sending Olivia a narrow look. 'You've not had a falling out on account of something other than Mr Kirkman, have you, Olivia?'

Olivia dropped her eyes. 'I have not heard from Max since last week when I elaborated on' – she drew her breath in through her teeth – 'my sins.' Faintly, she added, 'Nathaniel interrupted and although I wrote Max a full explanation I've heard nothing.'

'Then it's because he never received the letter.' Aunt Eunice's tone was comforting in its conviction. 'Doubtless that conniving, underhand clergyman intercepted it.' She patted Olivia's knee. 'Mark my words, Olivia, Mr Atherton wears his heart on his sleeve and is not the kind of man to let a mere misunderstanding stand in the way of true love. Once he knows you're no longer bound to Mr Kirkman he'll be on the doorstep upon the instant to beg your forgiveness and to make you an offer.'

*

'Dearest Olivia!' Cousin Mariah, resplendent in Pomona green and gold, ushered them into the drawing room of her fashionable townhouse in Laura Place. 'I was so hoping you would come. And you've brought the boy!' The peacock feather in her handsome gold toque swayed as she clapped her hands. A servant appeared and, after directing that the sleeping child be spirited away to a nice warm bedchamber, she waved them all to seats, settling herself amidst a noisy rustle of silk skirts. 'Your aunts have told me all about you! Marriage to a pillar of the church, no less! Your wisdom will be of great benefit to a certain younger member of this household.' Her expansive smile was followed by a look of deep concern. Lowering her voice, she added, 'Young Lucy has lost her head to a good-for-nothing so I am counting on you, my dear, to impart the salutary caution required. Your aunts assure me you have learned your lesson.'

Barely had she been admitted to the lavishly furnished drawing room than the sense of being welcomed once more into polite society evaporated. Olivia, the temptress, the scheming seductress, would never be allowed to die.

She saw Aunt Eunice and Catherine exchange looks before asking warily as she settled herself on the Egyptian settee, 'What else, pray, have you told Lucy about me?'

'That Lady Farquhar was the most captivating debutante the year she was presented and that she turned down at least a dozen marriage offers before she married Lord Farquhar,' came a breathless voice, as a young girl bounced into the room.

'Meet Lucy,' said her mother, adding in disapproving tones as she plucked at the sleeves of the girl's dress and smoothed a wayward chestnut curl, 'That's no way for a young lady to introduce herself. What must Cousins Eunice and Catherine think of you, not to mention Lady Far—'

'Please, call me Cousin Olivia,' Olivia begged, allowing herself to take comfort in the heavily censored description Lucy had obviously been given; though it appeared Olivia had already been held up as a warning to her lively cousin.

'You're every bit as beautiful as Mama said you were,' Lucy went on, irrepressibly, taking a seat beside her as refreshments were served. 'I'm hoping you can teach me a thing or two, Cousin Olivia, as my first season wasn't a great success, was it, Mother?'

Olivia didn't know how to respond to the embarrassment that crackled through the room. Clearly Olivia was the last person in the room, much less in Bath, who should advise Lucy on how a debutante ought to deport herself. Catching Mariah's eye, though she directed her words to Lucy, she said, 'I think perhaps I could teach you more about what *not* to do.' Her attempt at sounding self-deprecating had the desired result. Mariah sent her an approving look as Olivia added, 'And if you consider a season a failure simply because you didn't find a husband, perhaps the real reason was because there were no suitable suitors for you. One can't simply accept the first offer that presents itself just because the accounting is acceptable.'

'Bravo, Cousin Olivia.' Mariah offered her a plate of seed cake. 'Lucy has got it into her head she must make a spectacular match this year as if to make up for last season.'

'I'm sure I can make a match to please everyone.' The young girl tossed her chestnut curls. Though she wasn't pretty in the fashionable sense, there was a robust and engaging liveliness in her manner Olivia felt sure would appeal to some nice, steady young man. Not the sleek, dangerous rake her husband had been, but wasn't that just as well?

'Besides, I am far more agreeable to look upon now than I was last year,' Lucy went on, daintily picking out the seeds of her cake before her mother hissed at her to mind her manners. Lucy glared at her. 'You said those exact same words, Mama, if you recall—'

Mariah, relaxing her authoritarian bearing, threw her hands up in the air and everyone laughed.

'It seems only yesterday Olivia was Lucy's age,' said Aunt Catherine with a fond look at Olivia.

'I must confess,' said Mariah, 'I did, unwisely, tell Lucy that she'd bloomed in the past year and that—'

'What's wrong with giving a compliment?' Lucy interrupted. 'If it's the truth, I mean. I'm sure it hasn't turned Cousin Olivia's head being told she's beautiful.' She took a mouthful of cake, adding, 'I need compliments to remind me I'm no longer the plump, spotty ape leader I was last season.'

'You have a very well-used looking glass which seems to be constantly reminding you, Lucy,' said her mother. 'Now enough of your chatter. I must press Olivia and her aunts to accompany us to Lady Glenton's midnight masque, tonight.'

As Olivia opened her mouth to demur, Cousin Mariah held up her hand. 'There is plenty of time to rest, for surely Lady Glenton's marvellous annual event was the reason you came early?'

As revelry was the furthest thing from Olivia's mind, she put up strong resistance. She needed rest so she could be at her most radiant when she confronted Max tomorrow. All her senses strained towards this most important, momentous meeting of her life.

'Please, Cousin Olivia!' Lucy begged. 'Mama has a gown for you and now that I've seen you I'm dying to show you off.'

'I'm very tired—' Olivia began but Aunt Eunice cut her off. 'You can sleep a few hours and have plenty of time to prepare yourself for midnight. What you need is gaiety, Olivia, something to take your mind off your … grief.'

Cousin Mariah leant forward. 'I can think of no finer entertainment to end one's mourning year,' she said, decisively.

Reclining on the bed Lucy watched with avid concentration as Olivia prepared herself for the ball five hours later.

'Poor Cousin Olivia,' she sighed, 'you must miss Lord Farquhar very much. I know Mama disapproved of him, but then, she disapproves of most men.'

Olivia hesitated as she pushed a pin into her curls. Carefully she said, 'One must embrace the future rather than dwell on the past. And of course, your mama is right to be concerned that you meet the right man.' A vision of Max with his kind smile and the cowlick he was forever pushing out of his eyes swam before her and her heart spasmed with excitement. 'There are some wonderful and worthy ones out there. Find a good man to be your husband, not a dashing rake, and you'll not regret it.'

'The worthy ones are so boring.' Lucy grumbled, before brightening. 'I met a woman once who was green with envy when I told her that my cousin was married to Lord Farquhar. She said she was a debutante that same year and all the young ladies swooned over him.' Lucy kissed the tips of her fingers with a flourish as she rolled on to her back and gazed dreamily at the ceiling. 'She said he had the wickedest glint in his eye and was by far and away the most handsome of all the eligibles.' Hesitating, she added, 'But she said that since her mama had warned her against him she was not disposed to court his advances.' Lucy slid her appreciative gaze the length of Olivia's daring dress: a Madame de Pompadour gown Mariah had insisted she wear for the occasion. 'Of course she only said that to save face because he didn't look twice at her.'

'That's as may be,' said Olivia, striving for a note between sounding too censorious, knowing that if Lucy was anything like she had been at her age any warning would be like a red rag to a bull, and too dismissive. 'However, it's one thing if the young ladies consider a gentleman eligible and quite another if their mamas do. The latter,' she added pointedly, 'is all that matters.'

Looking downcast for just a moment Lucy whispered, 'I have a secret, Cousin Olivia.'

Disquieted, Olivia smiled her encouragement. Best to have any confessions out in the open. Lucy was such a fresh innocent it would be in everybody's interests if the girl chose to make Olivia a confidante, particularly if the confession was of an unsuitable nature.

The girl became suddenly coy. Tracing the outline of the fleur-de-lis on the counterpane she mumbled, 'A gentleman has made his especial interest quite clear. I want you to meet him.' With a look of earnest entreaty she added, 'He'll be at the masquerade tonight.'

'I'd love to meet him,' Olivia said. 'What does your mama think of him?'

Swinging her legs over the side of the bed Lucy smiled valiantly. 'I don't really know. He paid his respects so charmingly that I'm sure she was quite overwhelmed only I think she doesn't wish to influence me.'

Taking in the mutinous set to Lucy's mouth and the determined fire in her eye, Olivia decided Cousin Mariah had every reason to fear for Lucy.

CHAPTER TWELVE

—❧❦❧—

CLUTCHING JONATHON'S ARM, Amelia blocked her brother's attempted escape towards the front door. 'You need diversion, Max,' she said, holding her ground at the bottom of the stairs, 'and accompanying us to Bath is just the ticket.'

Halting reluctantly, Max sighed. 'Quite frankly, Amelia,' he said in clipped tones, 'I could think of nothing less diverting.'

'Max!' Releasing Jonathon's arm, Amelia hurried after him as he shrugged on his greatcoat in the hallway. 'It doesn't matter that you won't enjoy it but you need something to take your mind off Julian and …' She didn't say it and nor did Max allude to the fact that the name Lady Farquhar had been about to trip off her tongue.

Forbidden territory.

He stared at Amelia's pursed mouth, her pale, peaked face framed with dark hair, and imagined Olivia's vivid blue gaze and shiny coiffure the colour of newly ripened corn.

Longing ripped through him and he closed his eyes against the vision of the family he'd once believed would be his. But was Olivia an adulteress, a grand deceiver, and Julian, the boy he loved like his own, the result? An innocent usurper, but a usurper, nonetheless?

'You need a wife, Max, and Bath is full of lovely gels who'd be eager to fill the post,' Jonathan corroborated, as he watched Max pull on his riding gloves. 'Why not join us for a few days? It'd do you good.'

'Miss Hepworth is taking the waters with her mother,' Amelia said brightly. 'You were quite charmed by her the first time you met her and clearly she was struck by you.' She fixed Max with an imploring look. 'Whatever you might have said in parting can surely be undone.'

Max picked up his riding crop. Olivia's fear of the clergyman was greater than her ability to trust Max the confession she owed him: that her immoral actions had cost him ... everything! His initial shock and scepticism at Dorling's allegations had turned to contempt for the woman he loved. For the past week he'd believed his wounds were mortal.

He was thoughtful as he turned up the collar of his coat. Miss Hepworth was young and pretty *and innocent*. Isn't that, really, all he wanted in a wife?

His thoughts followed this train for but a second, obliterated by the memory of Olivia's lithe body pressed against his and her passionate avowal: 'I've never wanted anyone like I want you, Max'.

A sentiment wholly in accord with his own.

He flexed his fingers, no longer paying attention to Jonathon and Amelia's arguments. Hadn't he accepted that Lucien's cruelty was at the core of everything? The table dancing, the scandalous clothing. He shuddered ... Lady Farquhar's notorious butterfly.

Actions he had long ago forgiven.

Turning at the front door his mind was closer to the dower house in Mortlock than to Bath as he bent to peck Amelia's cheek. 'I'll consider it,' he said.

A cocktail of emotions flooded him as he strode towards the stables.

Olivia had not been married to *him* when she'd committed adultery. Lucien's cruelty had driven Olivia into the arms of another man.

But she had confessed that all was not as it seemed.

Lord, it had to be the reason she'd held back from committing herself to Max time and again, when her heart and body cried out for him.

Then he thought of Julian, the child who had usurped his birthright, and anger transcended all. For but a moment.

Olivia had promised to write. Perhaps her letter had gone astray. Perhaps she was awaiting his direction from at this very moment.

Odin nuzzled him as he adjusted the stirrups. Max patted his flank.

'Let's not give up on her just yet, eh, feller?' he said softly. Excitement that started as a slow burn was quickly thrumming through his veins as he mounted. 'Perhaps a night amidst vacuous, pleasure-seeking Bath acolytes before we see what the lady has to say for herself *is* just the ticket.'

When she met him in Lady Glenton's crowded ballroom dressed as a Roman senator, Olivia's fears were confirmed.

A Corinthian, to be sure.

'Mr Petersham arrived in Bath a week ago and has already extended his visit.' Lucy blushed prettily and Olivia was acutely aware of the power communicated to the young man in the gesture. His handsome mouth curved in the faintest of smiles, his eyes conveying a subtle subtext Olivia remembered from her youth: collusion; confident of his attractions.

Oh yes, Olivia had jostled for prime position amidst the ranks of rakes like this eight years before. Burnt like a moth at a flame she knew exactly what danger the heart-palpitatingly eager Lucy courted.

She inclined her head graciously, her smile distant. 'Delighted to meet you, Mr Petersham,' she murmured.

'You are a visitor to these parts, Lady Farquhar?' the young man asked, preventing her from making a gracious retreat, which would have obliged Lucy to accompany her.

'My first foray into society following my mourning, Mr Petersham,' she said. Once, the look in his eye would have thrilled her, now she was unnerved. She longed for Max's comforting presence, his straightforward manner and wished, heartily, she had pleaded a megrim and stayed at home, gathering her strength and reining in her excitement for tomorrow's momentous reunion.

'I am an excellent dancer, Lady Farquhar. If you are afraid of being sadly out of practise, it would be an honour to partner you on the dance floor later this evening.'

'Isn't he so kind and thoughtful?' Lucy demanded as they returned to the aunts. She tugged at Olivia's sleeve as if she would force her to concur and sanction Lucy's choice.

'He is' – Olivia searched for the right word – 'a charmer.'

Lucy seemed satisfied. After a pause, she said, softly, with a quick glance to ensure her mother was not listening, 'He told me the other night I was the most beautiful girl in the room. Can you believe that?' Her face shone. 'It was after he danced with Arabella Knight who is coming out this year and who everyone knows will snare a duke, she's so pretty, even if she has no fortune.'

'Unlike you, Lucy, who, I must remind you, is set to come into quite a fortune.' In a quiet corner Olivia stopped and gripped both her cousin's hands. 'Cousin Mariah told me that your Aunt Gwendolyn has made you her beneficiary. It's wonderful you are so well provided for, but if there is one thing I've learnt since I was a debutante it's to be aware of the hidden motive.'

Lucy looked hurt. 'You sound just like Mama,' she accused, pulling away. Her eyes glistened with unshed tears.

With a sigh Olivia followed her as she joined Mariah who was chatting to the aunts. She had barely reached the girl's side before Mr Petersham again presented himself with a bow and after a brief consultation with her mother, led Lucy on to the dance floor where a quadrille was forming.

Olivia nodded after the departing couple. 'Lucy seems taken with Mr Petersham.'

'She's been wearing her heart on her sleeve since he arrived a week ago.' Mariah didn't trouble to hide her disquiet. 'He's the eldest son of a baronet, comes from a respectable though impoverished family, and no one could dispute he's handsome and dashing. I just wonder what he sees in Lucy.'

'Lucy is a pretty girl.' However Olivia knew what Mariah meant. Lucy was not the dazzling swan-like creature one would have envisaged a man like Mr Petersham seeking out when there were in the room that evening a handful of far prettier girls.

Gazing at a couple of brunette beauties she did not fail to notice the flare of interest in Mr Petersham's eye as he passed them, Lucy on his arm. Olivia blinked. Perhaps she had imagined it, for immediately he returned his attention to Lucy, his manner full of gallantry.

'Pretty but penniless.' Following Olivia's look Mariah's tone was dry. 'Like you, my dear, and now I understand you have reneged on the clergyman. Was that wise?'

Taken aback by her bluntness Olivia replied, 'I could not commit myself to him when my heart was engaged elsewhere.'

Cousin Mariah cast her gaze around the crowded ballroom. 'Shall you find the object of your affections here?' she asked. 'Clearly, you have many admirers judging by the glances slanted your way. It is just as well my Lucy has not a jealous nature.'

Eight years ago Olivia's numerous admirers had fed her ego, bolstered her reckless spirit.

She wondered how many in this room knew who she was. The scandalous Lady Farquhar would be an object of prurient interest wherever she went. It was a dampening thought. A reason to conduct herself with the utmost restraint.

'A glass of orgeat?' Mr Petersham, returning to her side, offered her a glass of the sickly refreshment and Mariah drifted away.

Olivia wished she could do the same. Turning, she murmured, 'I only drink champagne.'

Poor naïve little Lucy courted grave danger if she thought this man a worthy contender for her affections and her considerable future fortune.

He chuckled. 'The moment little Lucy's mama left your side I seized my opportunity.' A head taller, he stood slightly closer to her than was decorous. 'I knew it'd not be long before some Johnny Likely came to pay his addresses to the most dazzling creature in the room.'

Olivia stifled the desire to take a step back. Instead she smiled, raising one eyebrow. 'And now he has.'

It took him a split second to digest what he could only interpret as a joke – unless he were to beat a graceful retreat.

'Then I must persuade you otherwise.' He offered her his arm. 'I've told you I'm an excellent dancer. Let me prove it' – he lowered his voice, his breath tickling her ear – 'amongst other things.'

As a debutante she'd revelled in being fêted as if she were a breed apart. As Lucien's wife the interest of other men usually meant sinister designs. She couldn't recall the number of times she'd had to bat away a man's insinuating hand in a dark corner. Lucien encouraged the perception she was a woman of lax morals. He punished her if she appeared too prim. She'd learned to tread a fine line; had in fact developed it to the highest degree.

Tonight she had intended to present herself a model of propriety for the benefit of those who might denigrate her.

Lucy, she now realized, must be her target audience.

Mr Petersham had merely to crook his little finger and Lucy would come running. One unfortunate encounter with the wrong gentleman could ruin the rest of her life.

The sun was low in the sky when Max saw the elegant town in the distance but a pebble in Odin's shoe forced him to stop at a hostelry two miles out.

It was while utilizing the light that spilled from the upper rooms and a knife to scrape out the hoof that a familiar voice made him raise his head.

'Reverend Kirkman?' The words were out before he could think better of it, for the man was disappearing into the inn and, really, Max had no desire to exchange pleasantries – or anything else – with him.

He swung round and Max could have sworn anger crossed his face before he asked with a narrow-eyed look, 'What brings *you* to Bath, sir?'

'Diversion, Reverend.' Clearly, the dislike he felt was mutual. 'And you? Enjoying a few days' gaiety before your nuptials?'

The words created a frisson of excitement. Olivia was not going to marry the man. Two hours of riding like the devil had firmed his resolve.

Kirkman grunted. 'I'm for my bed. Perhaps I'll see you at the Assembly Rooms tomorrow night, Mr Atherton. Good evening to you.'

Max stared after his disappearing back. He'd thought the man had planned to deliver a sermon at Nuningford where he was to spend a few days.

A light rain began to fall as he took the rest of his journey at a leisurely canter for Odin's benefit. Bounding up the stairs to his sister's townhouse he felt full to bursting with renewed enthusiasm for his future.

As he raised his fist to knock, Amelia and Jonathon issued from their front door, resplendent in masquerade.

'We'll see you at Lady Glenton's Midnight Masque, Max?' Amelia asked, adjusting her feathers and plucking at her gloves. The look she slanted up at her husband was smug. 'You said you enjoyed it last year and I've told her we're expecting you.'

His notion of pleasure-seeking had ebbed. All he could think of now was a good night's sleep so he could be refreshed for tomorrow's journey to Mortlock.

Amelia wasn't giving up. 'Lady Glenton's famous for her refreshments.'

Caging Amelia's hand upon his arm, Jonathon sent Max an apologetic look. 'Give poor Max a reprieve for at least this evening before you start playing matchmaker, Amelia.'

Grateful and exhausted, Max stepped across the threshold.

Within half an hour he was in bed.

Within three hours he was putting on buckled shoes and accepting that as sleep continued to elude him he might as well pass the time in congenial company rather than tossing and turning in a cold, hard bed.

Swept through the front door of Lady Glenton's by a jostling crowd of young bucks who had just come from a spirited game of faro, Max realized immediately what an error of judgement he had made. The clock chimed two. He was in no mood to mingle with the fabulously garbed crowd when all he could think of was hastening to Mortlock as soon as dawn broke. He felt out of place. The pretty debutantes with their shy, hopeful looks only reinforced how much he preferred Olivia with her experience and understanding of the world, pummelled into her at such cost.

Catching sight of Amelia with Miss Hepworth at the far end of the room, he turned. Far better to make his escape before his sister saw him and pounced.

Sidling towards the door he managed to avoid the attention of Sir John Smales, a near neighbour.

Nearly there, he thought with relief, just as another vision intruded into his peripheral vision. One that was far more appealing than the portly squire and which sent ripples of excitement through him: an elegant coiffure of shiny golden hair above a slender pale neck.

He'd have recognized her anywhere, though her face was half turned and she was dressed in masquerade.

In a small group beyond, her aunts chatted to a statuesque woman in a gold toque, but, as his gaze was drawn back to the stunning wasp-waisted creature sheathed in blue silk adorned with pink bows and roses, he could think only of crossing the room and leading her into some secluded arbour.

Madame de Pompadour? A daring statement for someone who usually dressed in sober colours, but Olivia was full of surprises.

Mesmerized, he watched as she raised her glass and spoke animatedly to her companion, a gentleman he did not know.

Candlelight reflected off the paste ear-rings that hung from her earlobes. The elegant sweep of her shoulders carried the line of her gown in far more alluring lines, surely even than Madame de Pompadour, the late French king's mistress. How he ached to caress the creamy length of her throat, feel the beat of her heart and murmur the words he had no doubt she longed to hear.

Timing had favoured him. How fortuitous he'd not ridden poste haste to Mortlock when Olivia was in this very room, resigned to a future with the clergyman.

Longing for Max's absolution ... his forgiveness....

'Why Max, I've been looking everywhere for you!'

Dear God. It was Amelia.

Max feasted his eyes a second longer upon Olivia before turning to his sister and her hopeful-looking companion, Miss Hepworth.

Olivia would have his absolution, his forgiveness, before the night was over.

CHAPTER THIRTEEN

'THANK YOU, DARLING Olivia, I don't think I'll ever know how to thank you *properly.*'

Lucy's eyes shone with excitement as she drew Olivia into an alcove.

'I can't imagine what I've done,' said Olivia, feeling at a distinct disadvantage. Was Lucy more cynical than she'd thought? Was she using irony as a precursor for the torrent of vitriol Olivia felt was justified?

Lucy lowered her eyes and her mouth curved into a secretive little smile. Olivia waited while the stirrings of disquiet escalated.

'At one stage this evening I confess I felt like clawing out your eyes or pulling out all your hair.' Lucy looked apologetic as she played with her sash. 'I shouldn't even say such things but there must be so many girls who would feel the same. After all, you're so very beautiful without having to work at it, and you make the rest of us feel like dowdy wallflowers while all the gentlemen clamour to ask you to dance.'

'Including Mr Petersham?' Olivia prompted, wondering where this was leading. It was unpleasant having Lucy put into words what she'd always suspected about her female rivals.

'Yes, and by two o'clock I was so in the dismals that when he passed by and said: "What ails thee, my pretty" I nearly burst into tears upon the spot.' As if galvanized by the reflection she reached up to whisper loudly, 'Then he touched my cheek and said, "Ah, so you do care.

You're jealous over my attentions to your cousin? Well, let me tell you, Lady Farquhar has only your best interests at heart and she is helping our plans to be together by deflecting your mama's attention away from ourselves, for we both know that she disapproves of me".'

Lucy clasped her hands and raised her eyes to the ceiling as if her thoughts were floating heavenward. Olivia stared at her, stricken, and wondered what else the young lovers had discussed in those impassioned few moments. 'Shall you see him tomorrow?' she asked.

Lucy looked at her a long moment as if weighing up whether to speak then said in a rush, 'We're eloping, and I was going to keep it secret because Mr Petersham said not to tell anyone, but as you've proved yourself the most wonderful and loyal of cousins I had to tell you.'

'Eloping?' Olivia knew the disapproval in her voice was not a good idea, but she was so horrified she couldn't help herself.

Checked, Lucy said with a frown, 'I believe you, yourself, eloped.'

'Eloping is a very drastic measure which will scandalize society and bring you much distress, Lucy,' Olivia counselled, sounding to her own ears very like Aunt Eunice. She took Lucy's hands in hers as she drew her further into the alcove. The girl refused to meet her eye, staring with trembling mouth at the carpet.

'Mama will never consent to my marrying him before the end of the season,' she said, in a small voice.

'Then have your season, dazzle society and in six months, if you and Mr Petersham still feel the same way and your mother still disapproves, *then* you can consider eloping with him.' She squeezed Lucy's hands, forcing her to look up at her. 'Promise?'

Reluctantly Lucy nodded. But when Mr Petersham appeared to lead Lucy once more on to the dance floor Olivia felt little consolation from the promise she'd extracted.

Or from the weight of her reticule with the coins that would soon transform her life. Olivia was about to embrace freedom and happiness with a man of forgiveness and compassion whereas Lucy …

She stared after the departing couple, Lucy blushing, giggling as her companion made some apparently witty remark.

It would take only Mr Petersham's impassioned declaration of eternal love and a request to climb into a waiting carriage and Lucy would be halfway to Gretna Green before anyone knew of it.

As she issued out of the alcove and went in search of her aunts she was waylaid by Mariah.

Her initial pleasure in her cousin's company had evaporated. Mariah's hospitality did not conceal her real feelings regarding Olivia: that her scandalous past could never entirely be erased.

Her cousin gripped her wrist, turning her in the direction of the dance floor where the young couple were positioning themselves. 'I fear Lucy's lost her heart to Mr Petersham and that any caution from me will do nothing but firm her resolve in his direction.'

'Eighteen can be a difficult age if one is not quiet and modest by nature,' Olivia murmured.

'Quite.' Mariah sent her a narrowed look.

Olivia dropped her eyes. She felt uncomfortable, as if Mariah were both condemning her and needing something from her at the same time.

'Cousin Mariah.' She sighed. 'I have told Lucy there is little happiness to be found by resorting to such impulsiveness. That a kind man makes a much better husband than a flattering buck.' Staring at the young people on the dance floor, at smooth, handsome, Mr Petersham and awkward little Lucy with their heads bent close together, her longing for Max redoubled.

'Such wisdom came to you too late, Olivia. Lucy, I fear, is similarly headstrong.' Mariah appeared not to realize how wounding her words were.

Olivia felt the tears forming and looked up as Mariah touched her arm.

'You've been given a second chance, my dear,' she murmured, 'but only because you are a widow. My Lucy may rue this week in Bath for the rest of her life.'

Olivia refused to be drawn. 'Lucy's good sense will tip the balance,' she hedged. She wanted no more part in this conversation. 'What more can I do? Besides, you know Lucy better than I.'

'I fear an elopement is in the cards.' Taking Olivia's elbow, Mariah drew her into the crowd so they would attract less attention. 'Her aunt Scrivener was here yesterday,' she said, 'roundly haranguing her for every sin in the book: loucheness, frivolity, obstinacy. Just the thing to whip up true rebellion in Lucy's heart.'

Stopping on the edge of the dance floor, Olivia followed her gaze. She wondered if she had looked that young, like Lucy, barely out of the schoolroom, eyes bright with infatuation as she clung to Mr Petersham's arm.

'It's clear she admires you enormously.' Mariah broke into Olivia's reverie, cool green eyes watching her intently.

In a low voice Olivia defended herself. 'I have counselled Lucy against following my deplorable example.'

'You cannot turn back the clock, Olivia.' There was an edge to Mariah's tone, a hardening of her gaze. '*You* can't and my Lucy can't.'

Olivia closed her eyes briefly and a tremor ran through her. Mariah spoke the truth.

Struggling to maintain her composure she replied in measured tones, 'What is done cannot be undone. But Lucy's behaviour cannot be put at my door.'

Mariah grew angry. 'Look at you, Olivia. You are magnificent in any sense of the word. No wonder Lucy holds you up as her model. She cannot see how you have suffered, for Lord knows I have heard it from your aunts. You do not need to pretend for me.' She put her hand to her pearl choker. 'To the ordinary eye you appear quite unscathed. You have a title, beautiful clothes, the freedom to move about at will—'

Olivia gaped. Is this how she appeared? With not a feather to fly with, her few clothes had been so mended and stitched to keep up with current fashions she had wondered if she would be mistaken for a lowly companion or chaperon fallen on hard times.

Apparently not.

'But Cousin Mariah, I have said everything in my power to deflect Lucy from following an undesirable course.' She was shaking. 'I flirted shamelessly with Mr Petersham earlier this evening and Lucy thought I did it merely to avert your scrutiny.'

'You can do more.'

Olivia had only heard such stentorian tones from Aunt Eunice.

'Really, I don't know what—'

Mariah sent her another kindling look.

'You have not even begun to utilize your powers of attraction, Olivia, to prove to Lucy that Mr Petersham is as fickle as we've all been at such pains to tell her he is.' Realizing that the strength of her grip had made marks, Cousin Mariah caressed the bruised white flesh of Olivia's arm above the glove. Her smile was brittle. 'If you believe in honour and atonement, Cousin Olivia, there is something I would ask of you.'

Miserably, Olivia stood by her aunts, her pleasure in the evening's gaiety entirely evaporated.

She didn't have to do this, she told herself. The day Lucien died was the day she should have been able to stop acting against her better judgement.

She managed a smile at some inanity Aunt Catherine directed towards her before the aunts resumed their animated conversation with an old acquaintance.

She had only just freed herself of Nathaniel's yoke. He'd used blackmail to bend her to his will, but she'd proved herself stronger than that. Now Mariah was appealing to Olivia's nobler instincts, pressuring her to perform an act of charity designed to save her impetuous young daughter from falling into the same trap that had all but ruined Olivia's life.

Swamped by her own helplessness, Olivia plucked at the embroidered silk of her reticule and tried to draw strength from the fortune it contained. What should she do?

Mariah's eyes were upon her. At her side, Lucy, pink-cheeked and radiant was gushing, 'Cousin Olivia! Mr Petersham has asked me to stand up with him twice already!'

With a smile for Lucy and ignoring Mariah, Olivia pretended to turn her attention to her aunts' conversation.

Her limbs felt heavy but she would do it. She had no choice if her conscience was to be clear. A clandestine kiss in a dark corner observed by Lucy was all that was required. How many men had kissed her when Lucien had been alive?

Revulsion soured her mood further while the memory of her seven long years as Lucien's wife galvanized her courage. If she refused Mariah's request and Lucy eloped with Mr Petersham, Lucy would be ruined and Olivia would be culpable, in part, through her inaction.

That was how Mariah regarded the matter.

Fingering the key at her neck a burst of excitement outweighed her present trials.

Elmwood. Elmwood was only two hours away.

Surely Max would still want her when she was returning more than she had taken away? Surely tomorrow's reunion would compensate for tonight's trials?

As she scrutinized her reflection in the empty ladies' withdrawing room a little later, she bolstered her flagging confidence with the thought of seeing Max again.

Satisfied by what she saw, she stepped back, smoothing the unaccustomed full skirts of her scandalous costume. Her eyes were bright and her skin still lustrous with none of the blemishes of age one might expect in a woman beyond her first flush of youth. She tilted her chin and fluttered her lashes. Her eyes flashed an invitation.

Tomorrow she could be herself, but tonight she had one final duty to fulfil: hoisting Mr Petersham by his own petard. A duty Cousin Mariah believed would change her daughter's life.

'Cousin Olivia?'

Mariah's voice floated from the passage and Olivia felt cold dread fingering her entrails. She was waiting for her, the noise of the ball filtering through the door at the end. With heavy heart Olivia turned to answer her summons.

'You will not fail me?' Cousin Mariah's mouth was a thin line as she drew Olivia back into the throng. 'In less than three years Lucy will have her entire fortune at her disposal.'

'Rest assured, Cousin Mariah,' she said wearily, 'that I shall persuade Mr Petersham three years is too long to wait when other rewards might be forthcoming faster.'

Mariah's green eyes flashed their gratitude. With a faint smile she laid her hand upon Olivia's arm. 'Deliverance and atonement, my dear,' she said, giving her wrist a squeeze before she left her.

Immediately Olivia was struck by the fear that Mr Petersham would fail *her*. Was she not too confident in her powers of attraction? This reservation was swept away as warm breath tickled her ear and Mr Petersham's voice, low and suggestive, asked, 'How many gentlemen have told you you're far and away the most beautiful woman in the room?'

'Too many to count, Mr Petersham.'

He grinned as they stood for the moment, alone, in an uncrowded corner of the ballroom.

'Your dry humour, Lady Farquhar, sits better with me than the endless chatter of a besotted schoolroom miss.'

Slanting an amused look at him beneath her lashes, Olivia remarked, 'I thought what a handsome couple you made when you addressed Lucy tonight. I hope you will not break her heart.'

Mr Petersham gave a short laugh. 'You have not a reputation for being tender-hearted. Besides, Lucy is a willing participant in the marriage mart. I am curious as to your participation,' he went on, caging her hand upon his arm as they made a leisurely progress. 'A widow surely grows bored and lonely in time.'

'I have too handsome a fortune to grow bored and I can assure you, Mr Petersham, I am never lonely.'

She said the lie as a challenge; recognized that he interpreted the subtext that she made herself available for dalliance on occasion.

And that right now she was contemplating him.

'You are a remarkable woman, Lady Farquhar,' he murmured, drawing her towards the dance floor. 'Very different from your cousin, Lucy, who I fear would make a dull bedfellow. Come! A quadrille?'

She could not deny the intoxication she felt as she preformed her moves though she wished Mr Petersham were not holding her so tightly.

Elation filled her. Dancing made her feel alive. She must put aside the horror of what Mariah required her to do. She was on a mission to save Lucy. A mere kiss when she had been forced to do so much worse in her life? It was nothing.

Dear God, rein in your temper, or you'll snap the stem of your champagne flute, Max exhorted himself as he gazed at the couple upon whom surely all eyes were fixed. By the saints in Heaven, she was dazzling. No wonder Lucien had needed to possess her. For this was the Olivia who had set his dissolute cousin's pulses racing. Not the demure, grieving widow she'd pretended to be when she'd made his acquaintance. Not the sincere, responsive damsel in distress who had avowed her love for him. The trouble was, Max was as susceptible to Olivia the dazzling beauty as he was to the maligned widow and damsel in distress.

He swallowed, uncomfortably conscious of his desire as he surreptitiously stared over Miss Hepworth's shoulder while trying to concentrate on the young lady's chatter about her pony.

Olivia fanned herself and whispered something in the ear of her handsome companion.

He had been on the verge of approaching her, bursting with expectation earlier this evening when his sister had thrust Miss Hepworth upon him.

Somehow a dance had been promised which had been followed by more conversation; it had seemed an eternity before he caught sight once more amidst the several hundred guests of the one woman who could stir his senses.

She was certainly stirring them right now. Breathless hope and anticipation had been replaced by white-hot anger as he observed the flirtation in her manner; the sly, colluding glance she slanted up at her companion beneath thick dark lashes.

What was she playing at?

Olivia's betrothed was tucked up in bed at the Duck on Puddle two miles away. Her behaviour made no sense. This was the false persona Olivia had decried; the coquette Lucien had forced her to be for his entertainment. Her humiliations had torn Max's heart in two yet here she was, behaving just as one would expect the notorious, brazen Lady Farquhar to behave – if one didn't believe her version of the truth.

'But I had to stop giving Misty apples because they gave him colic. And as a carrot isn't nearly such a tasty treat, Mr Atherton, what do you think I should give him, instead?'

He jerked his attention back to Miss Hepworth's earnest, pretty face. 'I beg your pardon.'

'What do you think would be a nice tasty treat?'

He nearly answered that all he could think about were devouring Lady Farquhar's luscious lips after he'd ripped her from the arms of her patently unworthy companion; that certainly fell under the heading of 'tasty treat'; when Miss Hepworth was joined by a companion.

'Look at them!' He recognized the young girl having seen her earlier with Olivia's aunts. In her distress she did not acknowledge him, clutching Miss Hepworth by the wrist and pointing to Olivia and her companion.

'Cecily! You must come! I trusted her, but she has betrayed me!'

Miss Hepworth turned to hush the girl, blushing as she slanted a look in Max's direction before introducing her distraught, chestnut-haired friend.

'Miss Lucy Snelling and I attended Miss Pinkerton's Seminary for Young Ladies in Highgate,' explained Miss Hepworth.

Max regulated his breathing as he listened to her soothe her friend's injured sensibilities before sending her off in the direction of her mama.

Turning back to Max she coloured prettily as she murmured, 'Mr Petersham has paid particular attention to Lucy during the past fortnight, however the arrival of her cousin, Lady Farquhar, appears to have set the cat among the pigeons.'

He should be admiring Miss Hepworth for her uncommon good sense. She would make an excellent wife. Every encounter with her merely reinforced this.

Unable to hide the thunder in his eye, he glowered at Olivia and her companion. 'Hardly surprising,' he muttered. He could taste the bile on his tongue. 'I am quite well acquainted with Lady Farquhar.'

CHAPTER FOURTEEN

'PERHAPS, LADY FARQUHAR,' murmured Mr Petersham, 'you'd care to admire the Roman busts Lord Glenton has displayed in the long gallery?'

Olivia was conscious of her fading bravado, felt it wilt her smile, felt the insidious progression of cowardice wrap itself around her vital organs.

She nearly said she would like nothing less, but how could she when Cousin Mariah was depending upon her?

As was Lucy.

She'd seen Lucy's eyes upon them several times this evening: luminous and uncertain, her smile so eager to please when Mr Petersham addressed her. He'd danced with Lucy to keep up appearances, but he'd done nothing but mock the girl to Olivia.

'She'll look just like her mother when she's forty.'

'Mariah is very well looking, if a trifle stout. And she's ten years older than forty.'

'My point exactly,' he'd said, stroking her cheek as the dance dissolved. 'Whereas look at you. Your dewy looks belie your experience.'

Had he thought she'd take it as a compliment and smile?

Certainly she smiled. It was expected, and she'd always done what the occasion demanded. What Lucien demanded.

But fear and trepidation gripped her. Oh! For this evening to be over! She wanted to be in her carriage on her way to Elmwood. She wanted to be telling Max that she had found his family's fortune and beg him to forgive her the deception that had brought about this impasse.

Girding her courage she said, 'You have a honeyed tongue, Mr Petersham,' taking his arm so he could lead her back to her aunts.

His eyes twinkled. She recognized his lust. It left her cold.

Caressing her hand, he murmured as they turned their footsteps towards Lucy who stood, lost and lonely in the centre of the room, 'I hope I may have an opportunity to prove to you just how accurate your words are. Perhaps in the gallery in ten minutes?'

The gallery in ten minutes. The thought made her ill with fear.

She met his eye. Slowly, she inclined her head.

After greeting Lucy with fulsome compliments Mr Petersham departed to procure refreshments. Lucy, quiet and uncommunicative beside her, fidgeted, while Olivia, conscious of her cousin's confusion, tried not to feel so traitorous.

'Perhaps tomorrow we can take a country ramble, Lucy?' she suggested. 'The weather looks set to be fair.'

Lucy jumped. 'Tomorrow?' Biting her lip she added, 'Yes, certainly.'

Olivia slid her eyes across to her discomposed cousin. So Mr Petersham's honeyed inducements had carried more weight than Olivia's cautions, she thought. And tomorrow was to be the day.

It was enough to banish the reluctance she felt at her part in Mariah's plan. Wouldn't any mother do all she could to ensure her daughter's happiness was not blighted by a misalliance with a fortune-hunter? Olivia's credentials equipped her perfectly for the part; she knew it, but how she railed against what her experience had cost her.

'You seem much taken with Mr Petersham, but I hope you have taken my cautions to heart.'

Lucy's pale skin took on a fiery hue as she struggled for a guileless smile. She looked too young for this sophisticated throng. 'He has been very civil to me.'

'Civil?' Olivia smiled, as she took Lucy's arm and began a leisurely stroll amongst the knots of exquisitely attired revellers. 'He is handsome but he is penniless, though I'm sure he thinks the title he one day inherits is compensation enough. Certainly he is charming, but I know his type.'

'Then why do you enjoy his company so greatly?' Lucy looked immediately embarrassed that she'd snapped out the words, and dropped her eyes from Olivia's face to gaze once more about her. Olivia saw her lip tremble.

'I enjoy testing my theories.' Olivia patted her forearm and lowered her voice. She hoped Lucy would take heed of her sober tone. 'I eloped when I was seventeen, Lucy. About your age. It was an act of naïve impulsiveness which I regretted every day of my marriage. I still regret it. I would hate you to make the same mistake for Mr Petersham reminds me very much of my late husband.'

'You know nothing about him!' Lucy ground out, her eyes glistening as she glared at Olivia. 'Why, Mr Petersham, thank you,' she added, with an unsteady smile as she accepted the glass of orgeat he handed her. Wiping her eyes she said in answer to his concern, 'Cousin Olivia's feather has just poked me. Otherwise, I'm perfectly well, thank you.'

'How careless of me,' Olivia apologized, skimming the length of the plume with her fingers as she slanted a knowing look up at him. She turned to Lucy, stifling her frustration at the girl's refusal to see sense; her fear at what she had agreed to do to ensure she learned her lesson. 'When you're my age, you can add to your consequence with such fripperies and be just as thoughtless of those around you.'

The words belonged to a woman with no feeling, no conscience.

Had she ever been a woman like that?

She tried to remember *what* she'd been like as a seventeen year old. Thoughtless? Self-absorbed? Heartless?

Disgusted, she forced a smile for Cousin Mariah and her aunts who had just joined them.

Like an excited child Aunt Catherine was enquiring of Lucy whether she was enjoying herself.

Olivia put her lips to Cousin Mariah's ear. 'The gallery in ten minutes,' she whispered.

When all things were considered, Miss Hepworth had the most charming little nose and a rosebud pair of lips, Max decided, grimly, as he led her in the stately steps of their dance. When he clasped her hands to dance down the centre of the room she gave a little gasp of excitement and her hazel eyes lit up. They were shining at him now as if he were the handsomest, most desirable man in the room.

Foolishly, he had imagined it was how Olivia thought of him. That his feelings were reciprocated with the same intense sincerity.

Now that his shoes had been filled, if only for this evening, it was some consolation to feel Miss Hepworth, with her great fortune, considered him a desirable catch.

His bubbling anger at Olivia made him say, perhaps unwisely, 'I am sorry, Miss Hepworth, if your last visit to Elmwood proved a disappointment to you.'

His sense of betrayal was acute. Olivia was not languishing, heart-broken, at the dower house, waiting for him to gallop back into her life and forgive her.

Clearly, she was trawling for an alternative future to marriage to Kirkman – *even if he was the father of her child.* Grimly, he wondered if she knew the clergyman was only two miles away. Or perhaps they had arranged to meet tomorrow and Olivia was making the most of her freedom tonight.

As he listened with half an ear to Miss Hepworth he struggled to comprehend Olivia's behaviour. Was she reverting to her true nature? Was her thirst for gaiety, her need for compliments, behind her incorrigible flirting?

And what of Max? Would she assume the mantle of damsel in distress the moment she set eyes upon him?

Miss Hepworth dropped her eyes, blushing. 'Mama explained matters,' she said, as they returned to the sidelines.

'You have every right to be angry with me.'

Fixing her gaze on the other couples performing their figures she said, 'I would not wish to throw myself at you, Mr Atherton. I ...'

She stammered and blushed some more. 'I am only just out of the schoolroom. There is so much I do not understand.' She raised her chin, proudly. It was such a guileless look; the innocent – uncorrupted – smile of a simple, inexperienced girl who makes no apology for what those more worldly may consider shortcomings, that he was captivated.

For a moment.

'Do you think I offended your mama?'

'I don't think so.' Her smiled broadened as she added with refreshing candour. 'But more to the point, you have not offended me.'

There was no time to dwell on the hopefulness and encouragement in her expression as he led her off the dance floor, for they were again interrupted by Miss Snelling.

'Cecily!' Miss Snelling came to a halt in their midst, her heaving bosom and flushed cheeks betraying her distress. 'Cecily, I beg of you,' she gasped, 'please accompany me to the long gallery.' Her voice held the edge of hysteria.

'But Lucy, I—'

'I cannot go alone and I must … confront my cousin who has gone there with …' – she gulped – 'Mr Petersham!'

Mr Petersham and Olivia?

Alone in the gallery? Max's anger blackened. He didn't care if Miss Hepworth obliged or not. He certainly needed to see what Olivia was up to in the gallery with this Mr Petersham.

Clearing his throat, he tried to sound fatherly though he heard the angry censure in his own voice. 'Shall we all take a turn about the long gallery, Miss Snelling? I've heard there are some very fine specimens.'

It was difficult to believe that Olivia was in Bath cuckolding, it would seem, the man she had promised to marry *and* the one she had professed to love.

'Please show us the way, Miss Snelling,' he said, offering Miss Hepworth his arm.

Lucy tucked an escaped chestnut tendril behind her ear and wiped her nose with the back of her hand before Max could procure her a handkerchief.

With a shaky breath she turned and led them towards the door in the panelling.

CHAPTER FIFTEEN

—◦◦◦—

OLIVIA'S INITIAL RELIEF that another couple was promenading in the long gallery was short lived.

'The library is through here.'

Mr Petersham's voice in her ear, low and intimate, made her stomach curdle. She resisted the squeeze of his hand as he tried to draw her towards a rear door, straining towards a Roman senator with the words, 'Aren't we in good company tonight?'

Did he sense her reluctance? Hear the fear in her slightly shrill tones?

If he did it made no difference for his grasp was firm as he ushered her before him into the library.

The door shut behind them and they were alone in a large book-lined room, unlit save for a fire burning in the grate.

'Aha!'

He must have seen the *chaise-longue* by the window at the same time as she. There was satisfaction in his tone. Olivia felt her knees begin to shake.

She should run. Pull out of his grasp and escape but her fear had translated into mute acquiescence which he interpreted as willingness.

'You drew attention to my honeyed tongue earlier this evening, Lady Farquhar,' he murmured, leading her to the *chaise*. 'And I promised to deliver, I recall.'

'Do you have an arrangement to elope with Lucy?'

She could not believe herself, how baldly she uttered the words. Shocked, he dropped her hand.

'Am I to be censured or applauded for my boldness?' he asked, halting in the centre of the room. The moment of uncertainty was over in an instant as his smile resumed its confidence. Staring into her eyes he raised her left hand, slowly circling the palm with his forefinger. His eyes bored into hers as he murmured, 'If you are jealous, Lady Farquhar, I assure you that I would infinitely prefer to elope with you.'

Stonily, she met his gaze. 'I prefer my widowed status, thank you.'

'As I thought.' He sighed, feigning disappointment. 'You have the freedom to' – he paused, recalling her sentiments of earlier that evening – 'enjoy your fortune as you please, and not be censured for the dalliances in which you choose to indulge.'

With a tug Olivia found herself stumbling the last few feet and then she was across his lap upon the gold- and blue-striped *chaise-longue*.

She heard herself shriek, a faint, cut-off sound, for Mr Petersham's mouth was covering hers while his arms had assumed the nature of tentacles. She could feel one of them insinuating itself the length of her thigh.

Was this what he thought of her? A strumpet all too eager for a quick fumble in the shadows?

She struggled but perhaps he mistook her objections for the writhings of passion? Just as she had mistaken speculation for admiration all these years in the hooded gazes of other women's husbands? Now she knew it was speculation. How far might scandalous Lady Farquhar be prepared to go with *them* given the right inducement?

Self-disgust united with her terror. What a fool she was. As much a fool as when she had been seventeen.

She tried to pull her mouth away but blind lust gripped him and even if he registered her resistance he did not heed it.

Horrible blackness clouded up behind her eyes, filling her head as she fought for control.

There was no finesse in his exploration. His groping hands sent shivers of revulsion through her but her protests were stifled by the single-mindedness of his quest for physical fulfilment.

Ineffectually, she tried again to push him away. Nothing was worth this foul indignity, this trampling of her sensibilities. His mouth was like a great sponge clamped over her lips, his arms like a vice caging her to his will. Did he not register her unwillingness? Was his mastery over her his enjoyment?

Like Lucien? Dear God, how could she have been so blind as to walk right into the trap set for her? Mr Petersham saw her as a conquest, nothing more. Just as Lucien had. No spark of feeling for her had ever burned in Lucien's breast other than the need to possess and vanquish.

How well she had read Mr Petersham. And she had gone with him willingly!

She twisted and writhed in her attempts to struggle free, but escape was not an option until Mr Petersham had had his fill.

Panic was overlaid with a desperate yet weary resignation that she had no one but herself to blame. There would be no rescue until Mariah had orchestrated the ghastly finale she'd planned for poor Lucy's edification.

And then a sharp, clear familiar voice cut through her horror. For a brief instant joy and relief pulsed through her as she registered the beloved voice of her rescuer.

Almost instantly her horror metamorphosed into a new form. Of all the people to witness her latest transgression: Max.

The shock of discovery caused Mr Petersham to release her. She wasn't sure if chivalry or devilry made him drape his arm possessively about her shoulders as he sat up on the *chaise*, pulling Olivia up with him. She felt the smug satisfaction conveyed by his caress as Max, eyes like flint, looked past her, his voice low and terrible as he demanded, 'Unhand that woman!'

'Who are you, sir, to interrupt a tryst between willing—'

He stopped as Lucy stepped out of the shadows and the stricken look she directed first at her erstwhile admirer and then at her cousin made Olivia wonder if any of this had been worthwhile – even had it gone more or less to plan.

Though the girl said nothing, Olivia thought she'd never seen the cruel effects of betrayal etched more poignantly on another's features. With a heartrending wail Lucy buried her face in her friend's shoulder.

Olivia darted a brief, guilty look at Max before she slid her eyes to the floor. The disgust in his tone was echoed by the recrimination in his slate-grey eyes.

He put a hand on the other young woman's shoulder. 'Miss Hepworth, I think you should escort your friend back to the ball-room,' he said, his hard gaze still encompassing the guilty lovers. 'I shall follow in a moment.'

As the weeping Lucy was borne away, Mr Petersham rose. His mouth quirked and he clicked his tongue.

'A disappointed suitor, perhaps? I do not believe we have had the pleasure.'

Max ignored the extended hand.

'Lady Farquhar is to marry Reverend Kirkman at the end of the week.' She had never heard his voice so cold. His gaze swept Olivia briefly. 'I am here to ensure she follows through on her commitment.'

'Max, no, I—'

He cut her off, seizing her hand and pulling her up from the sofa. 'Olivia, if you would kindly come with me.'

Mr Petersham did not even protest. Olivia's last sight of him showed clearly his amusement and his words followed her through the door. 'My pardons for having detained you from your obligation to the good reverend, madam. Do call on me when you are again in the market for dalliance.'

Dazed, Olivia could not even respond. It was only after she was hustled outside and pushed into a hackney that she came to her senses.

'Where are you taking me, Max? No, you do not understand—'

'Did my eyes deceive me?' Fury resonated through him as he thrust her ankle free of the door and leapt in after her, slamming the carriage door behind him.

Cowering into the corner her defences drained from her as he leaned across the small, dark, musty space, the once-kind grey eyes boring into her with revulsion.

'It was a mistake—' She grabbed at the window sill to steady herself as the carriage lurched forward.

'Only because you were discovered, Olivia!'

'I did not want to kiss him!'

As she put out her arms to appeal to him he grabbed her wrists, thrusting his face into hers. His eyes glowed with hurt pride and anger and her heart quailed.

'Do you love him?'

'Of course I don't!'

'Yet you compromised yourself out of – what, exactly? The dictates of your wayward body?' Like a wounded beast he was striking out. She winced as if his anger had taken a physical form. If she could just navigate her way through their current impasse all could be made right between them.

She opened her mouth to speak, but he cut her off once more. 'Perhaps it would *not* be so sickening if you admitted you cared for the gentleman. What was I, Olivia? Another dalliance to pander to your cravings and lusts?'

'I've only ever loved you!' Her voice sounded shrill to her own ears as she struggled to free her wrists, impulses warring between flight and the desire to soothe his injured sensibilities in her embrace.

But she lacked the courage, fear and desperation banishing her ability to use calm reason to explain away his misplaced anger. He crackled with it, his body stiff as he ended their contact with exaggerated revulsion, his eyes bleak and cold.

She made another attempt. 'You're the only man I've ever loved, Max! What you saw tonight was a mistake—'

'A mistake! How easily lies and excuses trip off your tongue,' he sneered, flicking away her renewed attempt to appeal to him as he retreated back against the squabs. 'You lied to me from the moment you saw me and it's been lies ever since. I was nothing but a means to an end: the return of your son.' His voice cracked. 'The son you would parade before the world as Lucien's heir! Well, now I know better!'

'Max!' She implored him. 'My ... my indiscretion with Mr

Petersham was part of a plan to save my cousin from the fate I suffered at Lucien's hands.'

There was nothing to signify he was at all mollified, much less believed, this confession. Scepticism dripped from his response.

'Really?' He regarded her from his dim corner. For a moment he looked frighteningly like Lucien but the pain in his eyes highlighted by the breaking dawn almost immediately erased this impression and gave her hope. Lucien had never looked so wounded in his anger.

'A shame your earlier indiscretions carried not the same thought for the future of others.'

The direct reference to Julian's parentage made her mouth dry. 'Please, Max!' she cried, 'I'm not ashamed of what I did, though I deeply regret hurting you. Nor am I marrying Reverend Kirkman. I am resolved upon it.'

Though he avoided her outstretched hands her misery was overlaid by hope. Right was on her side. She clutched convulsively at the reticule that dangled from around her wrist. She could give him so much more than he had ever dreamed. A fortune to go with her love.

Soon his eyes would kindle with a very different emotion from the hurt and fury that roiled there now. Yes, he was sickened at discovering her in another man's arms but there was ample evidence to vindicate her.

'What choice do you have?' The words crackled with contempt. 'You made your bed—'

'But I don't have to lie in it!' Olivia railed. Just because the reverend was prepared to accept her, sin and all, didn't mean another wouldn't.

She heard him let out his breath in a slow whistle while she rested her head against the window. 'I told you the truth, Max.' She strove for measured calm. 'I wrote to you and asked what you would have me do. I have been in torment at your silence.'

'So now the fault is mine.' His voice, disembodied in the shadows, was harsh. 'I never received the letter, but that doesn't change the fact that what you did can never be undone. Julian is a bastard yet you were prepared to parade him to the world as the rightful Viscount Farquhar.'

Wounded, she replied, 'Max, I never meant to hurt you. When I looked into Julian's eyes I didn't consider him a bastard. He was a tiny, defenceless baby … and Lucien was desperate for an heir.' It was an effort to speak through her tears. 'Do you know how many babies I had lost? And yes, I should have admitted the truth. I realized that the moment I met you' – she dropped her gaze. It was painful just to breathe – 'before I fell in love with you.'

His mocking laugh brought her head up. She stared at him. He truly did not understand. She wondered how she could have misjudged him. There was no forgiveness for replacing the babe she and Lucien had lost with Lucien's motherless bastard.

Gasping she cried out, 'Have you no compassion?'

'Not for scheming deceivers,' he ground out, snatching her hands and moving his face close to hers. 'Look at you, Olivia!' With his palms he contoured her face. 'You are without equal. Exquisite. What I wouldn't sacrifice to have you – if I did not know I would pay twice in pain for the pleasure you gave me.' He fell back against the squabs, wiping his brow with the back of his hand. 'Before you destroyed me, as you destroyed my cousin.'

The empty silence stung her ears.

Shocked, she whispered, 'I had no idea you hated me so much.'

'Not as much as I love you' – he gave a shuddering sigh and his voice cracked as he added, 'But self-preservation prevents me from succumbing to the lust that consumes me as we speak. For it is lust, only, Olivia. Tonight you proved there is nothing in you to love.' Raising himself he glared at her. Never had he looked so like Lucien. 'Besides, you are going to marry Kirkman. You know there is no other path open to you.'

Stung to indignation she wiped her eyes. 'Should I be compelled to atone the rest of my life for compromising myself before him?' Hunching herself into the corner the anger built within her. 'I can't do it. I won't,' she flung at him after a moment's silence.

'And Julian?'

Goaded, she muttered, 'He is Lucien's heir and as long as the world believes *that* he will be fine.'

'Is that a threat?' Max spoke quietly. After a moment he let out a humourless chuckle. 'So you would tell the world the truth only if I had been prepared to wed you and conveniently dismiss what stood between us?'

He was looking at her as if he could not believe it.

'I can manage very well without Mr Kirkman and if you choose to deny me my son on account of it, you are within your rights,' she said coldly.

'And I can manage very well without you!'

The anger drained from her. Sorrow took its place. They had once loved each other. It could have been so wonderful.

'Olivia.' There was so much pain invested in the word she nearly wept. She kept her head averted.

After a silence he shrugged and there was a distance to his tone as he said, 'A boy needs a father.'

'Mr Petersham would have done just as well.'

Max gave a sardonic chuckle. 'You really are trying to live up to your reputation.'

She made her tone deliberately careless. 'Since it was only you I wanted – yet clearly it is impossible for us to live with the uncomfortable truth between us – I no longer care what becomes of me. I shall make a point of enjoying my road to eternal damnation.' She smiled sweetly. 'When your worthy Miss Hepworth becomes too tiresome you can look to *The Tatler* for some diverting scandal about the latest exploits of the brazen Lady Farquhar.'

Clearly he did not share her self-deprecating humour for he said with a narrow look, 'The future Viscount Farquhar will not be brought up in such a manner. If you want to keep Julian, you forget yourself, Olivia.'

She heard his shuddering breath. 'At the end of the week you will marry Reverend Kirkman. He has been … good … to you. You deserve each other.'

'Oh God,' she whispered, covering her face with her hands. 'Would you really condemn me to torment by *forcing* me to marry him? Just because he knows the worst of me? I am not *so* far beyond redemption.'

'I have discovered too much, Olivia, to know what alternative you have.'

She nearly choked on her anger. 'You self-righteous beast!' she cried, lunging at him with flailing fists. 'You're no better than Lucien! I hate you!'

Caught by surprise as the glancing blow struck his jaw, he gripped her wrists while pain tore behind his eyes.

'You hate *me*?' he repeated.

He could not believe it of her. What did she expect? To allow her *carte blanche* to continue her reckless, ill-chosen path, dragging Julian along with her?'

Wincing, he acknowledged his love for the boy. How could he not? For more than a year they had been as close as father and son.

Her eyes were like blue thunder, her skin flushed and her creamy flesh tantalizingly bared by her sumptuous, scandalous dress; he thought he'd never wanted her so much.

But the price was too high. She would forever revel in the power she had over him. He did not think his manhood could sustain a lifetime of it.

She was straining across his lap as he caught her wrists. Holding them above her head caused her body to sag into his. He closed his eyes against the desire to place a kiss upon the flesh that swelled above her low cut bodice; fought the raging impulses that rushed through his body as anger faded beneath his yearning. Her hot breath on his cheek as he parried her blows quickly fanned the flames into full blown desire.

For an instant she stilled. He opened his eyes in the startled silence and saw that she felt it, too. She wilted in his embrace, her face inches from his, her eyes dark pools of need.

The thread that connected their two hearts from the moment they'd met tugged tighter. He was devastatingly aware of the soft contours of her body and for a second he almost yielded.

Of all the women he'd known, none had the power to stir his senses as the fascinating, faithless creature before him.

Common sense returned and he jerked back as if stung.

He turned his head away before the hurt and surprise on her face could weave their spell upon his all too susceptible heart.

'We're here,' he said as the horses turned into the stable yard. With enormous effort he kept his voice neutral. 'Kirkman is waiting for you.'

She did not want to go. He knew he forced her against her will; that he was abusing his power in this act of spite and self-righteousness.

He didn't care. If she hated him for it, all the better. He didn't know if he had the fortitude to hold out if it was any other way.

Smoothing her dress she sat back in her seat, glaring at him. 'I had not known such a fine line existed between the affection you've always extended towards me and' – she nearly choked on the words – 'the disgust you clearly feel for me now.'

When he didn't answer she whispered after a silence, 'Could I change your mind?' Then, more desperately, 'I do not wish to marry Reverend Kirkman. Since I have made that plain, perhaps you'd like to know my reasons.'

'I'm not interested in your reasons.' He knew he was being childish and pig-headed but he wanted to hurt her. Humiliate her.

The carriage jerked to a halt and Max rose over her in the small space. It was not a comforting thought that his domination and angry snarl: 'Perhaps confessing tonight's little dalliance might ease your conscience' could only remind her of Lucien. Yet perhaps Lucien's behaviour was not so reprehensible given all he had learned of Olivia. Opening the door and jumping out on to the hay-strewn cobblestones he added, 'If you have one.'

A stable boy ran up to enquire if Max needed fresh horses. Shaking his head he turned back to Olivia who remained seated.

'Please Max, I will go anywhere except back to him. Take me back to my aunts! Please!' Her disembodied, heartrending entreaty did not soften his resolve.

The dawn shouts of the inn servants as they began their work and the creaking of the water pump were reassuring. Cocooned in darkness the intimacy between them during the ride here had nearly undone him. Now daylight provided a welcome barrier. Yet as his gaze raked

her magnificent body and lingered on the perfection of her mutinous
face he acknowledged it would not take much before her charms overcame his hurt and anger.

If he were to accede to her reasonable request to be conveyed back
to her aunts the consequent confinement would be detrimental to his
resolve to sever all contact. He would be as enslaved as he ever had.

He dare not risk it. Reaching in he took her wrist. She gripped the
door and resisted. 'Take me back to my aunts! I'm not going!'

Releasing her, he glanced round, realizing the dangerous path he
trod. He could hardly drag Olivia kicking and screaming through the
inn and deliver her to a no-doubt still slumbering Kirkman.

Disgusted by his heavy-handed tactics he slumped against the
carriage door. What should he do now? He thought he heard her
sobbing until her shrill cry shredded all sympathy.

'Take me back and I will restore your fortune, Max!'

Her tear-stained face emerged from the carriage, her bosom heaving
above the enormous pink silk roses that adorned her dress. The dress
of a courtesan; and the lies of a woman who would debase herself to
the limits if she saw profit in it.

'I know where the gold is! Take me back and I'll prove it!'

'Mr Atherton?'

Relief surged through him at the familiar voice. He doubted he'd
have had the fortitude to parry Olivia's latest sensual onslaught had
rescue not arrived in the unlikely and unexpected form of The Rev'd
Kirkman. He did not for a moment believe her last desperate gambit.

Careful not to look at her he bowed to the soberly clad gentleman
whose shock at their unconventional arrival was palpable, and said
through gritted teeth, 'Lady Farquhar was anxious to see you.'

CHAPTER SIXTEEN

⸺◦⊙◦⸺

NATHANIEL'S ROOM WAS cold and Spartan. No fire had been lit as he'd intended spending the day in Bath searching for Olivia.

Oh, he knew where she was, but he was not so certain he'd have been received by the ladies who lived in the fashionable townhouse in Laura Place. Who knew what tales they'd been told about him? That's why he'd planned to waylay Olivia when she was out walking. He could think of no other way of managing it. Of making her understand marriage to him was her only recourse, despite the impulses of her foolish heart.

Until Max Atherton had kindly delivered her to him.

He shook his head, tempted to laugh at the way matters had played into his hands. Max, his greatest threat – his only threat, really – had delivered his quarry to *him*.

Olivia quailed at the menace in his eyes before returning his hard look.

'You ask what I have done to have so vexed Mr Atherton? Perhaps the truth is best, Nathaniel.' Clasping her satin gloves together she adopted a businesslike manner from the wooden chair on which she sat.

'I would hope the truth is always best, my dear.'

She was not deceived by the silken tone. Nathaniel, she had come to realize, was always at his most dangerous when he spoke like this.

In a few sentences she told him about Mariah's plan and Max's anger at discovering her in the arms of young Lucy's paramour.

Nathaniel's scorn turned quickly to amusement. Pacing the floor-boards in front of the empty fireplace, he shook his head as if unable to believe her tale. Finally, to her astonishment he began to laugh.

'By the saints in Heaven, Olivia, I cannot believe that you have been delivered to me, on a platter so to speak. And by Mr Atherton!' He could barely speak for chuckling. 'It reminds me of the lively entertainments Lucien staged in which you were the star attraction.'

She glared at him. 'How dare you speak of those days—?'

Grinning as he turned to face her, he cut through her objections. 'You realize Mr Atherton believes I am Julian's father.'

Her lungs deflated. Gasping, she leapt to her feet, the chair crashing behind her.

'He believes no such thing!' Blackness whirled before her as she grappled to back up her denial, a thousand truncated exchanges teasing her memory with their potential for misunderstanding. 'He couldn't! I wrote and explained everything surrounding the night I took Julian in.'

He quirked an eyebrow. 'Yet he still deposited you here.'

In a gesture of self protection Olivia's hands went to her throat as he slowly circled her before going to stand in the window embrasure.

'For someone who thinks herself so clever, my dear Olivia, you are remarkably credulous.' He chuckled again: a low, evil, gloating noise that made her insides resonate with fear.

She'd never been this afraid of him, before.

'My dear Olivia, of course that letter did not reach Max Atherton.' From his pocket he pulled an elegant wafer which he slapped upon the table. 'When I suspected a damaging little confession from you was forthcoming I was ever vigilant.'

The blood drained from her head as she stared at the letter she had written to Max. She could feel her self-control slipping. Desperately she struggled to keep up the bravado, her voice cool and imperious as she said, 'Since Max has deposited me here and I have no wish to remain, please be good enough to advance me a small sum so I can return to my aunts.' She drew herself up, wishing her dress did not expose so much flesh.

He stroked his chin, his expression thoughtful. Slowly he advanced. Her mouth felt dry. She could feel fear swelling her glands, making it hard to swallow; knew she must not let Nathaniel sense it. She tried to choke it back but it was too strong, too overpowering.

'I'm not going to marry you and you're not going to rear the future Viscount Farquhar,' she cried, recoiling from the hand he extended to stroke the side of her neck. 'That's what it was all about for you, wasn't it? The power you'd have as Julian's guardian.'

It was suddenly clear. Cursing herself for a fool, she railed at him, 'You wanted me to trust you, yet all you wanted was power over me!'

Nathaniel's smile was pitying. 'Dearest Olivia, what have I done that you suddenly hold me in such aversion? Four days ago you eagerly anticipated being a bride.'

'Not yours, Nathaniel.' With a shuddering breath she whispered, 'Never yours.'

He shook his head as if her words caused him sorrow while his eyes told a different story. They were black with anger. 'After all I've done for you, Olivia. The scandals I've had to deny, the lengths I've gone to protect you from Lucien's ill temper.'

'To shore up your own position.' Strange how the truth revealed itself only now.

His finger hovered in the air just below her breast. 'Lady Farquhar's butterfly has brought you notoriety, Olivia. If you continue to refuse my suit, if you won't accept the respectability I'm offering you, you'll not find it elsewhere.'

'I wouldn't marry you if you were the last man on earth!'

'Your Mr Atherton must have been very angry to have deposited you on my doorstep.' He pursed his lips in a parody of sympathy. 'Clearly he has withdrawn from the quest for your affections. Still,' he added, 'I've no doubt there are many other worthy, blameless young women eager to fill the breach.'

His hands caressed her throat, toying with the pendant, the key Max had threaded through the chain around her neck in the attic that night.

The key to Elmwood. The fact Max laboured under the most

ghastly of misapprehensions and that she had failed to convey to him so much that was important gave her courage. 'He will think differently when I tell him the truth.'

If she could only stop herself trembling. She wondered if her fear would fuel Nathaniel's malice as it once had her husband's. For the moment his manner was restrained, almost gentle. Lucien had used this tactic as a precursor to violence. She trembled even more as Nathaniel ignored her last remark, murmuring, 'Here you are, horribly compromised in my chamber, yet still you refuse to marry the only man who's prepared to pave your way back into society. You will be ruined, Olivia.'

'Marrying a man I detest is not worth my return to society – in the unlikely event the truth does not change Max's mind.' She held herself proudly. 'Regardless, my greatest comfort is knowing Julian will be well looked after by Max who loves him as his own son. For you surely never did, Nathaniel.'

He chuckled again, staring out through the greasy windows. With his dark, oiled hair combed back from his high, greasy forehead and his full, gloating lips, he looked more like a repulsive toad than ever.

She seized her moment. Leaping out of the chair she ran towards the door, gripping the knob as Nathaniel's voice floated from the window embrasure.

'You really have lost your wits, Olivia, if you think you can simply step out of this room and find your way home.'

'I shall walk if I have to!' she cried, as she tried to make the door yield.

'An attractive proposition for the first drunken rider passing,' he chuckled.

She must not buckle now, though she realized the door had been locked. The key, however, still protruded, though it was stiff. Relief flooded her as it ground its rotation. 'Goodbye, Nathaniel.'

'Not so fast, Olivia!'

How quickly he moved for such a heavy man, she thought as he gripped her elbow.

'Not when you've failed to give satisfaction.'

His words were ominous, but when he saw the revulsion in her face his lip curled. 'I admit I am disappointed to be denied your charms in the marriage bed, but the idea of forcing myself on you is even more repugnant.'

'Then let me go,' she whispered, looking at his fingers curled around her forearm.

'Not until you show me what's in your reticule.'

No sooner had Max closed the door of Amelia's drawing room than he found himself facing down a veritable regiment of women.

So much for a quiet sanctuary followed by the catharsis of sleep to calm his disordered wits, thought Max, as he was confronted by Olivia's aunts, flanked by a formidable-looking woman in a gold toque.

Oh Lord, and there was Olivia's cousin, Miss Lucy, too!

Amelia and Jonathan, he'd been told by the weary parlour maid who admitted him, had gone to bed.

'Where's Olivia?' Aunt Eunice's voice was strained as she peered past his shoulder.

On the sofa beside her, the young chestnut-haired Lucy raised a pale, blotched face, her mouth trembling as she wailed, 'So you were too late, Mr Atherton! They've eloped, haven't they?' Before he could reply she dissolved into tears against her mother.

Grimly, he said, 'There has been no elopement, Miss Lucy. I have just returned Lady Farquhar to Reverend Kirkman whom she is to marry at the end of the week.' He doubted he had the fortitude to answer any more questions. Especially ones that brought back the uncomfortably draconian manner in which he had handed Olivia over.

He was surprised at the reaction to his perfectly reasonable announcement. Surely it was the outcome everyone had expected; desired, even.

'The reverend!' gasped Aunt Catherine, springing up and clutching her bosom as if he'd just told her he'd returned her to Bluebeard himself. 'Oh dear me, no! Surely she did not request it?'

His discomfort grew. 'It would appear Olivia does not know her own mind, yet it is too late for her to withdraw without great damage to her reputation.' He picked up Jonathon's snuff box which lay on the mantelpiece. Distractedly, he added, 'Do you not think it better than facing the accusing stares of all of you in this room? It was a kindness.'

'A kindness?' repeated Aunt Eunice. Her thin frame trembled as she also rose. 'Olivia holds that man in great aversion. She ended matters between them quite decisively before she accompanied us to Bath.'

Aunt Catherine dabbed at her eyes with a scrap of lace. 'She did not deserve it, Mr Atherton. Not after what she did for Lucy.'

Silently, Max prayed for fortitude. Lucy?

'She ruined my life!' Lucy cried on a choking sob.

Aunt Eunice sank back upon the sofa. 'I really don't understand all this talk of betrayal, Lucy,' she muttered. 'And if Olivia has returned to Mr Kirkman, surely it proves her blameless?'

Aunt Catherine lent her argument to the cause. 'Why would Olivia steal away your admirer, Lucy, when her heart clearly belongs elsewhere?' She levelled an accusing look at Max as she settled herself beside her sister. 'Besides, she only met Mr Petersham this evening and your mama has tried to tell you Olivia is blameless in the whole matter.'

'Lady Farquhar has shown Mr Petersham up for what he is, Lucy!' said Aunt Eunice. 'It was very kind of her when she did not want to do it.'

Did not want to do it?

'She was not unwilling!' Lucy cried, close to tears. 'I saw them!'

Max had seen them, too. With distaste he recalled the vision: Olivia's body pliant beneath the onslaught of that … villain's … ardour.

Though, on reflection, it was difficult to gauge how pliant she had been. Yet he had jumped to the only conclusion possible, he defended himself, silently.

'No respectable woman would compromise herself like that if she did not want to!' Lucy persisted. 'I hate her! I never want to see her again!'

Aunt Eunice gave Lucy a gentle shake. 'You should never want to see *Mr Petersham* again, for Lady Farquhar has shown him up for exactly what he is.'

The lady in the gold toque leant forward. 'A fortune-hunter, Lucy, and it was only because I prevailed upon your cousin to … to compromise herself – though that is too strong a word for I ensured the assignation was in private so there was no risk to her reputation—'

Aunt Eunice turned on her. 'Cousin Mariah, I believe you were quite specific in your instructions to Olivia.' She glared, first at her cousin, then at Max. 'Atonement and honour, I believe were the words Cousin Mariah used to shame Olivia into helping her with her plan to ensure Lucy was under no illusions that her admirer was a philanderer.'

'How dare you accuse me—'

Aunt Eunice cut her off, her accusing glare still turned upon Max. 'Now my poor Olivia has been returned to Nathaniel Kirkman! Against her wishes, for I suspect your anger overruled your judgement, Mr Atherton, did it not?'

CHAPTER SEVENTEEN

L INED UP SIDE by side on the wooden table in Nathaniel's room the two gold coins looked surprisingly dull. Worthless, unless she had known otherwise.

They were to have been Olivia's passport to happiness; atonement to Max, they were to have won back his love.

'You're cleverer than I thought, Olivia,' Nathaniel murmured, tearing his gaze from the coins. 'After all these years you've found the fortune which sent Lucien mad.'

'But *only* I know where it is, Nathaniel,' she reminded him.

Nathaniel chuckled. 'It's a wonder we never bumped into one another, my dear, during our mutual nocturnal quest. For years I've searched every priest hole, nook and cranny I could think of.'

'I never believed the stories,' Olivia said stonily. 'I stumbled upon it by accident.'

His hand darted to the key around her neck. 'Then why this?'

She shrugged, then laughed. 'This is not the key Lucien gave me. It is the key to Elmwood where I shall soon return.'

Pressing against her side Nathaniel clapped her on the shoulder and gave a humourless laugh, his gaze returning to the gold. 'Ever the dreamer, Olivia. Still, no matter if it is not the right key as you are clearly able to lead me to the prize.' He took her arm. 'Besides, I was not leaving anything to chance. I had my own copy made.' Pocketing the coins, he turned. 'Time to order a carriage.'

'I have no intention of meekly leading you to the gold.'

'There is nothing meek about you, Olivia, when your blood is up.' He pinched her cheek. 'It's one of the things I've always liked about you. *Of course* you have no intention of leading me to the gold, just as I have no intention of leaving open the possibility of your escape, since leading me to the gold is *exactly* what you will do.'

He strode to the door. Grasping the knob he smiled at her. 'You must be patient, my dear, until I've returned. And save your breath if you've any plans of shrieking for help. I shall tell the publican you're a lightskirt who has stolen from me and that I'm off to fetch the magistrate.' His gaze travelled the length of her costume, so revealing and inappropriate in the light of day. With another chuckle he added, 'The way you're dressed they'll not disbelieve me.'

Olivia sank on to the bed and buried her head in her hands when Nathaniel had gone. Once, she had believed he had her interests at heart; that he had cared when Lucien had beaten or humiliated her. What a fool she had been.

Graft and gain had been his motive the entire time.

For a while she wept, curled upon the counterpane. It was a relief to choke out the sobs which racked her body until she felt it had no more substance than the clothes she wore.

And what clothes! How appropriate, she thought bitterly, that she should be dressed like a whore as her dreams exploded in her face. Yet what could Nathaniel do to her that her espousal of the truth to the world could not?

Sitting up, she sucked in a breath, trembling with the realization of what she must do. She had been waiting for direction from Max. Just as she had since the day she married Lucien, she had been waiting for a man to tell her what to do. The time had come to make her own decisions, and remain true to them.

Please, let there be time! she thought, as she ran to the desk where Nathaniel had been in the midst of writing a sermon when she'd arrived. How she wished she had done this the moment he'd left the room. She had no idea how long she'd been weeping.

She was scribbling upon the second page when Nathaniel returned.

Horrified, she tried to hide the parchment, but his gaze from the doorway took in her stricken, guilty look before it travelled towards the hand she concealed behind her back.

'You've shown admirable restraint,' he remarked, crossing the room towards her. 'The servants haven't heard a peep from you. Now, let's see what this drama-filled tale of imprisonment contains.' He put out his hand for the paper.

When she refused to give it to him he snatched it from her, reading it with interest and chuckling several times.

'You don't believe in half measures, do you?' His tone was admiring. 'A full and frank baring of the truth, no less.'

'It is not finished—'

'Yes, there is a little editing to be done.' Nathaniel continued to pace before the grate, still studying the parchment. 'If we dispense with the first paragraph in which you claim to be held prisoner against your will, I think it will do very well.' He frowned. 'Had you planned to throw this out of the window, my dear, in the hopes of being rescued? Foolish of me not to have thought of it, yet I am pleased you have so conveniently orchestrated an alternative future for yourself. I had not decided what was to be done with you once you'd furnished me with the gold.'

His cryptic words filled her with panic. She tried to snatch the parchment from him but he held it above his head, gripping her shoulder with his other hand.

'It is not finished, Nathaniel!' Olivia cried again, her hands tearing the air in her desperation to reclaim the document, so damning in its truncated state.

'But *you* are, Lady Farquhar!' he responded grimly, 'and so are your dreams of cosy domesticity with your heroic Mr Atherton.' He pushed her away from him as he made for the door. 'Where is he now?' he sneered. 'Where is the *hero* who delivered you into my very hands?' He tapped the paper before turning the door knob. 'You are confessing to the very crime of which he believes you guilty. He'll not disbelieve it when he hears your burdened conscience has prompted your flight far, far away where nobody will ever find you.'

She felt the knot of fear and hope pull tighter when he said cheer-fully, 'It would however appear Mr Atherton's conscience is pricked by his shabby treatment. He was asking for you a short while ago.'

Olivia stopped her pacing and gripped the bedpost for support.

Max was *here*? He had returned?

Surely it could mean only one thing? That he had realized the error he had made and had come to take her home.

She could not believe Nathaniel would resort to violence, like Lucien. Yet his insidious character had begun to frighten her more than Lucien ever had. Lucien's anger found its outlet upon the instant. He was not a man who would patiently plot his revenge.

She realized Nathaniel had told her so he could enjoy her suffering. 'What lies was he told?' she asked dully.

'I informed the publican that you were, on account of your nervous disposition, on your way home to Mortlock. Your outrageous rig-out helped persuade him you were not quite right in the top loft.' He chuckled. 'If you made no noise he may well have presumed you'd already left. Now!' Striding to the table he pulled out more paper and dipped his quill in the ink. 'To business, my dear. There are several letters for you to write in addition to putting your signature to the bottom of this delightfully damning little document.'

'Max will find me!' Olivia declared, firming her grip on the back of the chair by the still unlit grate, refusing his offer of a seat at the desk. 'Once he learns that infidelity is not amongst my crimes he will pursue me to the ends of the earth! And then *you*!'

'He'll have to be persistent to get that far!' Impatiently, he tapped the paper. 'Come over here, Olivia and take up your pen. Mr Atherton is on horseback so I'd give him an hour before he turns back after failing to pass us on the road. As soon as we've done this' – he picked up the quill and put it in her hand as he dragged her over – 'we shall leave, taking a more circuitous route. We should reach The Lodge by early afternoon.' He rubbed his hands together after pushing her down upon the seat. 'By this afternoon I shall be a rich man.'

Olivia let out a bold laugh as she shrugged out of his grasp. 'You think the gold is hidden *there*? Why, you have no idea where it is and nor shall you, for I swear, Nathaniel, I shall not reveal my secret unless you plan to murder me for it and then what would it profit you?'

He shrugged, as if her intransigence was of no account. 'You misjudge me, Olivia, if you think I had not considered I might have to resort to extraordinary measures to overcome your reluctance. Mary!' In response to his shout the door opened and across the threshold stepped one of the inn servants, a dirty, dishevelled girl bearing a squirming toddler in her arms.

A look of delight crossed the boy's face as he was deposited to the ground. Running across the floorboards he held his arms wide.

'Mama!' he cried.

She was allowed to hold him on her lap. Julian wrapped his arms around Olivia's neck and rubbed his plump rosy cheek against hers in a rare burst of spontaneous affection.

'When your touching reunion is over you can write the first letter to your aunts, reassuring them that you will be waiting for them at the dower house tomorrow. He held up his hand to stay her objection, his plump oily face twisted with malice. 'If you do not, Olivia my dear, this is the last time you will see your little bastard alive.'

Max was back in Bath by mid morning but with no stomach for the eggs and haddock on which his sister and her husband were no doubt sustaining themselves, judging by the smell which wafted out of the front door.

Wearily, he entered the house. He needed to take stock and decide what to do next before he walked the few streets to Laura Place to inform Olivia's aunts of his failed mission.

'Max! You look like the devil!' Jonathon greeted him cheerfully, looking up from his laden breakfast plate.

'Like you haven't been to bed,' Amelia added, dabbing her mouth daintily with her napkin.

'I haven't!' Max snapped, sinking into a chair, accepting the cup of coffee his sister poured for him.

'Surely you haven't spent all this time looking for Lady Farquhar?' Amelia grunted her disapproval. 'Miss Dingley was asking after you.

Apparently her niece took it into her head to return to Mortlock without informing anyone.'

Gulping down his coffee, Max leapt to his feet. 'When was this? Did she' – he hesitated, reluctant to speak the reverend's name – 'travel alone?'

Amelia shrugged, leaning back in her chair. 'Really, I've no idea. Miss Dingley merely said she was here to reassure you that Lady Farquhar's disappearance following Lady Glenton's masque had been adequately solved.' She slanted Max an assessing look. 'Was there some mystery, Max? And do you think Miss Hepworth enjoyed herself?'

Max grunted as he made for the door. 'Capitally, I'm sure,' he muttered.

'Where are you going, Max?' Amelia called after him. 'Not to see Miss Dingley, I hope. She said she was retiring to sleep for a few hours. And so must you, Max. You look terrible!'

'Your best behaviour, now, Lady Farquhar,' Nathaniel cautioned, as he led her past a couple entering the inn. 'You don't want to parade your insanity on top of your notoriety.'

Hating the feel of his fingers digging into her wrist, wincing as the cold wind hit her face once they stepped outdoors, Olivia hissed, 'By God, Nathaniel, you had better keep your promise.' She exhaled on a sob, squinting at the grey sky after the gloominess of indoors. 'If you won't tell me where you've sent Julian, at least swear to me he'll come to no harm.'

'He's perfectly safe and happy with Charlotte enjoying the hospitality of an old acquaintance of mine,' Nathaniel said, opening the door of the waiting carriage he had ordered. 'Someone who owes me a favour and will be too afraid not to follow instructions.'

Olivia bit her lip. She had not the fortitude to dwell on this cryptic reassurance. Better to concentrate on keeping her eyes open for an opportunity to escape. 'As for notoriety,' she added venomously, slipping on the wet cobblestones in her flimsy dancing slippers, 'that was not something *I* brought upon myself.'

'You thrust your charms at Lucien and he reacted with the

predictability of a trained puppy, bless him.' Nathaniel assisted her into the carriage, climbing in after her. It seemed the coachman already had his instructions for with a straining and creaking of harness the carriage lurched forward and began its lumbering progress along the rutted road that led from town.

'I was seventeen. A child wrapped up in foolish fancies.' Olivia glared at him. 'Am I to have that forever thrown in my face, Nathaniel?'

'You sealed your fate with the flutter of your eyelashes, my dear. Lucien could not resist you and I sanctioned it. I made you Lady Farquhar.'

In the dim, grey interior, she saw him close his eyes and shudder. Revulsion? When he raised his eyes to hers they glowed as if lit from within by some secret knowledge.

She felt her skin crawl with the caress of a thousand spiders' legs. It was her turn to shudder.

Why had she not seen the truth eight years ago?

'Lucien wanted me above all others,' she whispered. She had to believe at least this. It had been her undoing, but it upheld her powers of attraction. Without those, she truly was the empty shell Nathaniel derided.

'Lucien wanted a lot of things, my sister among them.' Though his voice was soft it contained a note of savage hatred she'd never heard before.

Convulsively, her hand went to the locket at her neck. She could have been living at Elmwood had it not been for the monster before her.

'You have a sister?' she asked. So the philandering had been going on long before she'd even suspected. When he nodded she said with dignity, 'I did not take Lucien from another woman.'

Nathaniel's look was shuttered. 'Dorothy was a sweet, virtuous child.' He tore his eyes from her, as if the sight disgusted him. 'So different from you, Olivia. I would not want to make comparisons with the woman who won Lucien's heart and the one who stole it.'

His voice dropped to a snarl. 'Had she lived, Dorothy's piety would have redeemed the monster Lucien became. The monster you turned him into, Olivia, with your vanity and pleasure-seeking and need to be admired.'

'You lie!' Shocked, she went on, 'Lucien never mentioned Dorothy during our entire marriage. Nor did you. *No one* did.'

'No one did because their love blossomed before Lucien went to London where he was corrupted by the society in which you thrived.' Nathaniel's voice rose. 'No one mentioned her because she died a miserable, unworthy death.'

'Is there no end to what you will blame me for?' Olivia whispered, turning her head.

'My sister was among the most virtuous women who ever lived. Lucien broke her heart. She poisoned herself, Olivia, because she could not bear his betrayal. The tragedy was that Lucien was coming back for her. He never got over the guilt, the grief.'

'I am very sorry to hear about your sister' – she spat out the words – 'but I did not steal Lucien from the arms of another woman. Certainly not a worthier one.' Who knew what women from the lower ranks he was consorting with at the time? It was something she'd not considered as a seventeen year old.

'Dorothy was already dead when Lucien saw you for the first time,' Nathaniel conceded. 'But his soul was black. Blackened beyond redemption for what he had done.' He pushed aside the curtain, his breath clouding the dirty windows. 'When I accompanied him to London he knew it belonged to the Devil, but he was not yet ready to go there. He turned to me for his salvation.'

She felt a terrible gnawing in the pit of her stomach. He had not been in jest, earlier? 'You *advised* Lucien to marry me?'

Nathaniel nodded. 'He needed an heir, and I knew what kind of wife would be best. Someone with a face and figure that would instantly appeal to him, but with a character that was' – his smile was so transparently gloating she felt ill – 'unformed. Someone who was so bound up in their own powers of attraction they could not see the danger they courted in a man like Lucien: a man who had lost all compassion.'

'Lucien wanted me!'

'Oh, yes, he wanted you. He was enslaved by lust' – Nathaniel grimaced – '*if* that's so important to you. And yes, Olivia, you were the season's most dazzling debutante. Why, I even wanted you myself.'

'I'd have turned up my nose at a low creature like you.' How could she not have recognized the evil in him before? Because she had been so bound up in her powers of attraction? Through dry lips she whispered, 'You'd never have had me willingly.'

'I'd have been a delusional fool if I'd thought I could.' Her barbs had no effect. 'As delusional as you, my dear, when you thought you could make something of your spectacular union with Viscount Farquhar. No, Olivia, I realized you would never have me willingly, but I sanctioned Lucien's union with you, nay, encouraged it, for I knew if I bided my time, I would be rewarded for my good advice.'

'But I'm no longer going to marry you.' For a brief moment she felt almost triumphant. As if she wielded the power. How pitiful she was.

'No,' he agreed, sadly. 'I must content myself with memories of enfolding you in my arms as I lifted you, all but naked, from the dining table after your titillating little performances for Lucien and his friends.' He reached forward and squeezed her hand. 'You needed me then, my dear. For most of your marriage, in fact, you turned to me for comfort. At the time it was enough, though I should have seen my dream would never be realized. Still' – he gazed once more through the window and sighed – 'I wanted the lost fortune more than I wanted you, so in that respect I have triumphed.'

'Through coercion and blackmail!' She had persuaded Julian to unclasp his arms from around her neck and go with the servant who would transfer him to Charlotte waiting in the carriage. She'd had no choice, but to what fate had she sent him? She choked back another sob. 'How can I believe you'll ensure Julian's safety? What will happen once you've got what you want?'

She had to give voice to her greatest fears, if only for the meaningless reassurance he would be forced to give.

'I am not a cold-blooded murderer, Olivia. No harm shall come to either of you unless something interferes with the careful strategy I've laid out.' He was thoughtful. 'Together we've laid the groundwork. Your aunts will not grow concerned for a couple of days; no one will look for you until at least tomorrow afternoon, giving me plenty of time to slip across the Channel, never to be heard of again.'

'What about Julian?' she asked again, though she knew her desperation bolstered his enjoyment in tormenting her.

'Julian's fate' – he leaned forward, putting his evil, oily face close to hers – 'and yours will be revealed in good time.'

She recoiled. 'Max will find me, and you!'

Nathaniel regarded her through hooded eyes. 'Mr Atherton will play the hero because it will be required of him,' he agreed. His fingers beat a tattoo upon his thigh as the corners of his mouth turned up. 'But *if* he finds you, will he still want you, Olivia? That is the question. Poor Mr Atherton is so confused over you and your lies I wonder if self-preservation is not more important to him than the transient pleasures of your fading charms. Once he's nobly deposited you with your aunts I suspect he'll attach himself to the first innocent, uncomplicated debutante who flutters her eyelashes at him.'

Miss Hepworth. If Nathaniel were not watching her so closely she'd hurl herself against the squabs and sob her eyes out.

Instead, calmly and quietly, she asked, 'Why did you bring me Julian?'

He answered as if he knew she referred to the night of his birth.

'For the same reason I brought him to you just now.' He smiled. 'The power it gave me over you.'

'You never loved the child and yet you would have me believe that only you could safeguard his future.'

'I never *dis*liked him. He was simply a child.' Nathaniel shrugged. 'Puling, puking and sniffling like most children his age.' Reflectively, he added, 'When I lifted him from Meg Dorling's cold dead chest I wondered how long it would be before he followed his mother into the grave. No one wanted him. And then I thought of you, Olivia.' He touched her cheek. 'I thought of all your suffering and feared, from what Charlotte told me, that it was about to be compounded. That's when it occurred to me I could give you the greatest gift possible: a living child.' He glanced out of the window as the carriage turned into the avenue which led to Olivia's old home. Smiling, he turned back to her with glowing eyes. 'So you would spend the rest of your life in my debt.'

The carriage ground slowly over the gravel and would have pulled up before the front door had Olivia not given the instruction to halt a few hundred yards away, near a grassy knoll.

The crypt.

What choice did she have? Nathaniel held her son hostage. Had just her life been in danger perhaps she'd have had the strength to resist. Max's respect was vital to her fragile sense of self, but the safety of her son was paramount.

They climbed out, Nathaniel craning his neck to ensure they were alone and well hidden from passers-by. The Lodge was unoccupied and there was no view directly from the dower house.

'The only place I never looked,' Nathaniel breathed as he outpaced Olivia in his quest to reach the iron door. 'Why, it's unlocked!' He gave a delighted laugh. 'Lucien's grandfather must have given him the key as a clue. The old devil was probably no longer coherent when he realized it was all up with him.' He was speaking to Olivia as a co-conspirator. 'Quickly! Show me the treasure! I have waited many years for this.'

Olivia hesitated halfway along the path which led from the gravel drive and cut across lawn to the family tomb. Where was the gardener who tended the hedges once a week? Or the milkmaid who took the common lane to the village?

Hidden from all directions, even the carriage would not be seen from either The Lodge or the dower house.

Wincing as Nathaniel hurried back and dug his fingers into her arm to drag her along, she stumbled to keep pace the last few yards.

On creaking hinges the door ground open and Nathaniel pushed her ahead of him. Turning, shivering, she saw his breath misting in fast, shallow bursts.

'Where is it?' The urgency of Nathaniel's demands cut into reflections of her treachery. She was about to sacrifice Max's fortune to a villain in order to preserve her own dreams.

Her entire life had centred around reclaiming Julian. When the unexpected love she'd found with Max foundered, the gold was to have shored up the intense, transient happiness that had gilded her life with hope.

Dashing away a tear she forced herself to attend to Nathaniel. She'd still have Julian, wouldn't she? Shouldn't that be all that mattered?

'You can see the hiding place,' she said, dully, her hands hanging limply at her sides. She did not bother to point; just watched as his greedy eyes darted around the gloomy cavern until they alighted upon the tiny disturbed crypt, its heavy stone lid awry.

With another burst of laughter Nathaniel ran towards it. 'Dear Lord, I mustn't forget to thank Mr Atherton for this!' he cried, thrusting his hand inside to withdraw a fistful of coins, some of which scattered upon the floor. The weak sunlight from the high window illuminated his joy, a manic grin twisting his mouth. 'You found it when you interred that cur I kicked to death – though if it's any consolation I never meant to kill it.'

'It's no consolation at all,' Olivia murmured, shivering as the damp seeped into her bones.

Nathaniel forced the lid open a few more inches and burrowed into the darkness. Transferring the entire cache of gold he filled the bag he had brought for the purpose, straining under the weight as he headed for the door.

'How fortuitous you considered the animal worthy of a Christian burial, my love.'

'Where are you going?' Her aversion to his touch was replaced by panic. Already he was on the other side turning the key in the lock.

She ran after him but the iron bars slammed against her face.

'To fetch blankets and sustenance for five days,' he said, unclasping her hands which she thrust through the bars. 'Time enough for me to make good my escape.'

'Nathaniel, don't leave me here!' she shrieked. No more than a square foot of iron grating in the centre of the door admitted light.

'You were shivering, Olivia,' she heard him call. 'I will not have your death on my conscience after all you've done for me. Have patience. I'll be back soon to load up the carriage.'

'I don't believe you! You'll let me die here, won't you?' she cried between panicked sobs.

He brought his face close to the bars, sliding his hands between them to cup her face.

'I'm too fond of you to do that, Olivia' he soothed, as if he meant it, 'and I owe you too much.' Kissing the tears which spattered the backs of his hands he said softly, 'This is a bittersweet moment. It reminds me of all those occasions you turned to me for comfort. Once, I had hoped we might share this discovery. That our joy would be mutual.'

'Five days! Nathaniel, I'll never survive it! I need to be with Julian!'

'Four days should give me ample time to disappear,' he conceded. 'And have no fears over Julian. I have given instructions for him and Charlotte to be released once I have secured a passage across the Channel.'

Chapter Eighteen

'Beautiful morning, sir!'

Max groaned and turned his head from the sight of sunlight bursting through clear blue skies as Frensham drew the curtains. Anything remotely cheerful was a reproach. Since the events of twenty four hours ago he seemed to have existed in some dark eternity.

Olivia might be safe, but he felt a villain, a cad, a traitor; his heavy-handed, bullying tactics a barbarous manifestation of his own jealousy.

Wearily, Max performed the necessary ablutions before presenting himself in the breakfast room.

He was chewing on a mouthful of haddock and thinking he needed to speak to Amelia about the quality of the food which tasted like sawdust when Jonathan burst into the room, waving the morning's news sheet.

'You haven't finished telling me, Jonathon!' Amelia's shrill voice punctuated the quiet of the early morning household. To Max's surprise she burst into the room in her husband's wake, her hair hanging undressed down her back, clutching a shawl over her nightdress.

'Lady Farquhar has left the country!' announced Jonathon, breathlessly, slapping the paper upon the table beside Max's plate and taking the seat next to him. Stabbing his finger upon the revealing paragraph he shook his head in astonishment. 'Gone to the Continent to begin a new life on account of her shame.'

Max's mouth went dry. He managed to swallow the remains of his mouthful without choking.

Amelia sank into the seat opposite and snatched the news sheet from her brother's grasp. 'Lady Farquhar has finally abandoned you, Max! Now you can ask Miss Hepworth for her hand!'

Max knew he was staring like an idiot; that he sounded even more like one when he repeated, stupidly, 'She's gone?'

Amelia's excitement grew. 'I've never understood the hold that woman's had over you, but it doesn't surprise me that some great shame has finally forced her from the country. Max, Miss Hepworth would make the perfect wife.'

He wouldn't argue that point, but the fact was he loved Olivia. He'd been on his way to tell her. He'd never considered jealousy one of his faults, but seeing her in the arms of another man had turned him into an irrational monster.

He jerked his head up at the sound of his sister's gasp. Amelia's eyes were wide with shock.

'What is it?' He seized the news sheet she was devouring, fighting her for it as she tried to take it back.

'Read it!' Conceding defeat, Amelia leaned across the table to point to the revealing article. 'It's a confession ... for the whole world to see.' She went towards the window, turning with a self-satisfied look. 'So Lady Farquhar has admitted her adultery to the whole world. I shall invite Miss Hepworth and her mother to our house party at the end of the month. If the weather is fine there will be plenty of entertainment to be had outdoors. Perhaps, Max, we should organize a picnic.'

'My matrimonial affairs are *my* concern, Amelia.' Max spoke carefully. There was too much too absorb. Miss Hepworth was the least of his worries, but Amelia had the capacity to cause a lot of trouble.

He shook his head, trying to make sense of it: Olivia's motives, the implications. Why had she confessed her adultery to the whole world before she'd confessed privately, in full, to him?

Amelia swept across the room and laid her hand upon his arm.

'Amelia is right,' said Jonathon. His voice quavered with excitement. 'You must think of your matrimonial duties, Max.'

Tossing back her hair, Amelia's eyes shone as she squeezed Max's arm. 'The world now knows Lady Farquhar for the adulteress she is and that I stand beside the true Viscount Farquhar.'

He finished his breakfast in silence while Amelia speculated upon the possible candidates who had participated in Olivia's misdemeanours, to extirpate any vestige of feeling he might still harbour?

Oh, he harboured plenty of feelings! He just wasn't sure what they were. Guilt. Desire. And fear for her safety.

'She danced upon her dinner table for the entertainment of her husband's guests!' Amelia's voice rang out with delighted horror before she whispered with exaggerated outrage, 'I'm told she has a birthmark on a very private part of her person which the men used to line up to kiss! Lady Farquhar's Butterfly, they called it!'

Studiously Max maintained his silence, even as his sister went on, taking no account of his feelings – or perhaps *because* she knew it would wound him. 'Can you imagine, Jonathon, how many men have seen it?'

Was it anger at hearing Olivia maligned, or simply that he must be one of the few men who *hadn't* sampled Lady Farquhar's Butterfly, Max wondered, as he fought the urge to hurl his plate across the table like a moonstruck calf and stamp out of the room.

'Visitor downstairs wishes to see Mr Atherton.'

The parlour maid who put her head around the door bobbed a curtsy.

'Who is it, Ellen?' Amelia asked.

'The lady wouldn't give her name, ma'am.'

'You didn't recognize her?'

'She were heavily veiled, ma'am.'

'You can stay here, Amelia,' Max told his sister curtly when she rose to accompany him.

Downstairs in the drawing room a small figure dressed in black wearing stout boots and an enormous bonnet festooned with black netting turned at Max's entrance before hurrying forward.

'Miss Dingley!'

'I came as soon as I read the lies, Mr Atherton!' she cried. 'Though Catherine would have dressed like this to hide her *shame* I have done so merely to conceal my identity.' Her eyes, when she raised the veil,

LADY FARQUHAR'S BUTTERFLY

were full of entreaty. 'Please, Mr Atherton, find Olivia and bring her back. She was forced to write this confession. That man made her, though I've no idea how or why.'

Max was reminded of the night Olivia's aunt had begged him in the corridor to champion Olivia. The night he'd seen Kirkman go into her bedchamber.

The night his faith in Olivia had been eroded. Yet he still loved her, Max thought, wryly as he ushered Miss Dingley to a seat.

If Olivia had only had the courage to confess her adultery to him, she and Max might have been looking forward to wedding bells at this very moment.

'How will I possibly find her if she wrote this yesterday and has probably already left the country?'

'I don't believe she has left the country, Mr Atherton. You were the last to see her' – she paused meaningfully – 'before you delivered her to the reverend.'

'I delivered her to the man she was to marry after I discovered her in a compromising situation.' Max began to pace. He knew he carried a considerable burden of both shame and blame for his part in Olivia's disappearance, but it needn't have been this way if Olivia had confessed her sins directly to him.

'I want to help, Miss Dingley, believe me.' He strove for patience. Olivia was not the wife for him. He could not afford to be in thrall to a siren who made him feel completely out of control most of the time and whom he'd learned not to trust further than the next platitude that tripped off her tongue. 'However, *The Times* states she has taken' – it was hard to say Julian's name without wincing – 'the child with her to the Continent. No doubt you'll be reassured in good time as to her whereabouts and safety. I'm sorry, Miss Dingley.'

Why did he feel like a limb had been lopped off when his suspicions about the boy's parentage had been confirmed by Olivia in the most brazen manner?

Taking a deep, controlled breath he turned to the mantelpiece, his tone and manner signifying that he considered he had nothing more to contribute.

195

He heard the rustle of skirts as she turned; her sigh of disappointment and her hesitation before her voice, thin and hopeful, 'This morning on her dressing table I found this.'

Would she never let up? Reluctantly he looked at what she proffered. Blinking to clear his vision, he looked again.

'Three gold coins, Miss Dingley? Worth a sum, but what of it?'

'Where did she get them, Mr Atherton, when they would finance more than just a new wardrobe? Olivia has lived in poverty since Lucien died. Recently she discussed with us the idea of taking a job as a companion.'

This was a shock. Max took the gold to study the coins better.

Miss Dingley's agitation grew. 'Why would she leave them on her dressing table if she were fleeing to the Continent and would be in need of immediate funds?'

Turning them over Max felt the flutter of excitement in his gut tempered by a wisp of memory: her last words which she had flung at him before he'd all but torn her from the carriage and thrust her at Reverend Kirkman.

'I've found the gold!'

He did not tell Miss Dingley this. Not when she would immediately have pounced and formed conclusions that needed more thoughtful deliberation.

Yet it was true the gold coins hinted at something deeper. Dismay lodged like a heavy stone in the pit of his stomach. Olivia had tried to make him believe she had found his grandfather's lost fortune, but he'd dismissed her words as more desperate lies.

He handed back the coins with a frown, but was saved from having to offer a sensible course of action for the door was flung open and Miss Catherine and a dirty, dishevelled young woman he did not immediately recognize stumbled across the threshold.

'Mr Atherton! Charlotte and the boy have just arrived!' Miss Catherine collapsed on to the settee while she caught her breath. 'I've brought them directly from Laura Place.'

Julian's nursemaid? The girl's hair was a tangled mess and her hands and face were dirty and scratched, as if she had crawled through black-berry bushes. She looked terrified.

'Charlotte!' Eunice Dingley rushed forward, as the girl's legs buckled. With Max's help they supported her to the sofa before Max went in pursuit of some reviving brandy, the obvious question hovering in the air.

After the girl had spluttered on the amber liquid, he could contain himself no longer. 'What happened? We thought you were with Miss Olivia,' he asked, bending over her, burning for answers and chafing at the need for patience for the girl was hysterical.

He poured her another tumbler of brandy and after she'd choked it down she calmed, collapsing against the back of the sofa with her eyes closed.

'I was taking Julian for a walk yesterday morning when the reverend stopped and told us to get into his carriage as the mistress were asking for us.' Her voice quavered. 'We drove a short while to an inn just out of the town. He told me to wait in the carriage and he took Julian inside.'

Gripping the arm of the sofa Max found it difficult to curb his impatience. 'What about Olivia?' The litany of fear kept repeating itself, over and over, in his mind. If Julian had been taken hostage, Olivia must be in grave danger.

Miss Dingley grasped his arm and drew him back. 'You'll frighten the girl, Max,' she warned. 'Let her tell her story.'

Supporting himself against the mantelpiece Max tried to quell the ferment in his heart and mind.

Dear God, what had he done? Where was Olivia and what danger was she in?

Charlotte sniffed before resuming in a querulous voice. 'One of the inn servants brought Julian back to the carriage. She didn't tell us nothing though I heard her talk to the coachman about a grand lady inside. Then the coachman just whipped up the horses and drove us what seemed like hours to a village I'd never seen.' She wiped her nose on her apron and hunched forward.

'Go on, Charlotte,' Miss Dingley prompted.

'When we stopped I asked the coachman where we were and where Miss Olivia was, but he ignored me. Then a man came out and took us inside his house though it were a hovel, really. He started to speak nice, but as soon as we were upstairs and in a room where he said we could rest, he snarled at us that we were his prisoners now and we better behave ourselves else great harm would befall us and our mistress. Then he locked the door.' Charlotte's small bedraggled form shook with sobs. 'I don't know where Miss Olivia is!' she wailed. 'When I took Julian to the privy we were alone after the man went inside, so I grabbed Julian and ran. There were a passing cart and we jumped in the back.' She turned to Max, her face reflecting the same hopefulness as Miss Dingley's that he would be the architect of Olivia's salvation. 'You'll find her, won't you, Mr Atherton?'

Still gripping the gold coins, Max muttered, 'If it's the last thing I do, Charlotte.' Never had he felt so called to action. He raked his hand through his hair. 'I'll bring The Reverend Kirkman to justice, too and when I've finished *he* will be the one facing the opprobrium of the world.'

He just wished he knew where to start. A double measure of the brandy which had revived Charlotte didn't seem such a bad idea.

As he paced, he turned the possibilities over in his mind. 'Why would Mr Kirkman do this?'

'Revenge, Mr Atherton!' cried Aunt Catherine in her first burst of anger. 'Olivia wouldn't marry him so he made her write a false confession and kidnapped her son.'

Miss Dingley added in a menacing undertone, 'He wanted to destroy what was left of her reputation and take away that which meant the most to her.'

Still puzzling over events in an undertone, Max shook his head as he muttered, 'Why would he kidnap his own son?'

The aunts gasped, their outrage competing for an audience.

Miss Dingley's eyes blazed as she leapt to her feet. 'Is that what you inferred from Olivia's confession?'

'How could you believe Olivia would betray her own husband?' cried Aunt Catherine, also rising.

'What confession, please, ma'am?' Charlotte's voice came out a strangled thread, but with enough intensity to cut through the mayhem.

Forcing himself to remain calm, Max said tightly, 'Today's newspaper reported that Lady Farquhar confessed that Julian is the result of adultery and not Lord Farquhar's rightful heir.'

'Oh, Lordy!' Charlotte clasped her hands to her bosom and the colour leeched from her face. She looked close to tears. 'He finally used it against her.' Her whisper was not directed at the others.

She jerked with surprise when Max snapped, 'What do you mean?'

Immediately he felt ashamed of himself. Charlotte's lip trembled and she exhaled on a sob. 'I can't tell you.'

Max covered the distance between the mantelpiece and the arm of the settee in less than a heartbeat. 'Charlotte!' He gripped her arm as he crouched before her. 'Tell us what you know about Julian and your mistress!'

The girl buried her face in her apron, pulling her arm free of his grip, shaking her head. 'I swore I'd never speak of a word of it and I never have. I never will!'

'Charlotte, please, you don't know how important this is!' He tried to sound soothing but heard the croak of desperation in his own voice. 'For Miss Olivia's sake, you must tell us. What secret did you promise your mistress you'd always keep?'

'It weren't a promise to Miss Olivia 'cos Martha and I never knew if she knew that we knew her secret.'

Max shook his head at this convoluted logic and tried again. 'What secret? And who is Martha?' Exasperation threatened to get the better of him.

Charlotte rubbed her swollen eyes. 'Martha were Miss Olivia's lady's maid before she married the publican of The Pelican and became Mrs Mifflin.' Her expression remained mutinous as she added, 'We promised each other we'd never say a word to *anyone*.'

Max rose and went to the fireplace, kicking a log that threatened to dislodge itself. Turning, he told Charlotte, 'Lady Farquhar confessed her adultery in this morning's new sheet. Everyone now knows Julian is not her late husband's legitimate heir. There is no point in keeping your secret any longer, Charlotte.'

The apron dropped. The girl's white face appeared above it like a frightened rabbit's just as Amelia bustled into the room, adding her contribution, 'Yes, Charlotte! Lady Farquhar's sins were made public this morning—'

She stopped short and looked uncomfortable when she saw Olivia's aunts to whom she'd been introduced so recently at Lady Glenton's, before exclaiming, 'Good gracious, Charlotte! What have you been doing?'

'Charlotte has come through quite an ordeal, Amelia.' Max spoke crisply. 'Please! It would be better if you left us alone.'

'No!'

Max turned back to Charlotte. 'If you wish her to stay then—'

'That's not the truth!' The girl started to her feet, her hands cupping her cheeks. 'Why would Miss Olivia say such a terrible thing when Julian is Lord Farquhar's son what she's brought up as her own? Her own husband's child what she's fought for so hard. It don't make sense!'

The log in he fireplace thudded from the grate with a hiss; the only sound in the confused silence. Max ignored it, concentrating on Charlotte's horrified expression.

There was no suggestion of play acting. Shock, outrage and confusion were etched into every soft, dirty feature.

Miss Catherine's quailed, 'I don't understand. If Julian is Lucien's son there is no secret, no sin—'

Her sister added her objection. 'I told you from the outset, this confession is a lie which Olivia's been forced to fabricate by Reverend Kirkman.' A flash of inspiration crossed her face. 'It would only be a secret if Julian were not Lucien's *legitimate* son.' Turning, she addressed Charlotte, 'This is no time for keeping confidences, however honourable your intentions, Charlotte. Only the truth will help us find Olivia.'

He heard Charlotte's quavering voice while he cursed himself for the arrogant fool he was. Gripping the mantelpiece he forced himself to remain calm. Charlotte was about to reveal the truth which had torn his beloved Olivia asunder. A truth which, he suspected, would turn his – and the world's – harsh judgement of her on its head.

'I were with my mistress the night the babe was born,' Charlotte began in a soft voice. 'I were to be the child's nursemaid, Miss Olivia said. My reward as I'd been with her since I first went into service.'

'Yes, yes! But what happened that night?' Miss Dingley asked impatiently. 'Where was Lord Farquhar?'

Surprisingly, Amelia intervened as the voice of restraint. 'With due respect, Miss Dingley, I think the girl needs to tell her story in her own words.'

Max cast his sister a grateful look as he took the fire irons and crouched to tend the fire, listening as Charlotte went on.

'Lord Farquhar had never been good to my lady and she'd lost so many babes. Her first went full term but died within the hour and he beat her for it.'

Miss Catherine let out a wail of distress. Turning, Max caught the dismay in his sister's eyes. He knew the story of Olivia's sorry treatment at the hands of her husband. It did not help hearing these abuses reinforced by Charlotte, but it might not be too bad a thing for Amelia to hear the truth.

'Miss Olivia was happy Lord Farquhar was on a hunting trip because she was afraid of what would happen if she gave birth to a girl, or if the babe died.' Charlotte blushed. 'Lord Farquhar was determined to have an heir. My mistress told it to me a hundred times the week before the babe was born. She were terrified something would go wrong.'

'And something did?' Amelia shook her head as she put her hand on the back of the sofa and looked at Max. 'I've heard such terrible things about our cousin—'

'Your sympathies didn't exactly extend towards his wife,' Max responded drily.

'She was the season's most outrageous debutante. They eloped, Max!'

'She was seventeen, Amelia! A child! Lucien was a dashing rake! Perhaps you've forgotten how smitten you were with Lord Sylvester when you were an impressionable debutante. If he'd crooked his little finger—'

'With due respect,' Miss Dingley cut in, as Amelia, embarrassed and outraged, turned away, and Max, ashamed, ceased his defence of Olivia at the expense of his sister.

'What happened to the child, Charlotte?' asked Aunt Catherine. 'The baby to which Miss Olivia gave birth?'

Charlotte smiled, dreamily. 'It were such a beautiful little thing. Perfectly formed with dark hair and eyes nearly black, just like his father. And it seemed so healthy. Miss Olivia were entranced.'

'But it died?' Max could barely contain himself, now, despite his earlier deviation. Here was the crux of Olivia's great secret upon which she would be condemned or otherwise. 'And where was Miss Olivia's physician during all this?'

'Attending a breech birth an hour away.'

'You delivered Miss Olivia's child, yourself?'

'Mrs Flannigan, the village midwife came. We sent one of the stable boys to fetch her but she were already overcome with spirits by the time she got here and soon sleeping in a corner so Martha and me did it. Martha had delivered her mother's last six so she knew what to do and I just followed orders.'

'When did the baby die?' Max asked.

Charlotte sniffed and wiped her nose with the corner of her apron. 'Within the hour. Martha and me were bawling our eyes out. The mistress were in shock. She kept saying, "My beautiful baby's dead. Another one gone to Heaven". She kept saying over and over, "He *has* gone to Heaven, Martha! He *has*!" ' Charlotte choked on the words, adding in a whisper, 'Then she said, "Lucien will tell me it's not true. He'll say if the baby was not baptized it'll be writhing in the flames of Hell and that it's my fault. Martha! Charlotte! One of you must fetch Reverend Kirkman to baptize him. We must beg him not to tell Lucien the baby died before he came".'

She took a shaking breath. 'Mr Kirkman arrived later the same night bringing with him another baby boy. It were Meg Dorling's from the village, 'is lordship's mistress who'd died birthing the babe. Everyone thinks her babe died as well, 'cept for the reverend, Martha and myself – and Miss Olivia, o' course – who only did what any good wife and mam would a' done – looking after the little one like her own.'

He brought his head round at his sister's gasp.

Dear God, Julian was *Lucien's illegitimate son.*

A weight like an iron bar rested across Max's shoulders. Why had he never considered this? Olivia had intimated Julian was illegitimate. Not for one moment had he imagined the boy was not *her* natural child. He had drawn the only conclusion that seemed to offer itself in view of her insistence upon marrying Kirkman.

Charlotte looked down at her hands in her lap. 'The reverend was Lord Farquhar's confessor and his lordship paid him well for telling tales on my mistress.' Her lip curled. 'Although he kept Miss Olivia's secret I knew he would one day use it to his advantage. I knew I should never have trusted him when he told us to get into the carriage yesterday. Oh, Mr Atherton, we must find Miss Olivia!'

'Yes, we must!' Max agreed, rising, his mind racing to answer the call to action. 'Finish your story, quickly, Charlotte,' he said, striding to the door. 'If there is something which casts light on the man's motives for forcing Olivia to make that confession and for taking Julian—'

'Oh, I know *that*, sir, because the man what was keeping us prisoner told us,' said Charlotte, blinking at Max. 'It's because Miss Olivia discovered Lord Farquhar's grandfather's fortune and he used Julian to blackmail her into telling her where it was. Reverend Kirkman spent years trying to find it himself, especially after my lord died.' Glowering, she muttered, 'If you ask me, that's why he wanted to marry Miss Olivia. So he'd have a better chance of finding it if he were living at The Lodge.'

The women gasped. Even Amelia.

Nothing surprised Max any more.

CHAPTER NINETEEN

DESPITE MAX'S URGENCY to reach The Lodge, he saw the merit in his sister's argument that local knowledge was always the best source of information. He also needed to speak to the publican's wife. If Mrs Mifflin could provide independent testimony of Charlotte's claims with regard to Julian's origins it would cast new light upon Olivia in the eyes of the world.

In the shadows of the tap room, Pat Dorling grinned a welcome from the settle as Max bent his head to step beneath the lintel.

'I 'ear the Merry Widow took to 'er pretty feet and scarpered leaving both you and the good reverend in the lurch, *my lord.*' He guffawed into his drink, as the publican handed Max his ale.

'Out with you, Dorling, if yer plan on speaking disrespectful!' The publican gripped the old man by the scruff of his neck and hauled him to his feet.

'Let him be,' Max protested.

Raking the old soldier with a scornful glance, he asked, 'If you're such a fount of knowledge perhaps you can tell us where the reverend and Lady Farquhar have disappeared to.'

Dorling shrugged and took another swig as if the matter was of no interest to him. 'Only 'eard the news this morning, didn't I? Whipped the village into a frenzy it 'as.' He looked thoughtfully into his ale. 'So the reverend's gone, too, 'as he?' He sniggered. 'And you're here to bring wicked Lady Farquhar to justice, are ye?'

'Any ideas you might have regarding her whereabouts would be much appreciated.'

Despite the old man's sour look Max could tell Dorling enjoyed being solicited for his thoughts. The old soldier tapped his nose, waving his mug to be refilled.

Max tossed the publican a coin and Dorling acknowledged Max's largesse with a nod. 'Reckon there's *more'n* a thing or two I could tell you about the reverend,' he said. 'Mean feller. Wouldn't like to get on the wrong side of him, but he's canny. Knows how to make things go his way.'

Max gave a short laugh as he shifted position on the hard wooden bench opposite the old man. 'Intimates, were you?'

Dorling grinned. 'Like I told you afore, I teached 'is late lordship how to hide a couple of aces up their sleeves and were well rewarded for it.'

In the dancing firelight he looked like an elf creature who had been admitted to the inner sanctum. 'Reckon he finally found the fourth viscount's fortune. Lady Farquhar led him to it and they've skipped to the Continent to enjoy the fruits of their greed.'

'Slandering my good mistress, Dorling? So you's heard all them lies today, too?'

The three men turned their heads. With hands on hips an enormous, ferocious-looking woman blocked the doorway: Mr Mifflin's wife, judging by the publican's cowed smile.

Thrusting out her impressive lilac-upholstered bosom, she sailed majestically into the centre of the room. 'If you're going to get gleeful about a good woman's fall from grace you can get out of this 'stablishment, *Mr* Dorling' – the woman pointed to the door, knitting beetling brows – 'or I'll get my Jeremiah to throw you out!'

Max intervened. He needed to keep the peace if he were to learn anything further. 'You'll find no more ardent champion of your mistress than me, Mrs Mifflin.' Bowing, he introduced himself before assisting her into a shabbily upholstered chair by the fire.

'Lordy! His lordship's cousin! Why, I can see it in yer face!'

Mrs Mifflin's mouth dropped open before she jerked her head in

Dorling's direction. The fruit display which adorned the top of her bonnet trembled perilously. 'Pay no mind to the lies others would have you believe. Miss Olivia were the kindest, gentlest lady and what that husband of hers did to her would make a grave robber cry.'

'That's as may be,' muttered Dorling with a baleful look, 'but she danced to her husband's tune! On the dining-room table all covered in cream before the men lined up to—'

'Get out!' screeched Mrs Mifflin, leaning forward and stabbing a stubby, beringed finger in the direction of the door. '*Your* Meg was a harlot, enticing his lordship into her bed. Well, she got her just deserts, didn't she?' She shook her head, adding sorrowfully, 'If you only knew how good her ladyship was to your Meg.'

'She slapped her face!' Trembling from outrage and too many ales, the old man rose to his feet. 'Lady High and Mighty slapped my Meg's face because she were jealous that my Meg knew how to please 'is lordship when *she* didn't!' His thin voice quavered while his ale splashed upon his boots. 'Not five minutes after she called my Meg a harlot Lady Farquhar were dancing naked on the table—'

'Because her husband ordered her!' Max championed, also leaping to his feet.

'Because the *reverend* ordered it!'

Surprised into silence, they stared at the old man. Shaking like he had the ague he dropped his eyes, muttering almost sheepishly, 'He were behind all the humiliations,' as he sank back on to the wooden bench.

They absorbed this in silence as the wind rattled the windows and the fire crackled.

'And did anyone think to have pity on her?' Mrs Mifflin exhaled on a sob. 'My beautiful mistress were forced to perform like a high-class whore so the reverend could wrap her up and whisk her away.' She turned an appealing gaze upon Max. 'Weren't no use telling her the reverend didn't deserve her gratitude. Not when he were so clever at making himself out to be her hero.'

Max recognized the passion that would see Mrs Mifflin defend her mistress to the death. If Charlotte spoke the truth there'd be no trouble getting the publican's wife to add her testimony to the evidence that would vindicate Olivia. Olivia's deceit with regard to Julian would be condoned; so would the behaviour that had branded her the notorious viscountess.

'Why?' Max waited tensely. It was the question behind everything. 'Why would he want to humiliate a married woman? The wife of his benefactor?'

The old soldier hunched into his seat. 'Why does it matter?' he asked, sourly. 'She were the one what danced naked on the table. Not the reverend. Not my Meg. *Oi!*'

With a squeal the old man dodged Max's fist. 'All right! All right!'

Recovering his bravado he grinned at their shock, chewing his gums a few seconds before adding self-importantly, 'Meg said it.' He lowered his voice. 'Said Lord Farquhar had sold his soul to the Devil and the reverend was paying his dues on his behalf. That 'is lordship could do whatever he chose so long as he did what the reverend said in return 'cos he were doing all the bargaining on 'is lordship's account with regard to the hereafter.'

The publican shifted his gaze from Dorling to Max. 'There's others what's made claims like this.'

'That my cousin was mad?' Max gave a hard laugh. 'I admired him when I was very young though he fell into bad company shortly after-wards—'

'After Miss Kirkman passed away.' The publican nodded his head sagely. 'A beauty she were, in a ghostlike kind o' way with her pale skin and staring eyes, though she were right queer in the attic. It were ever a surprise to hear 'is lordship's fancy had fell upon her.'

'Farquhar, the old devil, sent her to her Maker, just like he did my Meg and the child she bore 'is lordship,' Dorling said gloomily. 'Same night the young viscount were born.'

Mrs Mifflin clicked her tongue. 'The girl was introduced to society after convincing everyone she were better, but it were a big mistake.' Glowering at Dorling she added, 'Regardless of what we think of Mr Kirkman, his mother was a good soul. Let's not rake up the past. Miss Dorothy's in hallowed ground and that's all that matters.'

But Max was not so interested in Miss Dorothy or the efforts to give her a Christian burial despite the fact she'd taken her own life.

Shocked, he realized he sat opposite Julian's natural grandfather. The old man didn't even know it himself, thinking Meg's baby had been stillborn the night his daughter had died in childbirth. An irony that Dorling insinuated Kirkman was the boy's natural father, though he was now still talking of Miss Dorothy.

Max had a flash of inspiration: *Kirkman blamed Lucien for his sister's death.*

And Lucien accepted his guilt giving the reverend leverage over him. When his manipulation of Lucien proved so successful the clergyman made Olivia his next victim.

His veins seemed to ice up. Nathaniel Kirkman had brought Julian directly from Meg Dorling to Olivia. He'd brought her a living child, the fruit of her husband's infidelity, but a living child and an heir. *Olivia would be forever in his debt.*

'I can understand the benefits of having such a hold over my cousin,' he said, slowly, 'but why Lady Farquhar? Why would he orchestrate her humiliation?'

Mrs Mifflin drew herself up until she resembled a mighty galleon about to brave rough seas.

'Why, it were so Lady Farquhar's gratitude would know no bounds when he spirited her away after each debauch and she'd marry him after his lordship had drunk himself into his grave.'

She sniffed, adding, 'But it weren't Lady Farquhar the reverend wanted: it were the power e'd 'ave over the young viscount.'

Dorling cleared his throat. 'That is, what we all thought were the rightful viscount until Lady Farquhar admitted her crimes to the whole world.' Waving his tankard in the air to be refilled, he regarded Max. 'Like I told you afore, I reckon that lad you's looking after be the reverend's son. Stands to reason, don't you think?'

Mrs Mifflin gasped.

'How dare you charge my dear lady with such wickedness? I were with her during her entire marriage *and* the birth. The only reason I didn't stay after his lordship's death was because there was no money for me wages, which is why I finally said yes to Jeremiah, here.' She nodded at her husband who contrived a suitably grateful smile as she went on, 'Miss Olivia were the truest wife ever, and that boy is his lordship's son, I'll swear it on me grave.'

Dorling looked morose. 'The reverend wanted the boy, too. As much as he wanted Lady Farquhar, I reckon, though I dunno why he'd want to be leg-shackled to 'er when no doubt he could tup her anytime 'e liked, and I reckon he did.'

Max forced himself to breathe through his fury as the old soldier went on, 'That's why he got his lordship to change his will. So he could get power and influence over the new young viscount, have the beautiful Lady Farquar for his wife, and live in the house where the gold were hid.' Raising his head, he sent Max a challenging look through rheumy old eyes.

Like a fire-tipped arrow this information found its mark.

The Reverend Kirkman influenced Lucien to change his will, too?

'Like you'd know, Pat me old friend,' challenged the publican. 'His lordship died long after your Meg. Reckon yer makin' up what you think 'ud impress us.'

'It's true!' protested Dorling. 'Reverend Kirkman wanted Lady Farquhar that bad—'

'I didn't know you were such a confidante of my cousin,' Max remarked, drily, while his mind turned over the possibilities.

''Twere one of the housemaids what told me wife,' Dorling muttered. 'Daisy, what were a witness at the end.'

'Daisy's a good girl,' affirmed Mrs Mifflin. 'She'd not tell lies.'

'Did Daisy see it written down?' Max asked.

Dorling chewed on his gums. 'The girl couldn't understand what were writ, but she heard them talking when 'is lordship were on 'is deathbed and the reverend saying as how 'e'd be just the man as would look after the boy right and proper.' He sighed. 'If my Meg hadn't a' died she'd bin the next Lady Farquhar with the key to the hidden gold and I wouldn't be sitting here with you lot.'

The publican sniggered and Max leaned forward. 'So what *is* this great treasure?' he asked.

Dorling's eyes shone. 'A great cache of gold the late lordship's grandfather put together to fund the Jacobite uprising after hocking everything of value that he had. That's what the reverend were after – the key Lady Farquhar wore round her neck after 'is lordship passed away – and if he's found it, it's him you want to vent your spleen on, not me!'

The key.

Convulsively Max closed his hand around the key in his pocket he'd used to open the door of the crypt when he'd paid his respects to Lucien after leaving Olivia. The key with which he had replaced the key to Elmwood. The key he'd taken from around Olivia's neck when he'd asked her to marry him in the attic at the dower house.

Leaping to his feet he strained to see how much daylight remained. 'I know where Kirkman is – or has been!' he cried. He was, perhaps, half-an-hour's hard ride from The Lodge, from the crypt. For seventy years the cold, damp cavern dug into the side of the hill between The Lodge and the dower house had hidden the fourth viscount's secret treasure.

Perhaps it was about to yield another hidden secret. One much more important.

CHAPTER TWENTY

—◦◦◦○◦◦◦—

H ER BONES ACHED. Ached from the cold which seeped through her body despite the three blankets Nathaniel had brought and from the hard, cold stone of her bed: Lucien's sarcophagus. She'd have chosen any other except that his was closest to the light. After so many long hours, including the endless night, she craved daylight.

Her teeth chattered as she rubbed her hands together, trying to find rest and comfort beneath the insubstantial layers of warmth.

Dear God, Nathaniel would surely not leave the country with no clue as to her whereabouts? He couldn't hate her enough to let her die.

No … She shivered even more.

His revenge would be to orchestrate how she would be judged based on his lies and twisted truths.

Staring up at the ceiling she imagined all England gasping over her damning confession. Nathaniel had had it delivered to the printing press the night before.

Stiffly, she sat up and stared around the dim chamber. Her back ached; her stupidity mocked her. Nathaniel had orchestrated her fate since he had cast eyes on her eight years before.

What chance had she of convincing Max she spoke the truth, even if he did come for her?

The afternoon was closing in on her. Sobs rose up in her throat. Another night alone? How could she bear it?

She froze at the sound of a carriage. The slam of a door. Every sense moved to high alert, relief and desperation making her lightheaded as she swung her feet to the ground.

'Help me!' she screamed, the echo of her thin slippers resounding through the chamber as she ran across the flagstones and pushed her face against the bars. 'I'm here! In the crypt!'

The sound of purposeful footsteps followed the gravel path that curved beside the high grassy knoll. Her rescuer was out of sight but surely he could hear her?

'Help me!' she cried again, so hard her lungs hurt, while she rattled the bars.

She saw the black hat before the rest of him came into view. The black coat and breeches and, as he raised his head to look at her, the smug, smiling, satisfied countenance of Nathaniel.

Terrified, she leapt back.

'I was worried about you, Olivia.' His voice was soothing as he unlocked the door.

Horrified she saw his smile of satisfaction, heard the whine of rusty hinges as he closed the door behind him, stepping into the crypt.

'I left clues enough for Mr Atherton to have found you by now, Olivia, but perhaps he thinks you haven't yet learned your lesson and no longer cares.'

'Get away from me!' she shrieked, backing towards the far wall of the chamber.

Putting his head on one side, he studied her from near the entrance, his heavy body thrown into relief by the fading sun behind him.

'But *I* care, Olivia.' He advanced slowly, his voice heavy with intent as he murmured, 'That's why I came back.'

With her heart in her mouth, like a mouse staring into the jaws of a serpent, Olivia watched his approach. She was his prey, just as she'd always been.

'You left no clues, did you?' she whispered. 'You never intended Max to find me.' Tears trickled down her cheeks. She was the reverend's puppet, just as she'd always been.

He halted a foot away, close enough for her to see the parody of concern that twisted his features.

'Tears of joy?' His hand reached out, a finger extended to taste the salty evidence of her terror, her submission, before …

Before what? Before he led her to Lucien's sarcophagus to dominate and possess her?

'You bitch!' With a shriek of pain Nathaniel whipped back his hand, choking on another expletive as he sucked the damaged member. 'You'd bite the hand that feeds you? Where's your gratitude?'

He lunged at her, cursing as she slipped out of reach to hurl herself against the grating.

'Help me!' she shrieked, rattling the bars, cringing as his large meaty hands snatched her elbows, screaming as he pulled her into him.

'What do you want, Nathaniel?' she screamed, struggling. 'You have the gold. You've achieved my complete subjugation. You have damned me in the eyes of the world. Is that not enough?'

Gripping her chin roughly, he forced her face up as his other hand seized her round the middle.

'I want *you*! I want you to understand how much you need me!' he muttered, shoving his angry face close to hers as she convulsed with disgust.

She twisted her head out of his grip, clawing at his arms and face with flailing hands, stumbling free only to fall upon the sarcophagi, her body exhaling on one violent gasp as the air was forced from her lungs.

'Just say it and you shall be free!' he screamed. 'The gold is in the carriage. Just say that you want me, Olivia, and together we shall enjoy riches greater than in our wildest dreams!'

'Never!' Her voice broke on a sob. Her spirit was nearly broken, too, but she had to resist with all her might, or her mind would splinter into a million shards.

Then how could she be a mother to Julian?

Once again his large body filled her vision.

Eyes wide with horror, senses screaming with revulsion, breath and vitality returned in time for her to thrust herself off the coffin and on to the floor.

Immediately she was upon her feet, but her slippers caught in the lavish trimmings of her hem, tripping her up so that she was flung forwards, arms upthrust to break the force of her fall as the flagstones rose to meet her.

Nathaniel was upon her before she could rise. Knees pinned against her sides, one hand forcing her face down upon the floor, he grasped her wrists behind her back and jerked her body upwards. She shrieked with pain, tears blinding her as he rolled her over then scooped her up, before dumping her unceremoniously upon Lucien's sarcophagus.

Like a fly paralysed by the venom of a wasp, she felt his hands upon her collarbones, sweeping across the exposed skin to cup her now-bared shoulders.

She could smell his excitement: the oil from his hair combining with the familiar smell of animal lust and the arousal of power.

'I have your son!' Pushing his thumbs beneath the lining of her bodice he gripped the fabric and ripped, his eyes feasting greedily upon the sight of exposed flesh above her stays. 'You are in my power.'

'Foul murderer!' she screamed, twisting uselessly beneath him. 'Damn you to the ends of the earth!' She struck out at him with her right hand, but he caught it, pinioning both her wrists to the lid of the sarcophagus while his body came down to crush hers.

The fingers of his other hand dug into her shoulders painfully. 'Take what I'm offering you!' he shouted, as he pushed his face into hers. 'My love and the gold! Do you *want* me to take you by force?'

'Let me go!' she wept, twisting her head away. 'It's Max's gold!' Wincing at the pressure of his grip she sobbed, 'You damned me in the eyes of the world, but you will never get your final satisfaction for I love Max!'

His violence filled her with defiance. She would not give him the satisfaction of her submission yet again. 'I hate you, Nathaniel! You are cruel and evil and your power comes from threats!'

He laughed at her struggles, his lip curling as she spat out the words, 'Max is a thousand times the man you are and I will always love him for he is good and kind and he believes the best of people—'

Nathaniel drew in a venomous breath. She could feel the heavy beat of his heart and the oppressive thrust of his desire for her through her gown; the ultimate expression of his domination.

'He doesn't believe the best of you now, my love!'

She felt his hand fumbling beneath her skirts, his hot, foetid breath upon her neck as he panted above her.

Shrieking, she freed one hand and tried to push him away but he was too strong for her and his voice was triumphant as he delivered his verdict. 'The sight of you … the mere mention of your name—'

'Inspires me with love, respect and deep remorse! Get off her, God damn you, Kirkman!'

Sobbing, Olivia wriggled out from beneath her oppressor whose sweaty labours had been arrested by his shock.

'Oh, Max!' Tripping upon her torn skirts she fell to her knees as she tried desperately to reach him on the other side of the iron door.

Max had come for her.

Not only to rescue her from danger but to take her away … with *him*. Surely that was what his impassioned tone implied for his face had been in shadow and now she was on hands and knees like a cornered animal.

'She led me to the gold, Atherton!' Nathaniel crowed triumphantly as he whisked her up from the ground, her arms and legs flailing as uselessly as a cloth doll's.

'More lies, Reverend?' Max's tone was strained as he worked the key in the lock. 'I know the truth.'

The truth. She tried to wriggle free but Nathaniel was too strong.

Struggling to breathe, unable to move, she wondered how she was painted in the version of the truth Max claimed to know and if that was why he didn't close the distance between them now he'd gained access to the crypt.

Her answer came as she felt the cold press of steel against her breast; looked down to see the small silver barrel of a pistol digging into her flesh below where her bodice gaped open.

'No!' she gasped. Swallowing down her terror she strained towards Max, wishing she could see the look on his face, to be reassured by the concern for her wellbeing endorsing the tension in his voice.

Had he come to rescue her *despite* what he believed? Or did his love for her transcend lies and half truths?

'I shall kill her!'

She forced herself not to react. Fear motivated Nathaniel. It shored up his power; his belief in his invincibility.

'I wanted her since Lucien made her his,' Nathaniel snarled. 'For eight years I have worked towards this moment. I shall not let her go so easily.' He gave a humourless laugh. 'If I can't have her, you certainly shan't!'

Max did not move. 'You're vanquished, Reverend, and you know it.' His voice carried across the three yards that separated them, a low and controlled murmur. 'Drop the pistol and let her go.'

Nathaniel's left arm squeezed her tighter; the other pressed the pistol harder into her flesh just below her breast. Her neck was clammy from his foul, hot breath. She could smell his desperation and knew he would never relinquish her willingly.

'Right through the heart, Atherton. Or should I say, "my lord"?' Nathaniel sneered. 'You have me to thank for that! Where is your gratitude?'

'It is my birthright.'

Olivia trained her gaze on Max's beloved face. Anything to block out the fear engendered by the barrel of the pistol which stabbed into her.

The tone of his voice continued to reassure her. 'Olivia tried to tell me that a long time ago, but I was too obtuse to understand her.'

A ray of sunshine burned through the heavy cloud and slanted across Max's face, revealing the love for her that kindled in his eyes. He was speaking from the heart; here to save her and exonerate her in the process. Her fear of Nathaniel dissipated, despite the noxious smell of him that burned her nostrils and the painful, threatening hold he had upon her.

Not ten feet away Max represented her salvation. His expression confirmed her greatest longing: that in his arms she would bask in the loving warmth of his embrace, revel in the urgency of his kisses and glory in the knowledge that he was her future.

But Nathaniel held the upper hand and he was unpredictable.

'She considered her son more important than either you or the truth!' Nathaniel spat.

Max raised one eyebrow but said nothing.

'Max, I wrote to tell you …' she said, brokenly. How wicked, how venal the truth sounded when distilled. How calculating it made her when presented in its essence.

'Hush, sweetheart,' he soothed with a smile for her. 'I've no doubt that man intercepted it.' He took a step forward. 'Despite your lies, Reverend, and the lies you forced Olivia to publish to the world, I know what kind of woman Olivia is—'

'The kind who will dance naked on the table, who will let the men line up to lick the cream from her!' Edgily, Nathaniel pressed the barrel of the pistol harder into Olivia's flesh. 'Tell me, Mr Atherton, have you ever kissed Lady Farquhar's Butterfly?'

With a cry of shame, Olivia brought her hands up to her face.

'I look forward to doing so when it is not a sin,' said Max with a wry smile. 'I daresay you have not, either, Reverend.'

'Do you *want* me to kill her?' Kirkman screamed, pushing her so hard that her upper body snapped back over his supporting arm. 'Are you so arrogant you believe you can arrive like an avenging hero and everything will go your way?'

Ignoring him, Max's voice continued, low and mesmeric. 'At every opportunity you prevented Olivia from telling me the truth when she was desperate to unburden herself.'

Nathaniel laughed. 'The truth? You don't know what to believe! That's your eternal problem. Look at her!' Roughly he gripped Olivia's chin and turned her face upwards. 'Beneath this perfection lies a heart and soul more corrupted than mine! Olivia and I are soulmates, Atherton. I will *never* give her up!'

Olivia wrenched her face free. 'I would rather die knowing Max loves me and believes in me than suffer a lifetime with you, Nathaniel!' she cried, as she tore herself from his grasp.

'Olivia! No!'

She heard a dull thud, realized it was her head striking the edge of the sarcophagus and Max's cry, echoing through the chamber.

She heard the scuffle of feet; the heavy toe of a boot that clipped her ear before it was swallowed up by the darkness. A body thudded to the ground before hauling itself upright, disappearing into the gloom amidst shouts and scuffles.

She felt …

Nothing.

Certainly she felt no pain, but when she tried to raise herself she could not move.

Closing her eyes she listened to the muffled cries of fighting men: a wail of pain, a shout of anger.

A muttered curse. Max's voice, tight and desperate: 'Oh God! Olivia! You're bleeding!' followed by a cry, a snarl, low and heartfelt, 'I will never forgive you if she is harmed.'

Fearfully, she blinked open her eyes, orienting herself towards the fading daylight, the entrance to the crypt where she could see Max and Nathaniel locked in a violent dance of mastery over her.

Her life lay in the balance. She would belong to the victor. Nathaniel had a gun and if it found its mark and Max was vanquished Olivia would forever remain in Nathaniel's power.

She put her hand to the sting at her forehead. In horror she stared at her bloodied fingers. As she struggled on to her elbows she wondered how deep was her wound. If Nathaniel was to claim her she did not care. She'd rather die.

But while they fought hope remained. The possibility of a future with Max, lies and twisted truths untangled, confessed, accepted, forgiven and condoned was her greatest hope. As it always had been.

The cacophony of grunts and groans was pierced by a single cry. Something stung her knee. Her swimming vision came into focus. Upon Lucien's sarcophagus she saw Nathaniel stretched over Max who struggled beneath him, hands reaching up to clasp the other man's throat. Against the noise of labouring breaths and muttered curses Olivia could hear the rapid beat of her own heart, or so it seemed.

She struggled to her knees and nearly swooned. Blood dripped from her head wound on to her dress. Her life blood. Draining away before her very eyes. She had seen the same thing when her first baby had died. In her pain she had cried out that she wanted to die, too. Now, never had the need to live battled so strongly within her.

She had responsibilities she could not forsake: a child whose tenuous future only she could safeguard. A man she loved whose respect she would fight for to the death.

Trembling, she gripped the side of the sarcophagus and dragged herself to her knees.

She heard Nathaniel's gloating snarl, 'Too bad you were so ready to jump to the worst conclusions, ye of little faith, *my lord!*' He had the upper hand. Olivia could see Max struggling for air. She tried to heave herself to her feet, but pain shot across her vision and she slumped into a pool of weak, ineffective passivity.

The woman of strength and conviction was dying within the empty husk Nathaniel derided. The woman she so wanted to be would not be heard.

Her heart screamed out in pain. In the echoing cavern it came out a muted whimper.

Dear God, please give me one more chance, the fading, flickering voice of hope cried out within her. Let Julian and Max know the kind of woman I really am. The kind of woman I could have been all these years if Lucien hadn't stepped in to corrupt me. If Nathaniel hadn't manipulated and intimidated me.

'Olivia!'

She jerked her head up at the sound of Max's voice. In the dim light it was hard to see him. Already he was fading, though perhaps it was she who was fading. The dark stain on her skirt was growing. She no longer felt any pain but that's how it was when one bled to death. She knew that.

'The pistol!'

The pistol? she thought stupidly, straining to sharpen what reason was left to her, panic at her ineptitude surging through her as she continued to support herself against the sarcophagus. She winced at the pain in her knee and looked down.

She was kneeling on the pistol.

The pistol!

With trembling fingers she picked it up. Elation shimmered through her, despite the dulling of her senses. She stared at it. For the first time in her life she held the balance of power. Cognisance of the danger snapped her senses to alert. Raising the barrel, she pointed it in Nathaniel's direction.

'Release Max or I'll kill you.' Her threat sounded like a parody.

Nathaniel's mocking laugh as he forced his thumbs into Max's throat echoed round the chamber. 'The roof is in greater danger, Olivia, you're shaking so much.'

Struggling to see clearly she croaked, 'I *will* shoot straight, Nathaniel and I swear I shall get you through your rotten black heart.'

'Max or me. It'll be a lottery, my dear.'

The gloating confidence in his voice frightened her. 'Your life blood is draining from you until you staunch that wound.' With a grunt he forced his thumbs deeper into Max's windpipe. Olivia winced at Max's gasp, the struggle she saw in his eyes. Nathaniel was a much heavier man. Luck had favoured him when he'd hurled himself upon Max, the lighter-framed man buckling over the lid of Lucien's coffin beneath his adversary.

Dear God, she had to help him.

'I have the upper hand, as I always have.' Nathaniel sneered. 'Realize that fact, my love, and I'll realize your wildest dreams.'

'I wouldn't go with you if you were the last man on earth. If I can't be with Max I'd rather die.' Carefully she brought the other hand up for greater support, her eyes trained on her trembling grip on the pistol as she heard a grunt of effort and a bellow of pain. Jerking her chin up she saw Nathaniel sprawled across the floor of the chamber in the gloom some yards away. Max was struggling to his feet having brought his knee up to deliver a kick of sufficient strength to release him from Nathaniel's grip.

'Don't go to him!' Olivia cried. 'Let his blood be on *my* hands.'

Max halted his progress across the floor and Nathaniel rose slowly to his feet, a crooked smile twisting his mouth as he faced Olivia.

'What? Shoot me in cold blood?' He extended his arms wide before tapping his chest. 'Through the heart? Here it is, Olivia. I offer myself up as a sacrifice.'

'You think I jest—'

'There's no need, Olivia.' Max's voice, low and soothing, carried across the chamber. 'Give the pistol to me.'

She did not look at him. Her hands were shaking so much she felt a fool.

Nathaniel laughed.

'Not your heart, Nathaniel,' she said through clenched teeth, 'for I don't want your death on my hands. I just want to see you suffer a little for the misery you've caused.'

She lowered her hands, training the barrel of the pistol upon his groin. She was rewarded by the blanching of Nathaniel's face, the absence of mockery as he muttered, 'Think how you'd be judged, Olivia.'

'You've orchestrated how I shall be judged, Nathaniel.' She gulped, sweat and blood blinding her. 'And you've ensured I have nothing to lose.'

She swallowed and closed her eyes.

Nathaniel's mocking laughter rang out. "A coward to the end, Olivia. You'll never pull the trigger!" he cried.

She raised the pistol once more in his direction but her hand was shaking so much she nearly dropped it.

Turning to Max she saw he was smiling at her, bolstering her courage with further affirmation of his love. Of course he knew she could not do it. Dropping her hand limply to her side, she took a step towards him. Towards the man she loved; the man who was at last offering her the future she'd always wanted. She knew it from the expression in his eyes. Three more steps and she'd be in his arms. Nathaniel was vanquished. As long as she had the pistol, Nathaniel was powerless.

She was nearly there when alerted by movement in her peripheral vision. "Max! Be careful!" she shrieked, jumping back as Nathaniel swung high the lid of Molly's sarcophagus to bring down upon Max's head.

The crash of splintering masonry, of Max's angry triumphant shout as he leapt clear, was drowned by the explosion of the firing pistol and Nathaniel's ghastly scream.

Dropping the weapon, Olivia collapsed to the ground.

Nathaniel's taunts echoed in her head. 'You'll never pull the trigger.' Well, she had, and now she was drifting into blissful oblivion, reassured by Nathaniel's screams and the shouting of her name – it seemed a league away – confirming that Max was safe.

Boots rang out upon the flagstones. She heard a sigh, an urgent hiss of breath as strong arms slipped under her knees and shoulders, raising her from the cold stone floor. Max's voice, unsteady for the first time. 'Olivia! Open your eyes!'

She blinked them open, breathing in the wonderful smell of him; revelling in the hard strength of his youthful, vigorous body as he cradled her against his chest.

'Quickly! You're losing blood! We must attend to your wound!'

The concern in his slate-grey eyes nearly undid her. Chocking back a sob she whispered, 'Julian?'

'Julian is safe with Charlotte and your aunts.'

She exhaled on a sigh of relief. Settling himself on the lid of the sarcophagus he rocked her, dropping feather light kisses upon her brow as he staunched her wound with a wad of linen. His torn shirtsleeve, she realized as she blindly kissed the warm flesh of his arm.

At last he rose, still cradling her.

She whispered, 'Is Nathaniel going to die?'

'Exquisite aim, my angel. Maximum pain and humiliation but I doubt you'll have his blood on your conscience.' She heard the grinding of rusty hinges and winced at the light, almost blinding although it was dusk. 'I'll assume responsibility if luck goes against you.'

She curled her arm around his neck, basking in the warmth of his strong, hard chest. 'Why would you do that?'

He stopped on the gravel path. Odin was tethered to Nathaniel's carriage. The horse raised his head and whinnied, pleased to see its master.

'Atonement.' His face above hers radiated warmth and good humour. As if the battle over life and death just minutes before had never taken place though she could feel the urgent need for him pulsing through her body and felt his answering response. 'It's a good time to start affirming my faith in you.'

'Max,' she began through dry lips, 'the gold—'

'It doesn't matter, sweetheart,' he soothed, kissing her lips lightly as if to allay her fears. 'If Kirkman has taken it we may still find it. And if we don't, we're better off than we were before, aren't we?'

'No, it's—'

'Yes, we are, because everything's out in the open – the lies and the truth – and we still have each other.'

'The gold is in the carriage because he told me so.'

Checked, as he settled her carefully on to the carriage seat, his expression was thoughtful. A slow grin spread across his face. 'Then I may buy you diamond ear-rings and gowns worthy of a duchess sooner rather than later.'

'I don't want to be a duchess.'

Tenderly he brushed a strand of hair from the wound on her temple. 'A mere viscountess will do?'

She nodded, not trusting herself to speak.

He reached up and kissed her properly then, nuzzling her throat as he stood on the path by the crypt against the setting sun, Nathaniel's cries, more of anger than of pain, issuing from within.

Reluctantly he raised his head. 'It's time to take you to Julian. And then we'll all go home.'

She heard the catch in his voice. Gazing up at him, she drank in his look of love, and the hope he radiated for their shared future, knowing it would sustain her through all the trials she would face on her journey to acceptance.

'Home, my beloved Olivia,' he whispered as he climbed into the carriage beside her, closing the door against Nathaniel's threats. 'Home,' he added, softly 'to Elmwood.'